"My *house isn*

Maya saw where he

"I apparently need
over the word "—to make sure my headache
doesn't get worse and that I slap ice on my
shoulder periodically. You need a place to stay for
a while. I've got a spare room I never use. You'd
be doing me a favor."

What other options did she have? She wanted to
be with her son, and that would be difficult at best
in a hotel room. It could take weeks to find an
apartment.

"So, what do you say?" he asked. "Are we going
to be roommates, you and me and Joey?"

Maya hesitated. "Okay, but this is very temporary,
just until you're back on your feet and I find a
place to live."

"Temporary, right," he said, still smiling. "Got it."

But seeing the satisfaction on his face, Maya
wondered if he did.

Dear Reader,

Well, as promised, the dog days of summer have set in, which means one last chance at the beach reading that's an integral part of this season (even if you do most of it on the subway, like I do!). We begin with *The Beauty Queen's Makeover* by Teresa Southwick, next up in our MOST LIKELY TO… miniseries. She was the girl "most likely to" way back when, and he was the awkward geek. Now they've all but switched places, and the fireworks are about to begin.…

In *From Here to Texas*, Stella Bagwell's next MEN OF THE WEST book, a Navajo man and the girl who walked out on him years ago have to decide if they believe in second chances. And speaking of second chances (or first ones, anyway), picture this: a teenaged girl obsessed with a gorgeous college boy writes down some of her impure thoughts in her diary, and buries said diary in the walls of an old house in town. Flash forward ten-ish years, and the boy, now a man, is back in town—and about to dismantle the old house, brick by brick. Can she find her diary before he does? Find out in Christine Flynn's finale to her GOING HOME miniseries, *Confessions of a Small-Town Girl*. In *Everything She's Ever Wanted* by Mary J. Forbes, a traumatized woman is finally convinced to come out of hiding, thanks to the one man she can trust. In Nicole Foster's *Sawyer's Special Delivery*, a man who's played knight-in-shining armor gets to do it again—to a woman (cum newborn baby) desperate for his help, even if she hates to admit it. And in *The Last Time I Saw Venice* by Vivienne Wallington, a couple traumatized by the loss of their child hopes that the beautiful city that brought them together can work its magic—one more time.

So have your fun. And next month it's time to get serious—about reading, that is.…

Enjoy!

Gail Chasan
Senior Editor

Please address questions and book requests to:
Silhouette Reader Service
U.S.: 3010 Walden Ave., P.O. Box 1325, Buffalo, NY 14269
Canadian: P.O. Box 609, Fort Erie, Ont. L2A 5X3

SAWYER'S SPECIAL DELIVERY

NICOLE FOSTER

Silhouette

SPECIAL EDITION®

Published by Silhouette Books

America's Publisher of Contemporary Romance

SILHOUETTE BOOKS

ISBN 0-373-24703-6

SAWYER'S SPECIAL DELIVERY

Visit Silhouette Books at www.eHarlequin.com

Printed in U.S.A.

Books by Nicole Foster

Silhouette Special Edition

Sawyer's Special Delivery #1703

Harlequin Historicals

Jake's Angel #522
Cimarron Rose #560
Hallie's Hero #642

NICOLE FOSTER

is the pseudonym for the writing team of Danette Fertig-Thompson and Annette Chartier-Warren. Both journalists, they met while working on the same newspaper, and started writing historical romance together after discovering a shared love of the Old West and happy endings. Their seventeen-year friendship has endured writer's block, numerous caffeine-and-chocolate deadlines, and the joyous chaos of marriage and raising the five children between them. They love to hear from readers. Send a SASE for a bookmark to PMB 228, 8816 Manchester Rd., Brentwood, MO, 63144.

Chapter One

This was not the way it was supposed to happen.

None of it—the wind and sleet, the rotten, rain-slicked mountain road, the idiot driver swerving into her lane, forcing her to yank the wheel hard to avoid a collision. The baby coming.

Definitely not the baby coming,

Not now, not here and not six weeks early. Another contraction gripped her, and Maya Rainbow clenched her fingers around the musty car blanket she'd been clutching like a life preserver, fighting the fear that was threatening to become full-blown panic.

"Are you okay? Maya, are you still with me?"

The contraction eased slightly. Taking a shaky breath, Maya managed to fumble her cell phone close enough to answer the dispatcher who'd stayed on the line after she'd called out the paramedics. "I'm still here."

She didn't have much choice. Short of crawling out the window—and right now she doubted she'd be able to do anything more gymnastic than sit up straight—she couldn't get out. Her ancient Jeep Cherokee had skidded off the road, sideswiped a pine tree and ended up almost on its side in a narrow ditch. She'd blacked out. And when she'd come to, bruised and shaken, she'd managed to untangle herself from the seat belt only to discover the driver's-side door was jammed and the passenger door was wedged against a tree.

Before Maya could call 911, she also realized her baby was coming.

"The paramedics are on their way. They should be there in a few minutes. Try to stay calm and remember your breathing," the dispatcher's voice was saying in her ear. "Tell me when you have another contraction."

"I'm telling you now," Maya gasped.

It had to be the fifteenth time in the last ten minutes the woman had coached her to breathe, to stay calm, and if she hadn't been about to give birth sitting in the front seat of her wrecked car, Maya would have laughed. She'd spent the last seven years teaching others to cope with pain without medication, to release their stress and find an inner calm. For months she herself had been practicing all those focusing and pain-control techniques she'd touted to her clients.

But now all she wanted to do was scream, *I don't want to breathe! I'm not calm! It's too early, my baby isn't supposed to be this early. And where are those paramedics? It's been hours. They should have been here by now.*

What if they couldn't find her? She hadn't seen any lights from passing cars, nor did she know what had happened to the other driver other than his car had run off the opposite side of the road. She didn't know if they could even see her Jeep, wedged as it was in the ditch. In the cold darkness, with the rain battering the roof and whipping against the windows, Maya had never felt more alone.

"Less than two minutes apart," she heard the dispatcher say. "Hang in there. The paramedics should be there anytime now."

The tears she'd been holding back slid down her face as all

the worry and hurt and fear that had been building up for months now crashed her defenses. If only she hadn't stupidly decided to drive home tonight, if she'd just waited until after her baby was safely born, none of this would have happened.

At the time it seemed the perfect solution, a welcome escape from the stress of Evan's relentless campaign to force her out of the apartment they'd shared. It was less than a two-hour drive from Taos to her parents' house in Luna Hermosa. The weather had been clear when she'd left. She'd had a trouble-free pregnancy and she wasn't due for six weeks. It seemed nothing could go wrong.

And then everything had.

There was never a cat stuck in a tree when you needed one.

Sawyer Morente glared at the ringing cell phone he'd tossed on the desk beside him and, seeing his brother's number flash on the screen, wished he'd had enough sense to turn it off. Right now he'd rather talk to anyone but Cort—even elderly Mrs. Garcia, who summoned the paramedics nearly every week, always making sure she suffered her chest pains on a day when Sawyer was on duty because she said she liked the way he took her pulse. At least he'd have a reason not to talk to his brother.

Tonight, though, had been unusually quiet for a Friday, especially after a week of what seemed like almost back-to-back calls. Apart from the small electrical fire keeping the three-man fire crew busy for the last hour, there hadn't been any alarms at the main engine house centered in Luna Hermosa. The early-spring storm rumbling down across northern New Mexico from the Sangre de Cristo Mountains seemed to have kept most people off the roads and out of the kind of trouble Sawyer got called to handle.

His partner, Rico Esteban, slouching in one of the office chairs, his feet propped on Sawyer's desk, glanced up from the Sports section. "You gonna answer that? It's getting annoying."

"Tell me about it," Sawyer muttered. It was the fourth time

Cort had called this week, and Sawyer was getting tired of telling his little brother he didn't want to talk about the letter—the one that lay in a mangled ball somewhere in the vicinity of his kitchen trash can. Cort, for some reason Sawyer couldn't fathom, wanted to answer it.

The only response Sawyer wanted to communicate to the letter writer was, *Go to hell. After twenty-six years without a father, I don't need one now.*

On the fifth ring, Sawyer jabbed the talk button on his cell phone. "Go away, Cort."

"Nice to talk to you, too, buddy," Cort said, his voice slightly distorted by static.

Another streak of lightning slashed the sky, giving Sawyer hope that they'd suddenly be disconnected. "You know, it's no surprise you're the sheriff's golden-boy detective. I'd take jail time over being hounded by you any day. Isn't there someone else you can irritate this week?"

"Just you. And you've been doing your best to avoid me. Why bother having a house if you're never off duty?"

"Obviously not my best or I wouldn't be talking to you—again," Sawyer said, ignoring the familiar jab about his working hours. Already restless with the conversation, he pushed away from his desk and paced to the office window. "And I wouldn't be avoiding you if you would just let this go."

"You can't ignore it forever," Cort said, repeating the same argument he'd been making since Monday, when they'd gotten the letters.

Sawyer wanted to ask him why, but the question would be wasted on Cort. Instead his brother would patiently drive him crazy until Sawyer either finally gave in or relocated and changed his identity.

"Sooner or later, we're going to have to deal with this."

"I am dealing with it," Sawyer snapped. Rico looked up from his paper, then pretended he hadn't when Sawyer scowled in his direction. Sawyer turned his back on him to stare out the window. "I'm dealing with it just like he dealt with us all those years after he finally got tired of knocking us around. I'm pretending he doesn't exist."

Despite the static, Cort's frustration came through loud and clear. "The man only lives a few miles out of town. He does business here. Hell, we went to school with his son. Although if things had been right, Rafe wouldn't have grown up a Garrett—"

"Don't go there," Sawyer interrupted. "We had nothing to do with that."

"My point is, Garrett's not going away."

"Maybe that's where you inherited it from." Sawyer gave up trying to argue his point with Cort. Their father had never wanted them from the beginning. Big and rough, with a nasty temper made nastier by his love affair with Jim Beam, he'd made Sawyer the target of his rages early on. Then when Sawyer was seven and Cort barely five, he'd kicked them off his ranch and out of his life completely without a word of regret or explanation.

When Sawyer had asked about his father, his mother refused to talk about him, except to say that Jed Garrett loved his ranch above anything and anyone else and that Sawyer and Cort didn't need a father who didn't want them. And she'd made the break complete by legally dropping Garrett's name and giving her sons her proud family name, Morente.

Sawyer might have believed what she'd told him if he'd never known that his father had adopted Rafe, remarried and had another son with his second wife. But he did know. And because he knew, he'd wasted years wondering what made he and Cort so unlovable that their own father despised them and completely denied their existence.

Now their mother was dead and suddenly Garrett wanted a reunion with his two oldest sons.

Sawyer didn't know what had prompted Jed Garrett's questionable display of fatherly interest and he didn't want to know. He didn't want anything from Garrett, now or ever.

"If it's that important to you, then you answer him," Sawyer said at last. "But you're on your own, brother. I don't want anything to do with him."

The strident tones of the station alarm followed by the dispatcher's voice drowned out whatever reply Cort started to make.

Two-vehicle accident with injuries. Woman in labor. Mile marker 223, Highway 137 at Coyote Pass.

"Gotta run," Sawyer said, hanging up and cutting off Cort's exasperated curse.

The wail of sirens jolted Maya and she whispered a prayer of thanks as the flash of red and yellow lights broke into the darkness around her. She had been trying in the last few minutes to convince herself everything was going to be fine, but her attempts had been a miserable failure, underscored by visions of herself delivering a premature baby alone in her Jeep and everything going more wrong than it already had.

At least now she had a hope of safely delivering her baby in a hospital bed.

A man's face suddenly appeared at the window, blurred by the rain. He took a quick glance at her and around the vehicle, tried the driver's door and then flashed her a reassuring smile.

"Be with you in a minute," he called through the window.

Maya closed her eyes against another contraction, and about the time it eased, she heard glass break and the rear door open and then the Jeep creaked and shifted. It took her a moment to realize someone was climbing over the backseat toward her.

"How are you doing?" he asked as he managed to somehow maneuver himself around jumbled boxes and suitcases and into the seat beside her. Already cold to the core, Maya clutched her blanket closer and tried to keep from shuddering as his shoulder brushed hers, sprinkling her with the droplets clinging to his hair and clothing.

It was the man she'd seen at the window, and the small space suddenly seemed filled with him. In the dimness, broken only by the strobe of the emergency lights, she could only see he was dark, with a smile as potent as any remedy for terror she could think of right now.

Before she could answer him, he flicked on a penlight and began checking her over. "Now there's a stupid question. I'm going to have to work on my opening line." He worked quickly, asking her several questions about the accident and her pregnancy.

"This is not supposed to be happening," Maya said just as another contraction started.

"I figured that. Here—" he took her hand in his "—go ahead, squeeze tight."

She hesitated, torn between hating the weakness that made her want to cling to a stranger for comfort and needing someone to lean on, if only for a few minutes.

As if he knew everything she was feeling, he said, "You're gonna make me look bad if you do this all by yourself. That's it…"

Holding on to something—*someone*—besides a moth-eaten car blanket helped, but Maya had a crazy urge to ask him to go on talking. She wished she could bottle his voice and use it as a remedy for daily disasters. Rich and dark, with an intriguing hint of an accent, it—coupled with the reassuring warmth of his hand against hers—soothed some of the rough edges, distracting her from the bubble of panic waiting to burst inside her and making her feel a little less afraid.

She almost convinced herself she could relax a little when the growl of a motor followed by the crunch and shriek of metal being twisted apart next to her ear jolted her upward in her seat.

Gently he pushed her back. "They're just getting the door open," he said, gesturing at the firefighters outside. "Then we'll get both of you out of here and to the hospital."

Sawyer didn't add that he doubted they'd make it to the hospital before her baby arrived. She was obviously already frightened enough. Her small, cold hand trembled in his. The tracks of tears clearly showed on her face and she had a death grip on the blanket in her lap. But Sawyer admired the way she fought her fear despite being trapped, in pain and on the verge of giving birth. He could feel her strength as she tightly grasped his hand.

He wondered why she was alone. What kind of man let his pregnant wife drive by herself on a night like this? Pale and bruised, she looked like something delicate and finely made that had been treated roughly.

"What's your name?" he asked when she drew in a deep breath.

"Maya...Maya Rainbow." She hesitated, glancing down at her hand still in his, looking as if she desperately wanted to him to tell her that it would all be fine. But she didn't ask him for the comforting lies that would make it all the worse if things went wrong.

"It's okay," Sawyer said. "Nothing is going to happen to either of you if I can help it. Boy or girl, do you know?"

"Boy—Joey. I'm afraid he's either going to be very impatient or very dramatic, being born too early, in a storm, on the side of the...oh—"

The pain came at the same time the driver's door wrenched open and a draft of cold rain rushed into the Jeep. Everything happened so quickly that Maya couldn't have said exactly how she got from the driver's seat onto a stretcher and inside the ambulance. It all seemed to pass in a blur of people and lights and voices until she heard someone saying her name and looked up into the only familiar face there. Trying to focus, she heard enough to understand he needed to check on the baby.

"I don't even know your name," Maya said irritably, then thought how idiotic she sounded. Under the circumstances, she didn't really have the luxury of modesty. "Oh...never mind—"

"Sawyer Morente. And this will only take a minute."

The name momentarily distracted her from what he was doing. Of all people to come to her rescue, again. She hadn't thought about him in years, hadn't even known he'd come back to Luna Hermosa. And now...

From the business end of the stretcher Sawyer looked over at her. "Joey isn't going to wait until we get to the hospital, and my partner is busy with the guy who ran you off the road. So it's just you and me."

"Alone? Here? Oh, no, I—you can't. Not by yourself."

"Sure I can," he said firmly. "Don't worry, I've done this before."

When she just stared blankly at him, Sawyer reached over and touched her arm. "We'll do this together, Maya."

"I can't—" Her head twisted on the pillow, her whole body clenching. "Not, not here…"

"It'll have to be here. Has someone called your husband for you?"

For a moment Sawyer thought she couldn't or wouldn't answer. Finally, in a voice that sounded oddly strangled, she said, "There isn't one. Joey doesn't have…a father." Defiance flared with hurt in her eyes. "There's…only me."

Her words slammed Sawyer hard against the memories of the past, catching him off guard. He wanted ten minutes alone with the jerk who'd decided this baby and his mother could be abandoned like something broken and worthless. He wanted to comfort Maya and reassure her that she and her son were better off without a man who could turn his back on his own child. He wanted to tell her that it didn't matter—except that it did, and he understood that better than anyone.

A crackle of radio static snapped Sawyer back to the present.

With a stab of guilt he saw Maya was looking at him with something close to alarm. Immediately shifting his focus back to her, Sawyer didn't waste time with apologies or self-rebukes he could make later.

"Okay, Maya," he said, catching and holding her gaze. "Get ready, and when I tell you, push. Now—"

With all his attention focused on a safe delivery, it seemed hardly seconds from when he told her to push to the moment he cradled the tiny infant in his hands. Sawyer worked gently and quickly, and after a few moments the baby made a small mewl-ing sound and then started to cry.

"My baby...is he—?"

Sawyer looked up from the baby long enough to give her a brief reassuring smile. "He's small, but he seems to be doing okay."

Bothered by the hedging in his words, Maya anxiously watched him bend over her baby until Sawyer finally straight-ened and laid her son in her arms. The tears she couldn't hold back slid down her face unchecked as she touched the odd little tuft of red hair, the scrunched up little face, the tiny hands that flailed softly against hers.

"Welcome to the world, Joey," Sawyer said softly.

Maya couldn't think of any words powerful enough to express her feelings. He seemed to understand, and for a moment, as they looked at each other, everything felt right to Maya.

"I never knew," she whispered. "I never knew it was so... amazing. How could anyone not want—" She stopped. She wouldn't think of Evan, not now, not again.

Reaching out, she put her hand on Sawyer's, linking the three of them. She tried to say something, to thank him, but she couldn't find her voice. Meeting his eyes, she knew it didn't matter.

Her touch and the love for her child he saw shining on her face stirred again all the emotions Sawyer had pushed away after he'd learned Joey's father had abandoned her and her baby. In that moment, he almost said something stupid, almost admit-ted that after helping her through the birth he felt a connection to her and her son.

Then common sense kicked him hard. It was bad enough he'd had that momentary lapse earlier, he certainly didn't need to convince her he'd totally lost it by telling her this had been some sort of bonding experience.

He smiled at her before gently breaking the hold she had on him and focusing on doing his job. Because that's all this was, doing his job, and whatever else he'd imagined was the result of a long week of double shifts, too little sleep and that letter he'd wished he'd never opened.

Maya lay staring at the ceiling of the emergency-room cubicle, seriously considering getting up and going to find Joey and reassure herself he was okay. She wanted to find someone, anyone, and demand they tell her where her son was. But exhausted and aching all over, she didn't know if she could sit up, let alone do battle.

They'd whisked her baby away minutes after she'd been wheeled into the emergency room. No one since then had been able or willing to tell her anything about Joey or when she could see him again. Instead, after being questioned, prodded, probed, cleaned up and offered painkillers she refused, she'd been left alone in the curtained-off room to wait until someone could get her a bed in the maternity ward.

There was a murmur of voices just outside, and Maya pushed herself up on her elbows and then sat up, swinging her feet off the bed, determined to get someone's attention.

"Just a few minutes," she heard a woman say, and then the curtain was pushed aside and Sawyer looked in.

"Hey, I just thought I'd—" The smile she remembered vanished, and in two strides he was at her side, scowling. "What are you doing? You're not supposed to be up."

"If someone would tell me how my baby is, I wouldn't be. What are you still doing here anyway?" she asked, then immediately looked contrite for snapping at him.

"It's okay," Sawyer said, heading off the apology she started to make. He didn't have a good answer for her question and he didn't want to look too closely for one right now. Taking her by the shoulders, he gently guided her back down on the bed. "And Joey is, too."

"You saw him?"

"Right before I came to see you. The pediatrician is with him now—Lia Kerrigan. I know her. Don't worry, he's in good hands."

Maya closed her eyes and let out a long breath. "Thank you," she said. "I've been going crazy. No one would tell me anything and—" She stopped, looking up at him. "You've done so much for us. I—"

"Need someone to keep a closer eye on you."

"I can take care of myself. And Joey," she said, giving him a look that dared him to disagree.

Sawyer stopped himself from saying she didn't look as if she could have stood up without help. Except for the purpling bruise darkening her temple and cheek and the long tangle of dark red hair, she looked completely drained of color and strength. She shouldn't be alone, not now. She needed someone to take care of her, no matter what she said. "Isn't there anyone you can call?"

She raised her brows at his abrupt question, then shook her head. "I was on my way to my parents' house, but apparently they've either gone out or forgotten I was coming, because they aren't answering the phone." Even though she'd talked to her parents two days ago, reminding them for the third time she'd arrive today, their absence hadn't surprised her. It would be typical of her parents to have gone off to a party or some weird festival in the middle of the desert, expecting she'd fend for herself until they got back.

"Your parents…" Sawyer studied her a moment. "Of course, now I remember. You're the hippie girl."

Maya sighed. "That would be my parents. I grew up."

He grinned sheepishly at her. "Sorry, but I remember that's what all the kids used to call you. Your parents still live out at the old commune at the edge of town, don't they?"

"When they're not living in their van. They disappear every few months in search of spiritual enlightenment."

Maya didn't add she'd had no trouble remembering him once he'd told her his name, even though he was four years older and she'd never said more than two words to him the years she'd grown up in Luna Hermosa. She'd been the barefoot girl in ragged jeans whose unmarried parents lived in a run-down house with their cats and chickens and various people who'd stay for days or months, depending on their whims.

He, on the other hand, had grown up on the Morente family estate, excelled at everything, dared anything and been the object of many a young girl's fantasies. And she'd bet the fantasies had grown up with the girls. She didn't doubt his competence on the job, but the uniform looked out of place on a man who conjured images of a midnight rendezvous, and temptation whispered in that dark voice.

She realized she was staring and quickly looked away. "I'm surprised you remember me. You left town years before I graduated high school."

"How could I forget the only time I actually got to rescue a cat from a tree? Of course—" he flashed her that smile "—I ended up rescuing the girl along with it."

"Now there's something I'd hoped you wouldn't remember." She'd been twelve years old and had followed her favorite kitten up a tree only to find herself literally out on a limb and unable to get back down. Sawyer and several friends had been driving by and he'd stopped and climbed up, bringing her and the cat down. "You seem to have a bad habit of being there to rescue me."

Sawyer studied her with an intensity that made Maya blush. "I wouldn't say that," he said softly. Then he shrugged, and abruptly he was back to the competent professional again. "I was just doing my job."

"Luckily for me. That's twice you've been my hero," she said lightly.

The smile went out of his eyes so suddenly, Maya blinked.

"So," he said in a very obvious change of subject, "are you planning on staying in that house alone?"

"I'm sure my parents are around somewhere. I just talked to

them the other day. And if not, they won't mind if I crash there a while." She knew that wasn't what he'd meant, but right now she didn't want to think past making sure Joey was healthy. Her head was starting to pound, and all she wanted to do now was see her baby and then get some sleep.

Sawyer easily read the exhaustion in her eyes and the droop of her body. He didn't want to press her, but he knew the Rainbow house and he was surprised it was still standing. The idea of her there alone with a new baby, with no one to look after her, bothered him more than he wanted to admit.

It wasn't even remotely his problem. He didn't even know her, except as a memory of a scrawny girl with red braids and wide green eyes, a girl that everyone called weird. He'd done his job, gotten her and her baby to the hospital safely. There was no reason why he should care what she did or where she went.

Except that he did.

Before he could come up with a good reason why, Rico stuck his head into the cubicle. "We're up. Another accident on 137."

Sawyer looked at Maya. "I'll see you later."

She made herself smile. "Sure, and thanks again."

Then he was gone. A sense of loss stabbed her and Maya felt silly for it. He'd only been doing his job. And now that it was over, she doubted, despite his parting words, that she'd ever see him again unless it was an accidental meeting in town.

She and Joey were a family now. There wasn't going to be anyone else. And the sooner she accepted that, the better off they'd both be.

Chapter Two

A small noise woke Maya from a light doze and she stopped herself from groaning, wondering what the nurses wanted this time. In the past three days, she'd gotten used to being roused at odd hours to feed Joey, to answer more questions or to be poked, prodded, or tsked over because of her refusal to take any pain medication. Three hours of uninterrupted sleep had become a luxury. And she'd been tempted more than once to take the painkillers, especially the morning after the accident, when she'd awakened stiff as a hundred-year-old and with a thousand pains.

But no one should be here now. She'd been to the nursery less than an hour ago to feed Joey, and the doctor had already been by this morning to tell her she could go home tomorrow.

Forcing open her eyes, Maya found herself looking into a smiling face she'd hadn't seen in years. Though the woman's curves were more lush now and her dark hair shorter, her generous mouth and smiling eyes and a passion for brilliant orange and red hadn't changed. "Valerie? Valerie Valdez? Is that really you?"

Valerie laughed and bent to give her a hug. "In the flesh, honey, although there's more of it than you probably remember. And it's Valerie Ortiz now," she added, settling herself in a chair beside Maya's bed.

"But how did you know I was here?" Maya asked as she struggled to sit up. Running a hand over her tangled hair, she tried to force her brain to start functioning. "I haven't been able to reach my parents and I haven't talked to anyone I know since I got back." *Except Sawyer.* But she couldn't imagine him looking up her old friends and asking them to visit her.

"You can't have been gone so long that you don't remember how fast news gets around here. Your baby's day nurse is my sister-in-law. Rainbow isn't exactly a common last name. Cat told me about your accident and your baby and asked if I knew you and so here I am. Oh, and I have this," Valerie said and held out a crumpled and water-stained piece of bright yellow paper.

"I stopped by your parents' house first to see if I could find them for you but instead of them I found this stuck to the door," Valerie said with a look that said she was sorry to be the messenger. "It's a little worse for the wear, but the gist of it is they've gone off to some rock in Sedona to commune with like souls. Sorry, I tried."

"I know, and thanks. I'm not surprised. It's just—" Maya stopped, then made herself smile. "It doesn't matter. I'm just really glad you came. You don't know how wonderful it is to see you." After three days without seeing a familiar face or being able to share her joys and fears about Joey with anyone she knew, Maya felt close to tears seeing Valerie. She brushed quickly at her eyes, pretending to rub the sleep out of them.

"It's okay, babies do that to you," Valerie said, taking her hand and squeezing. "It's good to see you, too, honey. You look a little banged up, but from what I hear, you're lucky to be alive. You and your little boy."

"Have you seen him?"

Valerie nodded. "He's tiny and precious. But I hear he's doing just fine. He'll just need a little extra TLC for a while."

"So the doctor keeps telling me." Maya turned to look out the window into the bright sunlight, tears welling in her eyes. "He— he just looks so little and helpless right now. And they're not going to let me take him home with me when I leave here. They still won't tell me how long he's got to stay, and I'm just so worried about him."

"I know. But Lia Kerrigan is a good doctor," Valerie said, echoing what Sawyer had told her. "Before you know it, your baby will be a boisterous, rowdy little boy and you'll wonder how he ever could have been so small and quiet. Believe me, I know, between the twins and now the baby."

"You have a baby?" Maya remembered Valerie had married her high school boyfriend shortly after graduation. The marriage had gone wrong almost from the start, and less than two years later Valerie had taken her twin daughters and left. "New husband, new baby—wow, has it been that long?"

Valerie laughed. "It's been a few years since we were sixteen, dreaming up ways to cut algebra. I think my favorite was the time we took your dad's motorcycle and skipped school for two days so we could go to that music festival in Taos."

A flash of memories made Maya smile. "We were trouble, weren't we?"

"And proud of it," Valerie said. "Now I'm working to keep my kids in line. And not succeeding most days. If it weren't for Paul, I'd be a crazy person by now. This time I got it right." She hesitated, looking uncertainly at Maya before asking, "What about you?"

It was the closest Valerie would come to outright asking her what had brought her back to Luna Hermosa, unmarried, with a baby. And what could she say? She'd left shortly after high school graduation to find something her parents had never been able to give her—stability, commitment, someone willing to share responsibility. She thought she'd found those things in Evan, but she couldn't have been more wrong.

"I decided to come home to have my baby," she said at last, not ready to rehash the last miserable year with her ex-fiancé. "Unfortunately that turned out to be a really bad idea."

"Don't beat yourself up over it. You're here and you're both okay. And I hear it was our finest resident knight in shining armor, Sawyer Morente, who came to your rescue. You remember Sawyer, don't you?" Valerie prodded. "You know, Mr. Captain of Everything in high school, Air Force hero, the guy with the killer smile?"

"I remember him." Maya suddenly felt warm and restless. The memories of the accident, of giving birth, of the moment she first held her son, were as clear as if they'd happened minutes, not days ago. And they evoked the same uncomfortable mix of emotions, somewhere between embarrassment at having to be rescued and to give birth in the back of an ambulance and an odd lingering sense of intimacy with the man who'd safely delivered Joey. Avoiding Valerie's eyes, she fidgeted with the blanket, reached back to adjust her pillow. "I suppose everyone in town knows what happened by now."

"Well, it hasn't been in the newspaper yet," Valerie said, then laughed when Maya shot her a wide-eyed look somewhere between horror and disbelief. "Paul is a firefighter. He and Sawyer work the same shift most of the time. So—"

"So everyone knows I'm not married and that Sawyer delivered my baby on the side of the road. And next week it probably will be in the paper," Maya muttered.

"It's not that bad. I'm sure there are at least a few people who don't know what happened," Valerie said with a wink. "Oh, I almost forgot. These are for you." She reached over to the bedside table and tugged forward a plastic pitcher filled with an eclectic mix of brightly colored wildflowers. "I caught Sawyer bringing these to you when I was on my way up to see you. He didn't want to wake you, so I offered to deliver them for him. Sorry about using your water pitcher but it was all I could find."

"Sawyer? Brought these?" Maya almost couldn't believe her ears. Sawyer Morente had brought her flowers? The most drop-dead gorgeous guy in town, every girl's idea of the perfect romance hero, had picked wildflowers for the hippie girl no one ever wanted to be seen with? *Don't make more of it than it is.* "I suppose it isn't every day he delivers a baby by himself in a thunderstorm," she murmured as much to herself as Val.

"No, but it figures it was Sawyer. Paul calls him Zorro because he always seems to be the one riding to the rescue whenever someone's in trouble around here. Although…" Val turned thoughtful. "Paul said delivering Joey seemed to really affect Sawyer. Maybe it's because he understands what it's like."

"You lost me," Maya said.

Shrugging, Val didn't quite meet Maya's eyes. "I guess you don't remember hearing the gossip, but Sawyer's father abandoned him and his brother when Sawyer was about seven. He completely cut those two boys out of his life. He never acknowledged they existed ever again, even though he still lives less than fifteen miles from them."

An odd ache touched Maya, hurting her heart and burning her eyes with unshed tears. Whether for Sawyer's loss or her and Joey's, she didn't know, but she felt like crying, giving in to the sadness that had shadowed her since Joey's birth.

To distract herself Maya brushed a finger over a daisy, breathed in the fresh scents of lavender and sage. "I guess he thought wildflowers would suit me better than roses," she mused, still wondering at his gesture. "They do remind me of home."

"You are home now," Valerie said firmly. "And you're not alone, no matter how much it might feel that way sometimes."

Tears rushed to Maya's eyes. "Thanks Val," she said, reaching for her friend's hand. "I know we're going to be fine. I just need to get out of here and get settled at Mom and Dad's for a while."

"If you can call staying at your parents' place 'settled.' They haven't changed much."

"Changed from tie-dye to spandex and back again, but finding the next Grateful Dead concert is still their top priority." Maya sighed. "Maybe it's better they've taken off again. If they were here, I'd have three kids to keep up with."

"Well, don't you worry, Paul and I are here to help. And then there's Sawyer…"

"Oh, no—" Maya held up her hands "—don't even go there. He was only concerned about Joey. Like you said, he can sympathize. End of story."

"Oh, right, that's why he brought Joey flowers. I'm sure at three days old he'll really appreciate them. Yikes, look at the time. I hate to run *mi amiga,* but Paul's shift starts soon and I need to get home to the kids before he goes."

"Thanks so much for coming," Maya said, returning Valerie's quick hug. "I can't tell you what it means to me."

"Then don't, just invite me over when you break out of this place."

"You're on."

"Catch you soon." With a wave Val left.

The room felt cold and empty without her friend. Despite Val's comforting words, Maya had trouble shaking a sense of utter loneliness, although she guessed that would pass once she and Joey were out of the hospital and the drama of the last few days was a distant memory.

She reached out and touched the soft petals of a daisy once more and suddenly her whole being ached to be with her new baby. Moving carefully, she swung her legs out of her bed, grabbed a robe and headed down the hallway to the nursery.

Sawyer slammed the door of his truck and strode across the parking lot of Firehouse No. 1. The bee sting on his hand was annoying him. He turned his wrist over to look at the red swell. "Morente, you're a freakin' fool," he muttered under his breath.

What had he been thinking? Picking wildflowers for that girl—woman and mother now, he reminded himself. Maya Rainbow wasn't a scrawny kid anymore. Even bruised and disheveled and swollen with child, Sawyer had thought she was beautiful, so different from the pale girl with eyes too big for her face he remembered.

After three days he hadn't been able to shake the image of her struggling to hide her pain and fear, determined to bring her son safely into the world and to care for him alone. Those big green eyes seemed to hide lifetimes in them.

It was those eyes and the way she'd looked at him the other night when she'd told him Joey had no father, coupled with the miracle of her little boy, that had messed with his mind so much, he'd wound up in the middle of some field on the side of the road, picking wildflowers and getting stung by that damned bee.

As he yanked open the door to the station, he thanked the guardian angel of masculine pride that one of his buddies inside hadn't driven by and seen him with a handful of daisies.

Sawyer strode straight to the coffeepot and poured himself a mug, wishing it were a double espresso instead of Paul Ortiz's "lite" coffee. He needed to clear his head and he needed a jolt of caffeine to wake him up. He'd hardly slept since Maya's accident; the whole night kept turning over and over in his mind like a movie stuck on replay. Why that night, that accident, that birth should be any different from any of the others he'd dealt with over the years, he couldn't figure.

Lost in thought, he didn't hear Paul come into the kitchen until a slap on his shoulder nearly caused him to drop his coffee mug.

"Wildflowers, Sawyer? Wildflowers?"

Cursing under his breath, Sawyer refilled his mug to avoid Paul's smirk. "If Valerie wasn't your wife, I'd put a muzzle on that woman."

"Don't worry, your little secret is safe with me," Paul said, laughing. A few inches shorter and broader than Sawyer, his dark eyes seemed always to reflect a smile. "A little above and beyond the call of duty, though, wouldn't you say?"

"The kid could have died," Sawyer said, wondering why he bothered trying to explain himself. "They both could have. I— I just thought she needed a boost, you know, something to remind her it'll get better."

"Aw, that's so sweet of you. I never figured you for the sensitive type."

"Go jump," Sawyer muttered. Taking his coffee, he headed for his office with the idea of locking himself in. Unfortunately Paul followed. Paul was a great guy, the kind of guy you'd want watching your back when it counted. But he was also the type of guy who didn't know when a joke was old.

"I'll bet the next time you visit her, she'll have the flowers in her hair," Paul teased.

"I'm not going back. I saw the kid and he's doing fine. That's all I needed to know."

"Sure, that's what you say now." Paul said, leaning against the door to Sawyer's office. "But Val and I already have money on it. Once you see that dump of a house Maya's moving into, you'll be over there with a hammer and a paintbrush all ready to remodel the Rainbow love shack. We all know you can't resist riding to the rescue. Besides, from what Val says, your damsel in distress has grown up rather nicely."

"She's not mine," he said, then, unable to stop himself, he added, "So she really is going to move back to that rattrap of her parents'?" She'd told him so the night of her accident, but he'd put it out of his mind, half hoping she'd change her mind before the hospital discharged her and her baby.

"Val says so. Man, I remember that party we went to at the love shack right before graduation. The incense was so thick, my throat hurt for days."

Sawyer remembered he'd been glad to get out of the Rainbow residence before he caught something. He also remembered Maya, a thin girl with tousled hair, sitting against the railings of the upstairs loft, gazing down at the strange mix of revelers with a solemn look as her parents called and waved up to her, trying to get her to join the party.

"Her parents were something. They still are, from what I've seen," Paul mused. "I guess it shouldn't surprise anyone, Maya coming home the way she did."

"And what's that supposed to mean?" Sawyer said more sharply than he intended.

Paul held up his hands in mock surrender. "Hey, you're pretty quick to defend someone you plan on never seeing again." He grinned at Sawyer's glare. "I didn't mean to insult your flower child. It's just her parents were never married and everyone knows they basically raised Maya in a commune. Val says half the time they'd take off on that banged up Harley of theirs and leave her with whomever happened to be staying at their house at the time."

"She told me they're gone again," Sawyer said.

"Yeah, and Cat said Maya's doctor plans to release her tomorrow. So, just in case you want to drop by the old love shack…"

"Why, so you'll win the bet with Val? Wait a minute. If you two are so sure what my next move is, what's there to bet on?"

"That's for us to know and you to figure out."

Sawyer began sorting through the pile of paperwork on his desk, ignoring Paul's attempt to bait him. "Don't count on my losing any sleep trying."

"What, you sleep?" Cort, in his usual jeans and battered leather jacket, was standing in the doorway. He walked around Paul, greeting the other man before dropping down into the chair beside Sawyer's desk. "That's not what I hear."

"Superheroes don't need the rest we mere mortals do," Paul said, laughing. "I'll let you annoy him for a while. I've done my duty for the day. Oh—" he leaned back around the door before leaving "—don't forget to ask him about his flower girl."

"Now my morning's complete," Sawyer said. He rubbed at his temple, really wishing he had that espresso.

"Girl?" Cort looked expectantly at Sawyer. "Don't tell me

you're actually seeing someone. Although I've probably already missed it, since your idea of a long-term relationship is two weeks. So who is she?"

"There is no she. We delivered a baby the other night and I went back to check on the boy and his mother. Now Paul and Val have decided I'm ready to propose. So what are you doing here?" Sawyer asked, wanting to shift the conversation away from Maya before Cort got wind of his temporary insanity with the wildflowers. "As if I didn't know."

"You won't return my calls or come see me, so I came to you."

"This isn't the time or the place."

"C'mon, Sawyer, it never is with you," Cort said. "But we have business, like it or not."

"Not," Sawyer said flatly. "I need more coffee." Pushing back from his desk, he strode out of the office, hoping this would be the morning Mrs. Garcia would decide she needed her pulse taken.

The next morning, fed and content, Joey lay nestled in Maya's arms, sleeping peacefully. She rubbed her fingertip over his cheek, marveling at the softness of his skin, wondering how he could be so perfect.

"Looks like he's finished." Cat Ortiz walked over to where Maya sat in a padded rocking chair next to Joey's incubator. Maya liked the petite nurse, with her ready smile and gentle touch, but she dreaded her arrival in the nursery—especially today, because it meant leaving Joey in the hospital while she went home to her parents' house.

"I don't want to leave him," Maya said, holding her son a little closer.

"I know, but he needs to go back to the incubator now. It won't be long," Cat said as she rearranged the blankets in Joey's incubator. "Then he'll be able to go home with you."

Maya bent and kissed her precious little boy before grudgingly transferring him to Cat's arms. Joey sighed, wriggled a little, then let out a satisfied gurgle.

"'Bye for now, sweetie," Maya said softly. "I'll see you at feeding time."

"You'll probably want to give him a bottle for the next several feedings since you're going home today," Cat reminded her.

Maya bit her lip, watching as Cat settled Joey in the incubator. The last thing she wanted to do was leave her baby to the care of the nurses, no matter how competent and caring they were. But she didn't have much choice. Her insurance wasn't going to pay for her to stay any longer since her doctor had said she was fit to leave.

Cat had said she could visit Joey anytime, but it was a poor substitute for having her little boy with her.

"I know how you feel," Cat said sympathetically. "But Dr. Kerrigan says he's doing so well, he'll be out of here real soon. You'll see, the time will fly by."

Maya doubted it but she forced herself to smile at Cat before carefully levering herself out of the rocker. Her insides still felt weak and tender and her back and neck tended to stiffen up when she sat for too long. "I guess I'd better find something to wear besides this hospital gown," she said. Pausing by the incubator, she touched the glass, tears welling in her eyes as she watched her baby sleeping.

"Is someone picking you up?" Cat asked.

"No. Actually I hadn't thought about it." Val had come back yesterday afternoon and brought her some clothes from the suitcases packed in her Jeep, but the Jeep itself was still sitting in a local tow yard, useless. She doubted the doctor would release her knowing she was going to drive herself, anyway. That meant she'd have to impose on Val and Paul and hope they wouldn't mind giving her a ride to her parents' house. And first thing there, she'd have to arrange for a rental if she was going to spend as much time as possible at the hospital with Joey.

"Go ahead and call Val," Cat suggested. "Paul's off shift, he won't mind—oh, there's Sawyer." She waved, drawing Maya's eyes to the nursery window.

Sawyer stood on the other side of the glass, hands in the pockets of his faded jeans, watching her. In a leather jacket and boots and his hair wind-ruffled, he looked nothing like her rescuer of four days past and everything like those dangerous fantasies his voice suggested.

Maya's knees suddenly felt weak and she nearly sat back down in the rocker again. What was he doing here?

"You back again?" Cat asked him, going to the nursery door. She turned to Maya. "He's been here every day since the accident, checking on Joey." Grinning at Sawyer, she gestured to Joey. "He's fine, but his mom's not too happy about going home without him. Since you're here, maybe you could walk Maya back to her room."

"Oh, that's all right, I can…" Feeling her face grow hot, Maya wondered if Sawyer felt as awkward as she did about Cat's suggestion. She couldn't read his expression, but she guessed the last thing he wanted right now was to play nurse-maid to her. Then she realized she'd been staring at him again and quickly averted her gaze, deciding she couldn't do much more to embarrass herself at this particular moment.

"Actually I came to see you," Sawyer said easily. "Paul told me you were going home today, and since you don't have a car, I thought you could use a ride."

"Uh, well, I—" Maya began, but Cat interrupted.

"That's great," she said. "We were just talking about how she was going to get home. Now, problem solved."

Far from it, Maya thought, but not wanting to argue in front of Cat, she turned to caress the glass of Joey's incubator one last time before gathering her hospital-issue robe more firmly around her and walking out of the nursery to face Sawyer. "You don't need to rescue me this time. I'm sure I can find a way home," she said as they started walking back toward her room.

"Save yourself the trouble," he said shortly. "I just got off shift and I'm on my way home. I can easily drop you at your parents' house."

Sawyer told himself this was the last thing he'd do for her. He'd see her safely to her parents' home and that would be it. He was saving Val and Paul a trip to the hospital to get her, so his offer to drive Maya was really nothing more than a favor to friends. Besides, he'd been coming to the hospital anyway to check on Joey. It wasn't as if he was going out of his way.

He caught Maya looking sideways at him as they waited for an elevator and figured he probably looked more than a little tired and out of sorts. It was no wonder she was reluctant to go anywhere with him.

"Look, I'm sorry if I snapped. It's been a long week already and I haven't had my transfusion of caffeine yet this morning." He tried a smile. "Why don't we start over? I'll be glad to give you a ride home as long as we can stop for coffee and bacon and eggs on the way. What?" he said when she grimaced. "Please don't tell me you're one of those health-food freaks who only drinks weed tea and refuses to eat anything that used to breathe."

"Okay, I won't tell you," Maya said, flashing him a smile in return that lit up her eyes and temporarily banished the shadows from her face. The elevator opened and he followed her inside. "But I won't deny you your drug of choice."

"So does that mean we're outta here?"

"Just as soon as I lose this lovely hospital gown and sign whatever stacks of papers they have waiting," Maya said. The elevator shuddered to a stop and he walked her to her door, where she stopped him by touching her fingers to his arm. "One thing, though."

Sawyer looked down at her and decided at this point it didn't much matter what she asked. He'd committed himself to helping her, at least for today. "One thing?"

She nodded. "I'll accept your offer of a ride. But you have to let me do something for you in return."

And before he could ask what that might be, she smiled and ducked inside her room and closed the door.

Chapter Three

"This isn't exactly what I had in mind," Sawyer said nearly two hours later as he followed her, pushing a cart, through the organic-foods market. Instead of the café, she'd managed to talk him into stopping at this new-age excuse for a grocery market, offering him breakfast at her parents' house in exchange for helping her stock the shelves.

He'd agreed only because he figured she needed the supplies and, without a car, she'd have a hard time getting them. And she'd also reluctantly agreed to let him pick up breakfast at the café after shopping.

But watching her, Sawyer was beginning to regret giving in to her. She hadn't bothered with makeup, and in loose-fitting jeans and an oversize gray sweater, her hair loosely pulled back, she looked small and pale and unequal to a half an hour of grocery shopping, let alone the demands of time and strength raising a baby alone would take.

"You shouldn't be on your feet this much," he said. "You just got out of the hospital."

"That's the fifth time you've mentioned that," Maya told him as she reached for a container of yogurt. "Like I said, I'm fine. It's good for me to get up. If I sit too long, I get so stiff I can't move at all. Besides, it won't be too much longer and I'll be getting up all the time with Joey." She added a carton of soy milk, smiling as he winced.

"You weren't kidding about the weeds and sticks. It's a wonder you haven't starved to death."

"It's a wonder you haven't poisoned yourself."

"As far as I'm concerned, that stuff is poison," Sawyer told her. "Give me caffeine and cholesterol any day."

"Mmm...guess that's why you're so cranky."

"Who's cranky?" he grumbled. "I just don't like mornings without espresso." Catching the laughter in her eyes and the smile tugging at the corners of her mouth, he shrugged off her teasing. "Hey, I let you drag me here, didn't I? And this place is enough to make anyone with a healthy caffeine addiction cranky."

Maya laughed outright, remembering the look on his face when one of the clerks had offered him a sample of herbal tea. "*Healthy* and *caffeine* aren't two words you should use in the same sentence."

"If you're trying to convert me, you're wasting your time."

"Sorry," she said. "It's a bad habit I have, always working."

"What? Your job is helping hopeless caffeine addicts?"

"Some days," she said, laughing as she added bananas to the cart. "I practice alternative medicine." When he looked blank, she added, "You know, massage, aromatherapy, herbal remedies, meditation—that sort of thing."

She could see the effort he made to keep from rolling his eyes. "I guess that explains the weeds and sticks."

"That was pretty good," she told him. "Most people at least make a joke."

Maya remembered how embarrassed her ex-fiancé had been

whenever one of his friends or business associates asked what she did for a living. Evan had cringed every time the subject came up and had done his best to change it before she could answer. And when she'd gotten pregnant, he'd blamed her, saying it would never have happened if she'd gotten over her "fetish" about medication and taken the pill.

Her shoulders slumped and Sawyer noticed how she suddenly looked drained. Despite her continually telling him how fine she was, he'd been right and she'd tried to do too much too soon. But it wouldn't do him any good to tell her that again. The woman had a stubborn streak a mile wide.

"Let's get out of here," he said, touching a hand to the small of her back and urging her toward the checkout. "I think I'm crashing after going without coffee this long."

While she waited for the clerk to tally and bag her groceries, he used his cell to call ahead to the café and order breakfast, so it was ready by the time they'd stowed the bags in his truck. Making a quick stop to pick up the food, he easily found the road to her parents' house, and less than fifteen minutes later they were pulling up in the drive.

It was as bad as Sawyer remembered.

The story-and-a-half adobe house looked as if no one had bothered to do anything but live in it for the last fifty years. The peeling paint on the window frames revealed chips of about a half-dozen different colors, several tiles were missing from the roof and a crack in the front window had been mended with duct tape.

He switched off the engine but didn't make any move to get out of the truck. "Are you sure about this?" he asked Maya. "I mean—" He gestured to the house.

"It could be worse," Maya said with a shrug.

"How?" Sawyer wasn't sure he wanted to hear the answer.

She grinned at him. "We haven't been inside yet."

"Can't wait," he muttered as he pushed open his door and went around to offer her a hand out.

She looked up at him as she started to step down, and her foot slipped against the running board. Sawyer instinctively reached out and grasped her shoulders as she stumbled a little. Another step and she would have landed squarely in his arms. A jolt of awareness hit him of how close she was, the warmth of her against his hands, of how she looked at him, as if caught off guard by the same feeling.

In the next moment cold reality doused him. What the hell was he thinking? She'd just gotten out of the hospital after having a baby. He dropped his hands. "Are you okay?"

"Sure, fine—thanks." She didn't look at him as she stepped away from the truck. "Sorry, I'm not usually such a klutz. I guess I haven't gotten used to the sleep deprivation yet."

Sawyer tried to match her casual tone. "Take it from me, you never get used to it. At least I have caffeine to lean on." He glanced at the house. "You still have a key?"

That brought her eyes back to him and she laughed. "What key? Azure and Shem's doors have always been open to anyone the universe brings to their doorstep. Well, ready or not, I guess I'd better go in."

The bricked path leading up to the front door was overgrown with a tangle of wildflowers and vines. Blue paint peeled from the decades-old Spanish-style door that someone had embellished with a large yellow plastic peace sign.

"I don't think I'm ready," Sawyer said under his breath as Maya shoved open the door to a whirl of dust and a foul smell, some evil combination of sandalwood incense and neglect.

"I think they had a party in here before they left," Maya said, wrinkling her nose.

"For all we know, someone did, considering the way they let anyone walk in the place," Sawyer grumbled, fumbling for a light switch in the dim room. Finding one on the wall, he flicked it. Nothing.

"Don't waste your time. They have this habit of forgetting to pay utility bills."

Sawyer banked his growing irritation. He scanned the room for windows. Spying drawn curtains, he stopped Maya from going any farther into the room with a hand on her arm. "Wait here a minute while I let some light in this dungeon."

Maya groaned as morning sun streamed into the room. "Oh, you're going to wish you hadn't done that," she said, stepping carefully inside. "I think I was right about the party."

Empty beer and wine bottles, ashtrays, plastic cups and paper plates were strewn all over the house. All sizes, shapes and colors of pillows lay haphazardly flung about the small living room. Strings of brightly colored beads hung from the blades of the ceiling fan, and the air hung heavy and cold, as if no one had bothered to bring any warmth or light into the house for months.

"You're right, it's worse," Sawyer said flatly. "This place ought to be condemned. How could anyone live here?"

Maya shrugged as she bent to pick up a pink-and-green-striped pillow she almost tripped over. "Well, what do you know? My happy pillow. Azure made this for me when I turned seven," she said, absently hugging the worn pillow. "And she made that blue-and-yellow one over there, stuck between those two candles, when I was nine. Every year she made me a new happy pillow out of fabrics with the lucky colors for the number of my age."

"Nice," was all the response Sawyer could muster.

"Actually this isn't as bad as it's looked after some of their parties. A little elbow grease and a few dozen gallons of disinfectant and the place will sparkle."

Sawyer lifted a doubtful brow. "Sparkle?"

"Okay, so at least it won't stink."

Biting back a curse, Sawyer wondered how she could so casually accept her parents' complete lack of responsibility. He'd had an idea of what it was like for her growing up with parents like the Rainbows, but it hadn't come close to this.

"Maya—"

She turned from frowning over the mess as he strode over to

her. He took her shoulders between his hands. "You can't stay here. And you sure as hell can't bring a baby home to this. Besides the fact it's a man-made disaster area, you don't have electricity and probably no gas or water either."

"There's a well out back," she said steadily, although there were shadows of worry and doubt in her eyes. "And there's a butane tank for cooking. I'll get the electricity turned back on and things cleaned up. We'll be fine."

"Are you telling me you honestly want to bring Joey home to this?"

"Honestly?" Maya lifted her chin. "Of course not. But right now I don't have a choice. We'll make do."

Maya waited for his next argument, but instead he stood for a moment, still holding her, his expression clearly saying he wanted to scoop her up and carry her out of this place, compelled to rescue her once again. And it was tempting right at this minute to throw herself into his arms and let him do it. Since she'd been a kid, she'd been the one taking care of others, fixing their problems. It would be a new experience to let someone take care of her.

Someone with great hands and a killer smile, who could make her warm inside with just a look and who attacked her defenses with his determination to help her.

Tension breathed in the silence between them. From their argument. Had to be. From words, not feelings. Yet she was so close now that one step, the smallest move and she would be ing him and…

don't even go there. How crazy was she for even thinking like that? New single mothers with four-day-old babies and a life to reorganize had fantasies about undisturbed sleep and winning the lottery, definitely not about men who inspired wicked cravings.

Besides, there was no way she could believe that Sawyer Morente, who surely could have his pick of any woman in New Mexico, would ever see her as anything more than just a needy single mother. Even ignoring the fact he'd delivered her son a few days ago, in her baggy clothes, with her hair a mess, with her face colored with bruises and still moving stiffly, she hardly qualified as a temptation.

"Care to share the joke?"

Maya blinked, startled out of her musings. "Joke?"

"You were smiling," Sawyer said. He let his hands slide away from her shoulders. "I figured I was missing something, because there isn't anything remotely funny about this place."

"Give it up. I'm staying. Which means I need my groceries." She made to turn toward the door.

"Hold on a minute." Sawyer raked a hand through his dark hair, trying to quickly come up with a compelling reason for her to get as far away from this dump as possible. "You don't have to stay here. You have a choice. You and Joey can stay with me."

Maya stared at him. A faint pink flushed her pale skin. "You…I don't quite know how to answer that," she said finally.

Sawyer was beginning to feel he really had lost his mind where she was concerned. But it was too late to retrieve it now. "It wasn't a proposition. You'd be on your own most of the time. I'm hardly ever there, ask anyone. Besides, I've got the room and electricity and running water. It's a much better place for Joey than this."

"No retro decor, though, I'll bet." A smile tugged the corner of her mouth. She touched his arm. "Thanks for the offer, but I can't. Joey is my responsibility, not yours. Besides—" her smile broadened into a grin "—what would people think if they found out you were living with the hippie girl?"

"That she had more sense than to raise her son in a place like this," Sawyer snapped back, earning a frown from Maya. He took a breath. "I'm sorry. I know it's not my business and Joey is not my responsibility. I just wanted—" What? He couldn't find any words for what he wanted, because at this moment nothing made any sense anyhow.

"You've already rescued us once," Maya said, her eyes and mouth soft again, as if she knew what he didn't. "Listen, this is only temporary. As soon as I'm working again, I'll find us our own place. Trust me, I had enough of the love shack growing up. I mean, my parents were really good to me in their own way, but I don't want that kind of life for Joey."

Sawyer didn't understand her parents. But he kept quiet, not wanting to bring her frown back.

She seemed to read his thoughts all the same. "They weren't abusive. They're…who they are. They're good people. I have some really happy memories of this place. You just can't count on them for anything. But I always know they love me even if sometimes it seems they forget they have a daughter." She glanced around the room with a rueful smile. "I guess that's hard to understand, looking at this and comparing it to your family."

"There's no comparison," Sawyer said shortly. Avoiding her eyes, he started toward the door. "I'll go and get your groceries. I'm sure you're starving by now."

How could he compare living on his grandfather's estate with Maya's chaotic commune life? he thought as he hefted the bags out of the back and retrieved his own breakfast from the front seat of his truck. Somehow Maya had felt wanted and loved even though her parents had never bothered to marry or give her any stability.

His mother, on the other hand, had been the complete opposite of the Rainbows. She'd been a woman driven by her determination to provide her sons with everything their father would never give them. Teresa Morente could never have been accused of neglecting her sons, at least when it came to material things. But neither she nor his grandparents had ever been warm and nurturing, had ever looked at him or his brother with the soul-deep tenderness and love that he saw in Maya's eyes every time she looked at her son.

Joey would always have that even if he never knew his father. And that would be enough. Because it was obvious, as far as Maya was concerned, it would have to be.

Shouldering his way into the house, he found the living room empty. Sawyer followed the sound of banging and scraping to the kitchen, where he found Maya pushing the litter of cans, bottles and candle stubs off a battered oak table into a garbage bag.

"I think we might be better off eating in the living room," she said, indicating with a helpless wave of her hand the dirty dishes heaped up in every available counter space, along with what looked like dead weeds optimistically planted in clay pots.

Sawyer set the bags down on a square of table she'd managed to uncover. "I think you're right."

They carried breakfast into the living room, shoving pillows aside to share the slightly lumpy couch. Sawyer made short work of his bacon and eggs, and while Maya picked at her yogurt and banana, he moved to take a look at the fireplace. There was a stack of wood piled next to it and matches in a jar on the mantle, but he was unsure about what might be blocking the flue.

"It should be okay," Maya said, answering his silent query. She set her yogurt carton on an end table and drew her feet up, hugging her arms around her knees. "Since we couldn't always count on having gas or electricity, my parents made sure they at least had the fireplace to fall back on."

Sawyer didn't comment but set to work building a fire, and in about fifteen minutes his efforts paid off as the first tentative flames curled up between the chunks of wood.

"Much better," Maya said when he returned to sit next to her. Sighing, she looked at the flickering fire and wished she could be back at the hospital sleeping close by her son.

"You're going to need an army to get this place livable," Sawyer said, interrupting her reverie.

"Hardly. Just a lot of garbage bags."

"Come on, Maya, I can—"

She held up her hands, fending off his next attempt to convince her she needed his help. "Stop trying to fix everything. Just because I'm on my own doesn't mean I can't handle a dirty house. Your mom managed to raise two kids by herself."

"My mother lived with parents who didn't disappear into the

desert on a whim and who had a staff to take care of her kids and clean the refrigerator. It's hardly the same."

"Maybe not, but I'll survive anyway," Maya said firmly. She shifted on the couch, laying her head back. "I've got to do something about my car first. And then, once Joey and I are settled, I need to look for work. Maybe there's something at the hospital."

"Yeah, surely some department there needs an expert in weeds and sticks. Hey, just kidding," he said, fending off the pillow she threw at him.

Maya didn't feel like defending her work to him so she just smiled. "Don't worry, Joey won't starve."

His expression turned from teasing to serious. He hesitated a moment, then said, "Joey is lucky to have you. But it's not going to be easy bringing him up alone."

"I can't change that." Regret, sadness, anger mixed up inside her but she pushed them away. It was too late to cry over what might have been. Any love she'd ever felt for Evan was long dead, and it was very clear he'd never cared enough about her to stick by her when she needed him most.

"Where the hell is Joey's father?" Sawyer blurted out, then immediately held out a hand in apology. "Sorry, I didn't mean to pry that way."

"You have a better way?" Maya gently teased him. "It's okay," she said before he could say anything else. She looked away, plucking at a woolly strand on her sweater, not sure what, if anything, she wanted to tell him. Finally she raised her eyes back to his, deciding it would be better to say something. There would be enough rumors going around as it was.

"We were supposed to get married next month. But that was before he found out I was pregnant. Then he decided he couldn't handle being a husband and father all at once. So he walked out."

She didn't add that Evan at first had accused her of deliberately getting pregnant, then repeated his conviction she was a freak for refusing to take the pill. At one point he'd even questioned whether or not Joey was his. It was then Maya had given up on him, handed him back his ring and later gotten him to legally give up any and all parental rights, which he'd been only too happy to do after insisting he never wanted to see her or her baby again.

She would never regret that decision—Joey didn't need a father who resented him and didn't want him. But she could admit to herself, especially now when her emotions were so close to the surface following Joey's birth, that the idea of raising a child alone was more than a little daunting.

Something of her feelings must have shown in her face because Sawyer reached out and touched her hand. "You'll do fine."

She smiled a little. "I guess he'll survive me, one way or the other." Suddenly a wave of tiredness washed over her, and after a glance around the room she leaned back and closed her eyes. "I do wish, though, I could wave a wand and make this all go away. It's looking like a bigger job all the time."

"Nothing a bulldozer and a pit couldn't handle," he muttered.

"It's better than nothing. And it is home."

How anyone could call this "home" was beyond Sawyer. His irritation at the whole situation rose up again, making him angry with her parents for creating this dump, for bringing Maya up this way to begin with and then taking off when she needed them most.

He had to do something about it. He couldn't let her bring a new baby to this rattrap. Hell, anyone would feel the same way if they took one look at this place. Maybe he should talk to Val and Paul about it, get Val to convince Maya to at least accept help in clearing out this mess.

Sawyer turned to Maya with the idea of trying one more time to get her to see reason. But she'd fallen asleep.

The fire had chased the chill from the room and the warmth had put a slight flush on her cheeks. Her lips slightly parted, her breathing slow and even, she'd curled up, hugging her arms around her knees. Without thinking, Sawyer reached out and gently brushed an errant strand of hair from her face, his fingertips just skimming her skin. The bare touch of her tempted him to linger, to explore the soft curves and planes of her face.

It was a temptation he couldn't afford to indulge, not even for a stolen moment. Drawing back, he laid his head back against the couch, distracting himself from thoughts of touching with ideas for helping her.

It had been a long week and, despite the coffee, he could feel the string of nights with little sleep catching up with him. He closed his eyes and told himself he'd rest for just a minute or two. A minute or two and then he'd head home and get some real sleep.

A pounding in his head jerked Sawyer awake. He instinctively started up thinking it was an alarm, until he realized he wasn't in his bunk at the station but still sitting in the middle of the Rainbow living room, propped in a corner of the couch, with Maya sleeping snuggled against his side, his arm around her.

The feel of her pressed close to him was more disconcerting than being jolted awake. He didn't want to examine the weird combination of uneasiness and intimacy he was feeling, and the banging again, more insistent this time, gave him an excuse to ignore the sensations.

Someone was at the door and, from the sound of it, not going away anytime soon. Moving slowly, Sawyer tried to get up without waking Maya, but she sighed and made a little protesting sound when he eased her away from him and then opened her eyes enough to look at him.

"What—what's the matter?" she said, rubbing at her eyes as she straightened. "Did I fall asleep?"

"We both did, and now someone's trying to knock your door down. Stay here," he said. "I'll get it."

Sawyer almost groaned when he glanced out the window and saw Valerie. She stood on the front porch, three enormous bags at her feet, her hand raised as if she was about to start the pounding again. He seriously considered not answering the door, but with his truck in the driveway advertising he was there, leaving Val on the doorstep would only feed her already overactive imagination.

"The door's not going to be able to stand much more abuse," he said as he opened it to her.

"And hello to you, too. What's the matter, not enough caffeine this morning?" Val studied him for a moment, then glanced at her watch. "Ten minutes. Interesting."

"Not," Sawyer said flatly. "So don't go imagining something that never happened." The last thing Maya needed right now was more gossip about her.

Val laughed as she picked up one of the bags. "Why, Sawyer, I don't need to imagine anything. Your face says it all." And with a wink she walked around him and into the house.

Chapter Four

Hearing Val's voice, Maya scrambled to her feet, her legs still wobbly with sleep, and attempted to straighten her hopelessly wrinkled sweater and smooth her hair, then gave up, figuring she was only making her appearance worse.

A moment later Val came inside, followed by Sawyer carrying three overstuffed grocery bags. Maya avoided looking anywhere near his direction. The scent of him, clean and masculine, lingered on her and she wondered just how close they'd been sleeping. He'd been on his feet by the time she'd fully awakened, but Maya had a vague memory of his solid warmth pressed against her body as she slept. For some reason she felt vaguely guilty, as if she were a teenager caught by her parents making out with her boyfriend. Of course, her parents would have just smiled and told her to carry on. And besides, she and Sawyer hadn't done anything naughty enough to inspire even a raised eyebrow.

And Val knew she'd just had a baby. Surely she wouldn't imagine Maya being up to much more than heavy napping. Although the slightly amused smile on Val's face coupled with Sawyer's obvious discomfort made Maya squirm.

"What's all this?" she asked quickly. "Here, let me help."

"Hands off," Val said. "You don't need to be lifting anything heavy. It's just a few basics to help you set up housekeeping." She stopped and looked around. "*Madre de Dios,* this is worse than I imagined. I don't even want to see the bathroom."

Sawyer shifted the bags in his arms. "Good, I have an ally."

"Val, don't you need to put those down? In the kitchen? And you," Maya said, glaring in his direction, "let's not have this conversation again."

"Sure, not a problem," he said with an infuriating smirk. "But two against one, you're gonna lose."

"If he's talking about the state of this house, he's right," Val said. When Maya started to protest, Val held up a hand. "I'm sorry, I like your parents. I don't understand them, but to each his own. But this is just plain bad." Val planted her palms on her hips. "You're coming home with me."

Sawyer came back from setting down the groceries and stood in the kitchen doorway, leaning against the jamb, with every appearance of enjoying himself.

The smirk was still there but Maya decided to ignore him. Right now she had a well-meaning but misguided friend to contend with. "I know you're only trying to help, but—" She saw the line of her friend's jaw tighten as Val gritted her teeth.

"But nothing. You were just in a serious car accident and you have a newborn baby, a tiny premature baby, to think of. He's fragile, Maya. If you bring him home to this…this dump, who knows what he might catch."

Val almost succeeded in making Maya feel guilty. Almost. "You're exaggerating just a bit, don't you think?" She stepped closer to Val, laid a gentle hand on her arm. "I'm feeling better already. I plan to clean things up before Joey's released from the hospital. It'll be okay, really."

"Feeling better?" Val rolled her eyes. "Right. That's why you were dead asleep on the couch when I got here. I've had three kids honey, I know what you're feeling like right now and *better* isn't on the list."

"See how sensible she's being," Sawyer said, smiling when Maya answered him with a glower.

"I just had a baby," she said. "Of course I'm tired. But it's not terminal. And I'm not working right now, so I have nothing but time to clean up around here."

"Who are you trying to kid?" Val countered. "Let's see." She started counting off on her fingers. "You'll be at the hospital, say, eight, ten hours a day, if I know you. Sleeping and eating will take up another ten. So I'm figuring you ought to have at least an hour, maybe two every day to make this place livable. With that schedule you should be done cleaning up about the time Joey is ready for kindergarten."

Sawyer covered a cough that sounded suspiciously like a laugh.

Maya wasn't amused. Her patience wearing thin, she stubbornly stuck to her defense of her plan to temporarily move Joey here, even though a small part of her agreed with Sawyer and Val. Getting her parents' house into shape was probably going to be a much bigger job than she'd bargained for.

"Look, both of you, I appreciate your concern, I really do. But this is my home—Joey's and my home—for now. I know the pair of you would just as soon see it demolished, but believe it or not, this place has a lot of happy memories for me. And the *junk* has meaning to me. That hideous painting over there, for example," she said, pointing to a large framed painting of splattered colors. "I painted that for Shem when I was in the third grade. When he framed it and hung it on the wall right smack in the middle of the living room, I felt like a real artist. It might not look like much around here, but it's all we have and we *will* make do."

Val glanced at the picture, then at Maya. She shook her head, smiling a little. "You always were stubborn, girl. And you know you have me, too, *mi amiga*."

"And me," Sawyer said before realizing exactly what he was saying. Both women turned to stare at him—Val with speculation, Maya as if she wasn't quite sure what to make of him. What the hell, it was too late to back down now. "I already told you I'll help you get this place in shape for Joey. And I'm sure you can count on Val and Paul, too."

What he really wanted to say was he'd help her out of here as soon as possible and find her a place that didn't reek, wasn't a fire trap and didn't have an open invite to any vermin and vagabonds in the neighborhood.

Like my house he thought and then immediately squashed that idea. *Get a grip, Morente.* He'd had no business suggesting that in the first place and no business even thinking it now. *Man, do I need a good night's sleep.*

"Absolutely," Val said. "We're all here for you 24-7."

"Thank you, I know that." Maya smiled at Val and avoided looking at Sawyer. For some reason she didn't want to consider too closely, his words stung. *I'll help you get this place in shape for Joey.* Of course he wanted to do the decent thing and rescue Joey from what he considered a disaster. Not her, Joey, she thought with a pang.

In the next instant she felt ashamed at herself. How ridiculous was she, feeling disappointed because gorgeous rescue-hero Sawyer Morente was more interested in her days-old baby than in his less-than-stunning mother.

"I'm really grateful for all you're trying to do," she told Val. "But we have to find our own way from the start. Actually it's probably better that Shem and Azure aren't here. They'd only try to tell me how I should be nurturing Joey's spirit and trying to read his aura and chart his stars." She couldn't help but laugh. "Then they'd just mess the place up even worse by throwing me a big congratulations party."

"All the more reason to get out of here before they come back," Sawyer muttered.

"All the more reason you should accept a little help from your friends," Val said. "You and your little boy are going to need all the help and support you can get. It's not going to be easy for either of you."

Maya looked at Sawyer, and for a moment Val wasn't in the room.

Sawyer could hear Val's unspoken message: *Raising a father-less baby is going to be hard—for both of you.*

Still looking at him as if she understood exactly, Maya said, "Joey has me and I'll love him enough for two. He doesn't need a father who doesn't want him."

From the recesses of his memory, Sawyer heard his mother saying the same thing to him. *You don't need a father who doesn't want you.*

He recalled the times, as a boy, he'd gotten into fights because kids at school had teased him about not having a father come to watch him play baseball or because he was clumsy in shop class. He'd never had a father to teach him how to use tools the way the other boys had. His mother had always chided him and reminded him that he didn't need a father who didn't want him.

And all his life he'd told himself the same thing. Until he'd looked into Joey's innocent blue eyes and seen a reflection of himself. Now the idea of that little boy growing up with the same doubts and fears he'd had bothered him more than he cared to admit.

Fighting off a surge of unwelcome emotion, he abruptly turned back into the kitchen and began unloading groceries.

There was a silence and then he heard Val say, "Well, how about this? Why don't you stay with us, just until we get this place into shape? It'll be cozy, but we don't mind if you don't."

"Val, you are not listening to me. I'll have a job soon and Joey and I will move into our own place. Try and understand. "

Val heaved a sigh. "I don't understand, but obviously I can't change your mind right now. But I'm not taking my groceries back, so don't even start with me on that. Speaking of which, I'll give you a hand putting them away."

"I can do that," Sawyer said as they walked into the kitchen. He hoped Val would take the hint and leave. "Why don't you stay and let me make you lunch?" Maya asked, unaware of Sawyer's wish. "It's the least I can do after all this."

"I'd love to but I have to get back home. The girls have ballet class and Paul's taking our little one for his checkup." A feline smile slanted her lips. "But maybe Sawyer is hungry."

The woman didn't know when to quit, Sawyer decided. Fantasizing about a good use for duct tape, Sawyer resisted telling her to give up on her very obvious and misguided attempt at matchmaking. "Actually I'm more tired than hungry. I think I'll take off as soon as I put the last of these away."

"I'll get those," Maya said, reaching for a can. He caught her gaze, her eyes brimming with a combination of sympathy and apology.

"Fine, then I guess I'll head back to my place," he said, inwardly wincing at the brusqueness in his voice, especially when Maya looked a little taken aback.

She followed him to the door, and when he turned to tell her goodbye, she averted her eyes, her face a becoming pink. "Um, thanks for everything," she said quickly. "I really—"

"Appreciate it, I know. Forget it," he said roughly. He looked down at her upturned face, those wide green eyes locked with his, and wondered why he couldn't just walk away and forget about her.

"I should go," he said. Fishing around in his pocket, he pulled out his sunglasses and shoved them on. "Call me if you need or want anything." He opened the door and stepped out, paused and turned back. "You know where to find me."

She smiled at that, soft and full. "And you know where to find me."

His arms laden with a pile of dirty clothes he'd kept throwing in his truck from the station but forgetting to bring home, Sawyer kicked his door shut with his heel. Regina had come this morning, and the place smelled fresh, of lemon oil and floor wax. His housekeeper would ream him for bringing her the heap of sweaty, smoky clothes from work, but he was used to that.

Regina Cortez had been taking care of him and Cort one way or another since they'd moved to the estate. She'd been working for his grandparents for a couple of years before his mother had come to live there with her two young sons and asked Regina to be their part-time babysitter. From the beginning Sawyer and Cort considered Regina family rather than hired help. Even now she fussed over the both of them and had made it her life's work to find them both nice girls to settle down with, since she was firmly convinced both of them were overdue for marriage and family.

Tugging off his boots, Sawyer left them by the door, lest she have another reason to curse him out in Spanish for leaving black scuff marks on *her* shiny beige ceramic tiles.

Sawyer strode to the gleaming kitchen and tugged open the stainless-steel fridge. "Beer, beer or beer?" he muttered to himself, rummaging through shelves largely empty except for the bonanza of imported beers. "Come on, Reggie, didn't you leave me some of your world-famous tamales? Ah, there they are." He pulled a tray from behind a six-pack. "Atta girl, I knew you wouldn't hold that gouge in the coffee table against me forever."

He snapped the beer and drank it while he shoved the tamales in the microwave to warm, then wandered into his living room and snatched up the TV remote. He sat back in his favorite leather chair and propped his legs up on the coffee table. He began channel surfing, not really watching anything. His thoughts weren't here in his gorgeous, custom-decorated hacienda. His thoughts were back at the Rainbow love shack. His thoughts had never left Maya.

Why was she so attached to that run-down excuse for a house? Maybe because it was a home, he mused.

Sawyer looked around him at the beautiful Spanish antiques, Indian rugs, pottery. Most of it, including the rich leathers and upholstery, had been given to him by his mother from the estate house furnishings. His mother had bought the house shortly after Sawyer had joined the Air Force, with plans of finally moving off her parents' estate. But she'd always found a reason not to make the move, and when Sawyer came back to Luna Hermosa, she had insisted he move in to this house. She had offered the house to Cort, but he had flat-out refused to live there. Sawyer hadn't been excited about a house, either, because he thought it was too big and too fussily decorated for his taste. And if his mother hadn't been ill at the time and determined he accept, he would never have agreed to live here.

The house had every amenity money could buy. And yet it was still only a house, a shell. Impersonal. Cold. The house had almost nothing of him in it except his old leather chair—and that he'd had to fight his mother tooth and nail to keep after she'd consigned it to the junk pile.

He smiled, thinking of Maya's grade school painting on the wall. Hardly the Gorman that hung over his fireplace. But it was a part of Maya, like her mother's pillows and heaven knew what other trinkets and odd junk. All of it worthless, except to Maya. He took another swig of his beer, his other hand still impatiently surfing his hundred-plus channels of cable service for something worth watching.

Hell, if that place means so much to her and she won't leave it, then at least it's going to be up to code and safe for her to bring Joey home to.

Sawyer dug his cell phone out of his jeans pocket and punched in his brother's number. "Hey, Cort, you wanted to talk, right?"

"Yeah, but—"

"How about now?" Sawyer suggested. He figured Cort would make the time for a brotherly heart-to-heart, especially since Sawyer hadn't bothered to tell him what their talk would be about.

Half an hour later Sawyer slung a towel around his waist and went to answer the doorbell only to nearly get hit in the face by the door when Cort shoved his way through the entrance. "Come on in," Sawyer said.

"Sorry. I got tired of waiting for you to answer," Cort grumbled. He looked harried and not at all glad to be there.

Sawyer pulled the towel from his waist and dried his chest. "Go grab a beer while I throw on some pants," he said, heading for the bedroom, where he tugged on a fresh pair of black jeans.

"Where's my brew?" Cort yelled from the kitchen.

"I don't stock rotgut beer." Sawyer strode into the kitchen, still bare-chested, and prodded his brother away from the fridge.

"You used to. But that was when we saw each other once in a while."

"Stop bellyaching. Here, I found one." Sawyer handed the bottle to Cort, thinking he must have been working out like a fiend. His younger brother had always had strong arms and broad shoulders and he'd always worked out, but he looked a size larger in the faded black T-shirt and worn jeans.

"So, you finally ready to at least talk about this?"

Sawyer fingered his damp hair back from his face. "Yeah, whatever. But first I need a favor."

Cort set his beer down, leaned back against the counter and crossed his arms over his chest. "I knew it. The invite was a ploy. And I'll wager it's another Sawyer-to-the-rescue stunt, isn't it?"

"It's a worthy cause."

"And does that cause have green eyes and red hair?"

"Actually he doesn't have any hair yet."

"What?"

"Her baby, Joey."

Cort looked unconvinced. "Like I believe that. Saving babies in distress isn't exactly your style. You usually prefer rescuing someone when it requires you to jump out of a plane or climb a mountain through ten feet of snow or— What's that latest rescue group you're heading up now? The mounted saviors, led by Zorro himself? Last I heard, you were riding poor old Diablo through the rapids of the Rio Grande to drag some drunken rafter out of the river."

"Diablo likes adventure," Sawyer said, not bothering to defend himself. Cort didn't exactly spend his time in sheltered safety.

"He told you that, did he?"

"I know my horse."

"Sure you do," Cort said, smirking. "The poor beast doesn't have much chance to avoid potential loss of life and limb with you around. So, anyhow, what's with this baby? I'm guessing this is the kid you delivered the other night."

Sawyer nodded. "He was premature and he needs a safe place to come home to after he's out of the hospital."

"And this is your responsibility because…?"

"Because he's a helpless baby and his mother doesn't have many options right now. Besides," Sawyer said, searching for some reasonable explanation that would cut short Cort's questions, "we went to school together."

"Oh, well, that makes perfect sense then," Cort said. "I'm sure the other dozens of women you went to school with would love to hear about this."

"Will you cut me some slack here?"

Cort took a lazy swig from his bottle. "Okay, okay, so I've heard. Maya Rainbow is back in town, unmarried and unemployed, and she's moved into the love shack. And you're so taken with this baby that you've decided it's your duty to rehab the place for her. I get the picture."

Ignoring the heavy sarcasm in Cort's tone, Sawyer said, "You haven't seen the place lately. It ought to be condemned, but she's determined to live there with Joey. So, will you help me?"

Cort shoved away from the counter to toss his empty bottle in the trash can. "Of course I'll help you. Don't I always?"

"Thanks, I knew you'd see it my way, little brother."

"I'll help," Cort added, "on one condition."

Sawyer's grin faded. "I figured that was too easy. As if I have to ask what this condition of yours is."

"After you're done with this latest rescue mission, we set a date to go see Garrett. I want to get this over with once and for all." Cort hesitated, eyeing Sawyer as if he was trying to gauge his reaction, then said, "I talked to him a couple of days ago."

Sawyer looked at him in disbelief, then shook his head. "Great, good for you. So, what, you're all ready to forgive and forget now?"

"No, but I'm ready to listen. How about you?"

"Listen to what?" Sawyer moved past Cort and went to the refrigerator for another beer, not because he particularly wanted one but because he wanted an excuse to break off the conversation and get his temper under control. Getting mad at Cort wouldn't solve anything, but he was getting tired of Cort's campaign to bring about a family reunion.

"I don't know," Cort said. "And we're never going to know unless we talk to him. If nothing else, maybe we can finally bury it."

"Talking to him isn't going to make *it* any deader for me than *it* already is." But even as he said the words Sawyer knew that they weren't quite true. A small part of him still did want answers, if only to know what had been so wrong that his father despised his oldest sons.

"Will you at least think about it?" Cort asked quietly. "I told him I'd call back in a couple of weeks and let him know."

Sawyer started to refuse outright, but Cort had always been there for him and obviously this was important to his brother for some reason Cort hadn't bothered to reveal yet. "I'll think about it, okay? That's all I can promise."

And as soon as he'd said it, Sawyer began to wish he hadn't agreed to even that much.

Joey's big blue eyes fluttered closed and Maya shifted him in her arms. He'd just finished nursing and now he lay contented against her breast, his little breaths coming in short, even puffs.

Maya pulled her blouse down and shifted her small bundle

to her shoulder. Gently, her hand covering his entire back with each pat, she burped him. His tummy full, he let out a satisfied sigh and drifted into a deep sleep.

The door to the hospital room opened quietly and Dr. Kerrigan stepped in. "Is he finished?" she asked quietly.

"Yes, he's been nursing for the last half hour straight. Here—" Maya moved Joey back to her arms "—touch his belly. It's hard as a rock."

Lia reached over and laid a palm on the rounded pink mound. "Well there's certainly nothing wrong with his appetite. He's gained five ounces already."

"Really? That much? Does that mean I can take him home?"

"Patience, Mom." Lia moved her hand from Joey to lay it on Maya's arm. "He's on a roll here, so let's not interrupt it. You see, there may be latent effects from the trauma of the accident that haven't surfaced yet. I want to keep him under round-the-clock observation a little longer."

"I know, it's better for him." A tear welled in Maya's eye and rolled down her cheek. "I miss him every minute of every hour of every day I'm not with him, but right now I have nothing to offer him to come home to."

"Hey, you have you. That's all he needs." Lia pulled up a chair and sat next to Maya. "What's going on here? This doesn't sound like you. Has something happened?"

"Something *else,* you mean?" Maya tried to laugh. She impatiently swept the tears from her face. "No. It's probably just postpartum depression."

"Maybe. Maybe not. In your case, I think maybe not. Why don't you tell me what's really bothering you?"

Maya's pride warred with her need to release her pain, her fears, the emotions she'd been keeping bottled up, hiding from everyone, herself included. "It wasn't supposed to be this way," she burst out at last.

"Well, no, having a baby in the middle of a storm after a car accident isn't ideal, but you both came out of it basically unscathed," Lia said, smiling a little. "Joey is thriving, and you're recovering from the accident and childbirth faster than just about anyone I've ever seen in similar circumstances."

"I know. We are very lucky. But I wasn't talking about the accident. I was talking about everything else. I was supposed to be married, with a loving husband, a job, a nice, clean home to bring our baby back to."

"Oh, that."

Maya managed a laugh between tears that now flowed freely. "Yeah, that. The reality is Joey has no father, a sad excuse for a home and an unemployed mother who bursts into tears at every opportunity."

Lia laid a gentle hand on Maya's shoulder. "Maya, listen to me. Do you know how many women I see who are bringing their babies back to homes where they wind up abused, neglected, abandoned?"

Maya shook her head. "I can't even think about that."

"Believe me, I don't want to. Especially when there's little or nothing I can do about it. But my point is Joey has more than a lot of kids I see every day," Lia said firmly. "He has a mother who adores him and who knows how to take care of him. He has a mother who will get a job, who will make a home, who will be there for him. That can be enough. If you let it be."

"I hope so," Maya murmured, gazing down at her little boy. She took a deep breath and started to thank Lia, but a slight noise turned them both to the door.

Sawyer stood there, his eyes on her and Joey, and Maya had the sinking feeling he'd just overheard way more than she had ever wanted him to.

Chapter Five

Great, just great, Maya thought as she turned away and hastily rubbed her fingers over her face. Of course, any pitiful attempt to pretend nothing was wrong would be wasted since it was obvious from the way he was looking at her that Sawyer had overheard her crying on Lia Kerrigan's shoulder. She didn't know which bothered her more—him seeing her in tears or that he always had to see her at her worst.

He already thought she needed constant rescuing. Now this probably made him more determined than ever to fix everything in her life.

"Well, you've got company and I've got to finish my rounds. Don't worry," Lia said, patting Maya's shoulder, "I promise this little guy is going home very soon and then you'll have him all to yourself."

As Lia started past Sawyer, she smiled up at him. "Good to see you again, Sawyer."

"Yeah, you, too," he said, his eyes on Maya and Joey.

Lia hesitated, but Sawyer seemed not to notice, and after a moment she moved out into the hallway—disappointed, Maya thought. Her competition was Joey, Maya wanted to tell her, since Joey's mom wasn't likely to figure in any man's fantasies right now.

Sawyer came over to stand close, looking down at her gently rocking Joey as her little boy began drifting off to sleep again. Maya looked up and caught an odd expression on his face, something both soft and fierce, that made her throat tighten and her eyes blur with tears because it echoed her own feelings about her baby.

"Hi," he said quietly. This near to her, Maya could feel the warmth of his body, almost touching hers.

"Hi, yourself. I wasn't expecting to see you here again."

Sawyer shrugged, shifting his focus to Joey. "I wanted to see how the two of you were doing." Almost as if it were an involuntary gesture, he reached out and very gently brushed a finger over Joey's cheek. Joey gave a little gurgling sigh and seemed to look in Sawyer's direction.

Sawyer smiled and Maya blinked, swallowing hard.

"I think he remembers me," Sawyer said.

"Well, you do make a pretty good first impression," she managed around the lump in her throat. "And I think you've been here with him as much as I have."

"Not quite." He went down on one knee, draping an arm over the back of Maya's chair and reaching out to touch Joey's tiny hand. The baby latched onto the end of his finger. "Hey, you've got a pretty good grip for a little guy."

Oh, she was not going to cry again. She'd swear she'd shed more tears since Joey's birth than in her entire life. But why couldn't Joey have had a father like Sawyer? A man strong and protective and sharing her awe at the new life they'd created?

It would be so easy right now, with Sawyer's arm pressed lightly against her shoulders, almost embracing her as he watched Joey, to indulge in a few fantasies of her own. To pretend it was real, that she'd chosen the right lover—

Maya cut off the thought before it bloomed into full-fledged insanity, hoping Sawyer was too absorbed with Joey to notice the flush she felt washing up her face.

"Maya?"

No such luck. She glanced up to find Sawyer looking at her with a slight frown. He started to say something, but Maya, uncomfortable with his closeness, spoke up first.

"Joey's going to be fine. Dr. Kerrigan says he can go home in a couple of days and that'll be wonderful." She cuddled the now sleeping baby a little closer. "Then we can finally get settled in and I'll get a routine established and we'll be just fine." She was rambling and she knew it, trying to pretend everything really was fine.

And Sawyer wasn't buying any of it.

Gently tugging his finger free from Joey's grip, Sawyer moved so he was in front of Maya, forcing her to meet him eye to eye. "How are you doing?" He held up a hand when she started to answer. "I know, you're fine, just fine. Now how are you really doing?"

"Do you ever take no for an answer?" She sighed. "Really, I'm okay. I just need to get used to…everything."

"It's a lot of everything," Sawyer said. He hesitated, searching her face as if he was trying to make up his mind about something. Then he got that determined look and Maya could guess what was coming.

"You're back to the house again," she said. "Can't you just let it go?"

"No. In fact, I've made plans to do some work on it next weekend," he said quickly, not giving her time to interrupt. "Paul and a couple of guys are coming over to help. We should be able to get enough done to make it livable. Don't bother telling me no. Paul and Val agree with me that you can't bring a new baby home to that mess. And I bet I could get Lia to refuse to release Joey if I told her what you were bringing him home to."

"You wouldn't dare."

"Try me."

"I thought we already settled this," Maya said, trying to damp down her annoyance. "I appreciate everything you've done and what you're trying to do for Joey but I told you, more than once, I can take care of him and myself. I'll get the house in order before I bring him home."

"It's ridiculous to tackle that job on your own when there are people willing to help you."

"You mean you're more than willing and you talked Paul and Val and who knows who else into working with you."

Sawyer stood up, pacing to the door and back. Maya could almost touch his frustration with her. "A lot of people heard about your accident and Joey. It's not a crime to accept a little help from friends. Why can't you take it without fighting me every step of the way?"

"Because I can't depend on you or anyone else to rescue me every time something goes wrong!" Maya blurted out. As if sensing her agitation, Joey wriggled a little, and Maya stood up and laid him back in his incubator, tucking his blanket around him before facing Sawyer again. "This isn't the first time I'm going to have to fix things. I'm a single mom now. I've got to be able to rely on myself to solve my problems because there isn't going to be anyone else around to do it for me. I know how you feel about Joey growing up without a father, but I can't change that. Any more than you can change what your dad did to you."

That was the last thing Sawyer wanted to hear. The man that fathered him hadn't ever been and would never be *Dad* to him, and the way he felt about that didn't have anything to do with his wanting to help Maya. "It's not about me," he said tightly. "And it's not about you either. It's about what's best for Joey. And living in that excuse of a house isn't what's best. You know it and I know it."

"I grew up there and I'm still here," she shot back. "It's not that bad."

"It's not that good," he countered. "Just because you survived the commune life doesn't mean that's the way your son ought to live."

"I moved out of the 'commune' as you call it, a long time ago. That's not the way I live now."

She looked as if she wanted to hit him, but Sawyer refused to back down from this. He'd gone too far to stop now even though the small part of him that remained sane kept telling him to quit while he was behind. He ignored it.

"But you're back, aren't you? And still doing the incense-and-weed thing." Sawyer wanted to take back the words as soon as he'd said them. It wasn't what he'd meant. Comparing her to her crazy parents and criticizing her lifestyle wasn't going to win him any concessions from her. "I'm sorry," he said, working to bank his frustration. "I just can't be comfortable with the idea of a baby living in that place the way it is now."

"I told you it was only temporary," Maya said, her voice chilly enough to create frost.

"Even one day would be too long." Sawyer took a deep breath and tried to think of something, anything, to make her see reason. He realized he'd started pacing again and stopped, facing her. "Look, I'm not trying to run your life. I'm just trying to make sure you don't bring a new baby home to a house that ought to be condemned."

"I know that," Maya said more softly. "But—"

"But you want to do everything yourself. Fine. After next weekend, it's all yours."

"Sawyer—"

He headed for the door, not giving her time to start arguing again. "After next weekend, you won't see me again. But I am going to get that house in shape, whether you like it or not."

Maya managed to push her argument with Sawyer to the back of her mind for the next three days, deliberately ignoring the approaching weekend while she tried to make some progress on cleaning up the house in the few hours a day she spent there. When the ringing of the phone jolted her awake the fourth morning, she was almost regretting her determination to do everything herself. Right now, easing herself stiffly off the couch where she'd fallen asleep to dredge up the phone, refusing Sawyer's help was beginning to seem like sheer stupidity.

"I'm sorry to wake you," Valerie said in her ear. "I wanted to call you before I started running today to talk to you about Saturday."

Maya inwardly groaned. "Do you have to? Saturday was Sawyer's idea, not mine. I'm sorry he talked you and Paul into it."

"I'm not," Valerie said. "After seeing that house, I agree with Sawyer that it's going to take a small army to make it livable."

"It's bad, but I can handle it," Maya said with more confidence than she felt.

"Get real, girl, and quit giving Sawyer such a hard time. Take it from me, after a few months of sleep deprivation with Joey, you won't be so quick to turn down help."

Maya sighed. "I know you mean well and I do appreciate what Sawyer is trying to do. But like I told him, I can't get used to depending on him." Even if she could get used to the idea of having a hero with a killer smile waiting on her doorstep whenever she needed him.

She could almost see Val shaking her head. "Oh, I know you're independent and capable and all that. But that doesn't mean you can't accept help from your friends once in a while."

"Sawyer and I aren't exactly friends."

"Mmm…if you say so."

"I do," Maya said firmly. "He's a nice guy—"

"Nice? Please. I think you bumped your head too hard in that accident. My seventy-five-year-old neighbor is nice. I love Paul, but I'd have to be blind not to know Sawyer is a walking fantasy. That wicked smile of his alone is enough to start a fire."

Secretly Maya agreed with her. Not that she'd ever give Val

the satisfaction of admitting it. "Well, Mr. Wicked Smile and I aren't exactly friendly right now. I can't get him to give up his one-man campaign to renovate my parents' house."

"You might as well give up," Val said, laughing. "Nothing stops Sawyer when he's on a crusade, and you seem to be his latest."

"Joey, not me," Maya said.

"Right. If you say so. Of course, nobody believes that but you."

Maya couldn't help thinking about it after she hung up. She hadn't seen or spoken with Sawyer since that day at the hospital, although Cat told her Sawyer had visited Joey a couple of times, always in the evening after Maya had gone.

The more she thought about it, the more uncomfortable she was with the way they'd left things. She thought of calling him and even reached her hand out to the phone only to pull it back. Maybe Val and Sawyer were right and she was taking her fear of depending on anyone too far.

Then again, she'd tried that for the first time with Evan and it turned out to be a big mistake. She couldn't risk leaning on someone again and then suddenly waking up to find him gone when she needed him most.

She didn't doubt Sawyer's good intentions, yet she also didn't kid herself into believing his interest was in her. And she doubted his concern for Joey would last past making sure her son had a safe place to come home to.

Perhaps there was some way she could make him feel better about Joey's homecoming. Maybe if she could see him, talk to him…

She was still doing the wishy-washy thing on her way to the hospital to start the morning with her son when she spotted Sawyer's truck parked in back of the fire station. Impulsively, Maya turned into the lot and pulled her car up beside his.

This is probably a mistake, she thought. But she'd rather risk another confrontation with him than leave things unsettled and unsaid between them.

The moment she saw him, though, unsettled and unsaid seemed like a pretty good option.

The equipment-bay doors were open and Maya saw him standing by one of the ambulances, apparently doing inventory with his partner. He looked up and straight at her when Rico nudged him, and Maya's stomach clenched and her pulse skittered.

Pasting on a smile, Maya forced herself to walk up to him. "Hi. I saw your truck and I thought maybe you'd have a minute to talk."

"Go ahead, take him," Rico said, flashing Maya a grin and ignoring Sawyer's scowl in his direction. "I can count bandages on my own. Besides, you're doing me a favor. Somebody apparently hasn't had enough caffeine for the last three days."

Sawyer turned his focus back to Maya, his expression unreadable. "Yeah, sure. Let's go to my office."

Maya followed him to the small room and he closed the door behind her, then leaned against it, arms crossed. "If you're here to talk me out of this weekend, don't waste your breath."

"I know you—" Maya stopped herself and started over. "Sawyer, I don't want to argue with you again. I just wanted to… Oh, I don't know what I wanted! Why do you have to make things so difficult?"

"Me? I'm just trying to help. You're the one who's too stubborn to accept it."

"*I'm* too stubborn? What do you call your refusal to take no for an answer?"

"Sensible."

"Frustrating is more like it."

"If you want to talk about frustrating…" He straightened, eyeing her up and down.

"Frustrating, stubborn." Maya stepped up to him and poked a finger in his chest. "You're driving me crazy with your—"

Her sentence broke as she suddenly realized they were inches apart and that he was looking at her intently. Something between them shifted, the tension from their building argument subtly changing so Maya became acutely aware of the intimacy of being in the small closed room alone with him, of the way his gaze touched her and his breathing quickened.

He moved closer, the barest distance keeping their bodies from touching. "Yeah," he said, his voice low and rough. "You're driving me crazy, too. Crazy enough to…"

Closing the space between them, Sawyer pulled her up against him and kissed her.

If she'd had any time to think about, Maya would have said she was too aggravated with him, too stunned by his boldness, to respond to him with anything approaching desire. That she hardly knew him and she couldn't want this less than three weeks after having a baby.

She would have been wrong.

Instead of pulling back, she leaned into him and shamelessly invited him to deepen his kiss.

Her response kicked hard at Sawyer's control. He'd already lost his mind where she was concerned anyway, and with her soft body pressed against his, her scent of desert flowers and incense filling his head, he could feel himself sliding fast.

Too fast. The moment he envisioned letting himself fall, he also pictured Paul and Rico and the rest of the crew taking notes on the other side of the door.

And what was he doing anyway, when she, less than a month after having a baby, was hardly ready for this.

As gently as he could, Sawyer drew back. Maya made a little sound of protest and he nearly lost it again. Instead he gritted his teeth and let her go.

She looked at him, at first in bewilderment and then in confusion as she flushed and dropped her eyes. Sawyer didn't know what to say. And he sure as hell didn't know what to feel. "Maya, I—" He stopped. What? "That. . .shouldn't have happened. I'm sorry."

"Thanks for the ego boost," she muttered. Turning a little away from him, she pushed trembling hands through her hair.

Then she looked straight back at him, her face still flushed but her expression determined. "You're right, it shouldn't have happened. But I'm not sorry."

Now he really didn't know what to say. She took advantage of his hesitation to head past him for the door. "I have to get to the hospital to see Joey. We can talk later," she said. She started past him but he stayed put, stopping her escape.

"I don't want to leave it like this."

She shook her head impatiently. "How would you like to leave it?"

Sawyer flexed his hands and deliberately raked her body up and down so she blushed even hotter. "I don't think you want me to answer that."

Finally he stepped back, keeping a hand on the doorknob to stop her from going out. "I lied," he said before swinging the door open. "I'm not sorry either."

She opened her mouth to say something, then apparently changed her mind. He followed her as she walked outside to her car. She opened the driver's door before turning to him. "I guess I'll be seeing you again soon."

"Count on it," he told her.

"I'm beginning to believe you're the one thing I can count on," she said. Not giving him time to reply, she got into the car and drove away, leaving Sawyer standing there, watching until she'd disappeared up the street before he let go the breath he'd been unconsciously holding and went back inside the station, hoping to slip back to his office before anyone noticed.

Paul met him at the door. "So, did you two kiss and make up?"

"No, and none of your business," Sawyer said shortly. He made a U-turn and headed for the kitchen, praying there'd be coffee.

"Come on, fifteen minutes alone in your office," Paul persisted. "The yelling stopped after five. Wait until Val hears—"

The alarm sounding cut him off. They both listened as the dispatcher gave the address of a house fire with two persons trapped.

Sawyer and Paul exchanged a look. "That's Maya's house," Sawyer said.

They both headed to the equipment bay at a run.

Maya rocked Joey, softly humming a lullaby as her baby wriggled and cuddled a little closer to her, almost smiling in his sleep. Sawyer's kiss had stirred up something inside her, but she wasn't ready to admit what it might be. She only knew it made her feel—*he* made her feel—restless and edgy.

Joey seemed to feel it, too, and he squirmed, his face crunching up. Maya quickly soothed him and made herself use a relaxation technique to quiet them both.

As Joey settled back down, her thoughts went straight back to Sawyer.

She couldn't pretend everything was the same between them. She also couldn't pretend she didn't want him to touch her again. And that unsettled her more than anything.

Looking down, she saw Joey sleeping peacefully and she bent to kiss his forehead before putting him back in his crib. She was just finishing tucking his blanket around him when Cat rushed in looking so rattled that Maya knew immediately something was wrong.

"It's your parents' house," Cat blurted out. "It's on fire."

Maya stared. "Fire? But how—" She pawed through her memories trying to recall if she'd done something that could have started a fire.

"I don't know everything, but apparently a couple of boys broke in while you were gone. Somehow they started a fire and one of them got trapped in the loft."

"Is he okay?" Maya asked. "Did they get him out?"

Cat nodded, her face white. "He's okay. But Sawyer's not. The floor apparently gave way when he was getting the kid out. They're bringing him into Emergency now."

Chapter Six

Maya got to the emergency room just as Sawyer was wheeled in. She had a brief glimpse of him strapped to a backboard, apparently unconscious, before he was pushed into one of the treatment rooms. Rico stayed by his side. A few moments later Paul came in, sweaty and smudged with soot.

Spotting Maya, he came over to where she stood. "It's not as bad as it looks," he said, although Maya saw his worried glance toward the treatment room. "Rico says—"

"Hey, Paul."

From his strong resemblance to Sawyer, Maya knew the tall, dark man striding over to them had to be his brother, Cort. Paul introduced them and Cort gave Maya an odd look before turning to Paul. "How's Sawyer?"

"They just took him in. Rico thinks he did some damage to his shoulder and maybe he has a concussion. The fall knocked him out cold. He's been in and out of consciousness for the last half hour."

Cort blew out a breath. "Well, he's survived worse. What happened?"

"A couple of kids broke into Maya's parents' house, apparently looking for a party. They were smoking and somehow started a fire in the front room. The place is such a dump, it didn't take much for it to spread to the loft. Sorry, Maya," Paul said, looking at her. "But—"

She waved off his apology. "How did Sawyer get hurt?"

"Stupid kids were high on something and one of them panicked and ran up to the loft instead of out the front door and got trapped up there. Sawyer got him out, but when they were starting down the stairs, the floor gave out and took Sawyer with it."

Even though she knew it wasn't her fault her parents' house needed serious work, guilt stabbed Maya. Paul had said the kids broke in, but *walked in* was more accurate. Her parents had never bothered with locks, and were used to living with an open door, Maya hadn't even thought about adding one. Maybe if she had, Sawyer wouldn't be here now.

Something must have showed on her face, because Paul touched her shoulder and said, "It's not your fault."

"Yeah, if there's trouble, Sawyer's going to be in the middle of it," Cort added. But he sounded distracted and he didn't look at her but kept watching the treatment room curtain.

Paul turned to Maya and started telling her about the damage to the house when Rico came out. "They're getting ready to take him down to X-ray," he said. "Doc thinks he's got a mild concussion and that his shoulder isn't too bad. It's probably a sprain. He's awake now, although he's not too happy."

Maya let out the breath she'd been holding, a sweet rush of relief washing over her. She barely heard the three men talking about the fire as she drifted a little away from them and sank down in one of the chairs lining the wall.

She supposed she didn't have any real reason to be here. After all, it wasn't as if she and Sawyer were friends exactly. She just hated the idea he'd gotten hurt in her parents' house, especially after all he'd done for her and Joey. That was it—concern, nothing more. In fact, there wasn't any reason for her to stay now that she knew he was okay.

But she didn't move, waiting for the next hour with the rest of them until finally the doctor arrived to confirm what Rico had told them. "He can go home tomorrow as long as it's not alone. He'll need someone to stay with him for a couple of days at least."

"Yeah, like that's gonna happen," Rico muttered after the doctor had left.

"As soon as they let me see him, I'll try and talk him into staying with our grandparents for a while," Cort said. When both Paul and Rico looked at him in disbelief, Cort held up his hands. "Hey, I can try. I better go and call them now so they know what's going on."

"We've gotta get back to the station," Paul told Maya as Cort left to make his call and Rico went to finish filling out the paperwork for Sawyer's treatment at the nurses' station. "Will you be okay?"

Maya nodded. "I'm not the one in the hospital bed this time. I just wanted—" She stopped, then said, "I need to go back up and check on Joey. Then I guess I should take a look at the house."

"I'll give Val a call when I get back. Maybe she can go with you. We'll figure something out," Paul said before he and Rico headed outside.

Left alone, Maya stood there for a few moments before going back upstairs to the nursery. Joey was still sleeping peacefully. She caressed his cheek as she looked down at him, disconcerted to find her hand shaking. Sitting down in the rocker next to Joey's crib, she tried to breathe slowly and deeply.

It was just a relief knowing Sawyer was okay. But she wished she could have seen him so she could know for sure he was all right. All she had now was an image of him lying on that stretcher….

"There you are." Lia came into the room, smiling. "I stopped by earlier to talk to you, but you weren't here. I wanted to tell you Joey can go home Friday. He's really doing well. Two days and he's all yours."

Maya mustered a weak smile. "Um, that's great. Really. I've been looking forward to it."

"You could've fooled me," Lia said, eyeing her critically.

"I'm sorry, it's just been a bad morning," Maya said and quickly told her about the fire and Sawyer.

When Lia left, saying she wanted to check on him, Maya got up to look at her baby again. It was wonderful her little boy could finally leave the hospital and that she could finally have him with her and take care of him herself.

The problem was, where was she going to take Joey home *to?*

Sawyer shifted uncomfortably as the nurse fussed around him, getting him settled in the private room they'd stuck him in. He'd protested about having to stay the night but the doctor had insisted. And since he felt as if he'd been run over twice by a large truck, Sawyer didn't have the energy to argue.

The nurse was just finishing when Cort poked his head into the room. "You're alive," he said, coming in as the nurse left and pulling up a chair next to Sawyer's bed. "You had me worried, big brother."

"I'm indestructible," Sawyer said lightly. "You should know that by now."

"It looks like they're holding you together with tape right now," Cort said, nodding at Sawyer's bandaged right shoulder and the sling immobilizing his arm. "Look, I called the grandparents. They want you to come and stay for a while, until you can use your arm again. Before you start complaining, the doctor said because you decided to land on your head, you needed someone with you for at least a couple of days. Besides, last time I checked, you were right-handed—although, knowing you, now you'll become left-handed just to prove you can."

"There's an idea," Sawyer grumbled. "And I'm not going to complain, I'm just saying no. If I spend more than an hour there,

I'll have a relapse. I'll just take my drugs and go home tomorrow. I'm sure I can manage to feed myself for a couple of weeks."

"Well, you could stay at my place." Cort ignored Sawyer's frown. "But I've been pulling a lot of extra hours lately. That doesn't solve the problem of having someone around."

Sawyer could see Cort was going to keep at this until he talked Sawyer into a babysitter, and right now, with his head splitting and his shoulder hurting every time he breathed, he wasn't up to sparring with his brother.

"Maybe you can get your girlfriend to look after you·for a while."

"My what?" He stared at Cort, wondering if the knock on the head had caused him to start hearing things.

"Maya. She was there when they brought you in," Cort said. "And she looked really worried about you. And since you've probably rounded up everyone you know to work on her house by now, I figured there was something going on between you."

"I told you, I was just helping her out because of the baby."

Cort looked skeptical. "Yeah, that's what you said."

"That's what I meant. We're…friends," Sawyer said, although the word seemed inadequate to explain his confused feelings for Maya and her son. "But that's it. I've already got Paul and Val making up stories about us. Don't you start, too."

Cort reminding him about the house made Sawyer suddenly realize that Maya no longer had a house to worry about. There was no way she could get the fire and water damage repaired in less than a few weeks, let alone a few days. Which meant she was literally on the street now with nowhere to go with Joey.

"I need to talk to her," he said so abruptly that Cort looked taken aback.

"The fire. She doesn't have anywhere to go now and she's supposed to be bringing her baby home in a couple of days."

"And this is your problem." It wasn't a question.

"She and that baby don't have anyone right now. Do you expect me to just ignore that?"

"I don't know." Cort eyed him thoughtfully. "Does this have something to do with that letter?"

Sawyer cursed and shook his head. "No, it has something to with a homeless mother and baby. Could you just do me a favor and tell Maya I need to see her?"

"Sure, I'll do what I can. And I'll work on that babysitting problem for you," Cort said, getting to his feet. "But right now it looks like you need those drugs and about two days' sleep."

Sawyer didn't argue with him, and although he appreciated Cort's concern, for his head's sake, he was glad of the silence after his brother left. Unfortunately he was also left alone with his own thoughts. And thinking of Maya and her predicament didn't improve his headache.

Maya stood in the remains of the living room and tried to tell herself it could have been worse. Not much worse, but at least the house was still standing. For the moment.

The fire had blackened about half the floor and two walls of the living room and destroyed the floor of the loft. Though the firefighters had been able to quickly contain it, what hadn't been burned in the living room was soaked and soot-covered, and the whole house reeked of foul-smelling smoke.

Seeing her seven-year-old happy pillow on the floor, Maya bent and picked it up, tears pricking her eyes. Waterlogged, flattened and streaked with black, it seemed as beyond repair as her life right now.

She had nowhere to bring her baby to now. Practically everything she owned smelled burned or was soaked or charred. Her parents weren't there to make any decisions about the house, and Sawyer was in the hospital. She had no idea what she was going to do next.

On the verge of giving in to a serious bout of self-pity, Maya suddenly stopped herself. She wasn't going to fix anything standing here, clutching a soggy pillow and feeling sorry for herself.

Mentally she started making a list: find somewhere to live,

find her parents, do something about the house. She had no idea if her parents were insured, but she seriously doubted it. She had doubts, too, whether or not the house could be made livable again, but if it could be salvaged, she thought she'd invest in a couple of locks. First, though, she had to find a temporary home.

She was going through the house gathering up her and Joey's things when her cell phone rang. She answered it, not surprised to hear Val's voice.

"Come and stay with us, at least for tonight," Val said after commiserating with her over the fire.

Maya knew Val and Paul would gladly take both her and Joey in. But with two young kids running around and a baby, there wasn't much room in their small house to begin with. "Thanks for the offer, really, but I'm going to find a hotel room tonight and then start looking for something more permanent. Maybe you could point me in the direction of a good rental."

Val argued with her but in the end, when Maya refused to back down, grudgingly agreed to help Maya in house hunting. "Just let us know where you are, okay?"

"Yes, Mom," Maya teased. "I'm heading to the hospital just as soon as I get these suitcases crammed in the car. I'll call you afterward, once I find a room."

"Tell Sawyer we're thinking about him," Val said. "He's in 204 by the way."

"Joey, I'm going to see Joey. In the nursery."

"Give him a kiss for me."

"Joey or Sawyer?" Maya flipped back without thinking and immediately regretted it.

Val laughed. "Both of them."

Tempting, Maya thought two hours later as she pulled into the hospital lot. She figured Sawyer might not be overjoyed to see her. After all, he had sustained his injuries fighting a fire at her parents' house, a house he hated.

Still, after checking on Joey, she made her way to the second floor, determined to see for herself he was okay.

No one answered her light knock on the door, so Maya pushed it open a few inches and peeked in. Sawyer appeared to be sleeping. Maya hesitated a moment, then slipped inside, crossing quietly to his bedside.

He hadn't bothered with—or had refused—a hospital gown, and the blanket was bunched up around his waist as if he'd gotten irritated with it and shoved it aside. She guessed he'd been irritated from the start by the bandaging on his shoulder and the sling on his arm. Even sleeping, slight frown lines creased between his eyes.

Without thinking, Maya reached out and gently smoothed back a lock of dark hair from his forehead.

The light touch brought him instantly awake. For a moment he looked disconcerted to find himself in a hospital bed. Then he focused on her and his expression softened. "Hi, there."

"Hi, yourself," she said. "Is this your way of getting a vacation?"

The light teasing didn't fool Sawyer. She looked pale and tired and she watched him as if she worried he'd break. "Everyone tells me I work too much." He tried to shrug and regretted it. "I've survived worse than this. Although right now I'm questioning whether this thing on my shoulder is meant to cure or kill."

"I don't think I want to know what's worse," she told him, shaking her head. She reached behind her and pulled a chair close, resting her arms on the bedside. "Do you make a habit of falling through floors?"

"I fell out of a plane a lot in the Air Force, but that was on purpose." He smiled a little. "I told you that house should've been condemned."

Guilt flickered in her eyes. Her voice shook slightly as she said, "You didn't have to put yourself in the hospital to prove it."

Sawyer could so easily read her thoughts at that moment that she might have been speaking out loud. For some reason she blamed herself for his accident. But if anyone was to blame, apart from the kids who'd stupidly started the fire, it was her parents for living and raising their daughter in that dump to begin with.

Reaching out, he took one of her hands in his. "Stop trying to take responsibility for this."

"I'm not," Maya began hotly, then stopped and gave him a rueful smile. "Okay, maybe I am, partly. I should have gotten some locks for the place and maybe then none of this would have happened. But I'm so used to the doors being wide-open to anyone, I didn't think about it."

"It doesn't matter," Sawyer said. "It's you I'm worried about."

Maya laughed a little. "Now there's something new."

"Seriously what are you going to do without a house?"

"That's the last thing you need to be worrying about," she said, giving his hand a squeeze before letting go. She stood up and went to the window, looking out at the fading light as if by hiding her expression from him she could also hide her emotions. "I'll figure something out." She turned back to him. "What about you? Surely the doctor isn't going to let you go home alone. You're going to need help."

Sawyer grimaced. "You sound like Cort. I'll figure something out," he echoed her words.

"Meaning you'll do it all yourself."

"Look who's talking," he said with a grin.

She smiled back, and when he beckoned her back over to the bedside, she came easily, sitting next to him again.

"I guess it's a draw," he said.

She shook her head at him. "You never give up, do you?"

"Never. You might as well get used to it."

To his surprise, Maya flushed and suddenly seemed to find the edge of the blanket intensely interesting. "Maybe you could stay with your brother," she said.

"Cort's busy hunting bad guys. And besides, we'd drive each other crazy in less than a day in that cell he calls an apartment. He's trying to push me on the grandparents."

"You don't look exactly thrilled about that idea," she said, looking at him again. "I'm sure they'd be happy to have you. You said yourself they have all kinds of help and that house is huge. I doubt you'd be in their way."

"We've always been in each other's way." Sawyer stopped, not sure he wanted to say anything more despite the questions he saw in Maya's expression. She wouldn't ask but he guessed she was curious.

With a sigh he shifted on the bed, wincing as pain stabbed his shoulder. "My grandparents have never exactly been the warm and nurturing type. They're very—" he searched for the word and finally settled on "—traditional. The Morentes settled here in the 1800s, opened their first restaurant in 1882 and, according to my grandfather, have been nothing but successful since then. Both of them expected Cort and I would go into the family business, and when we didn't, we were criticized for blackening the family name. But after working in the kitchens for several summers when we were kids, neither of us had a burning desire to spend the rest of our lives worrying about the perfect plate presentation."

"What, the proper alignment of parsley doesn't excite you?" Maya teased.

"Want to know what does?" She blushed and he laughed. "We'll keep that one for later. Anyway, apart from my lack of culinary interest, my grandfather isn't impressed by what he calls my 'foolish risk-taking.' According to him, I've wasted my education and most of my life. I'm not interested in spending a week listening to him lecture me again about breaking another bone."

"Another?" She raised a brow. "Do you do this often?"

He grinned at her. "I've had more than my share, I guess. And that means I'm used to taking care of myself."

"Which means you're going home alone tomorrow." Reaching out, she put her hand over his. "Sawyer, that's dangerous."

But as soon as she touched him, Maya knew she was the one in danger. He slowly shifted his hand so his was on top, twining their fingers together and using his thumb to rub light patterns against her skin. "I like living dangerously," he said softly, the hint of an accent more pronounced. "Are you going to tell on me?"

Maya tried to work up some measure of firmness, but it was difficult to do with her focus on the warm, rhythmic slide of his skin against hers. "I should. What if you need something?"

He smiled, slow and easy. "I'll ask for it. What about you?"

"What about me?" she asked.

"Aren't you bringing Joey home in a couple of days?"

"Ah, Joey." *Get it together,* she told herself. How ridiculous was she, with him in bed and her a homeless single mom and all she could think about was the last time they were together and the way he'd kissed her.

"Joey's coming home on Friday," she said. "And before you ask, yes, it's a little overwhelming considering I don't even have the rattrap, as you call it, to bring him home to. I went there this afternoon. It's even more of a mess now, if you can believe that. It'll take weeks to make it livable now."

"Bulldozing and starting over would be quicker," he muttered under his breath but loudly enough that Maya caught the words.

For a few moments neither of them said anything. Sawyer seemed to be distracted by his thoughts, his fingers still making absent patterns over hers, making it hard for Maya to focus on anything else.

"You know," he said finally, "my house isn't a disaster."

She saw where he was headed even before he said it. "Sawyer—"

"Before you say no, at least think about it. We can help each other out. I apparently need a babysitter to make sure my headache doesn't get worse and that I slap ice on my shoulder periodically," he said. "You need a place to stay for a while. I've got a spare room I never use, so you're not forcing me onto the couch. Actually you'd be doing me a favor."

"Right," Maya interrupted. "And you expect me to believe that?"

"Sure," he said, looking straight at her without even a blink of guile. "With you there, I won't have to endure the grandparents and Cort'll get off my case. And you'll have time to find a better place for Joey."

"I don't think you think there's any better place for Joey," Maya muttered. But she stopped herself from making the automatic refusal on her lips. What he proposed started to sound reasonable to her, which was scary.

On the other hand, she could just imagine the reaction from his family and friends if she and Joey moved in with him. Val and Paul and who knew who else already believed something had started between them, and them living together would only give people more to talk about. And then there was the little problem of living in such close proximity to Sawyer. That seemed more impossible than anything. He couldn't even get close without her feeling like a hormonal teenager, and right now that was just wrong.

Still, what other options did she have? She wanted to be with Joey and that would be difficult at best in a hotel room. It could take weeks to find an apartment.

And she could be of help to Sawyer, maybe make amends for him falling through her parents' floor. No matter what he said, he obviously was going to need someone with him for a week or so at least, and she had skills that could help him with the pain and recovery. Maybe it could work…

She looked up from her internal argument with herself to find Sawyer watching her, a triumphant expression in his eyes.

"So what do you say?" he asked, looking smug, as if he already knew the answer. "Are we going to be roommates, you and me and Joey?"

Maya hesitated, then nodded, giving him his victory. "Okay, but only for a while. This is very temporary, just until you're back on your feet and I find a place to live."

"Temporary, right," he said, still smiling. "Got it."

But seeing the satisfaction on his face, Maya wondered if he did.

Chapter Seven

The next afternoon Maya searched the hospital lobby for Cort. They were supposed to meet to take Sawyer home. She caught sight of him standing near the front window, out of the hustle and bustle, watching everything and everyone.

Cort spied her immediately and nodded. She hurried over to him, a little uncomfortable with his attention fixed on her, feeling as if he was sizing her up.

"Everything okay?" Cort asked as she approached him.

"Fine, thanks. I've fed Joey, so he'll be set for a few hours, although I'll probably check on him again before we go."

"Great." He flicked her a smile, not attempting to hide the head-to-toe once-over he gave her. "Don't take this the wrong way, but it's hard to believe you just had a baby. Sawyer was right. You've grown up."

"Thanks, I think," Maya said, not quite sure how to take him.

"It was a compliment. When I first saw you yesterday, I

wouldn't have recognized you if Sawyer hadn't described you so…accurately."

Unabashed, Maya looked directly at him. "I don't even want to think about what he must have told you about me."

"He said that not only had you become a beautiful woman but a strong one, too. You've really been up against it lately, but you're still smiling."

Maya shrugged. "It's either that or jump off a cliff."

"Not much of a choice there," Cort said, laughing, a deep, throaty sound, more subdued than his brother's but every bit as sexy.

"I didn't have any trouble recognizing you either," she told him. "You look enough like Sawyer to be his twin."

"Don't tell him that. He likes to think he's the good-looking one."

"Telling her lies already, I see." Sawyer spoke up behind them. The nurse pushing his wheelchair parked him next to Maya and Cort, and Sawyer immediately stood up, ignoring the nurse's frown. "They wouldn't let me go unless I rode in that thing. Can we get out of here now?"

"You go ahead. I'll be there as soon as I say goodbye to Joey," Maya said and quickly started toward the elevator.

"I'll help you with Joey's stuff," Sawyer said, catching up to her in a few long strides.

"Um…thanks, but—" she nodded at his sling "—I don't think your shoulder is going to let you be much help. Besides, I've already loaded most of it."

"Oh." Sawyer stood a moment, silent. He felt a little embarrassed in front of his brother for rushing to Maya's aid. "Sure. I'll catch up with you out front," he mumbled, turning back to face Cort's smirk. "Shut up."

"I didn't say anything."

"You didn't have to."

They stood side by side watching the sway of Maya's hips as

she walked into the elevator. She was still wearing a loose blouse, but it didn't cover the back of her slim-fitting hip-hugger jeans.

"She's hot," Cort said, eyeing her appreciatively.

"Dammit, Cort, the woman just had a baby. Have some decency."

Cort shrugged. "She's still hot."

"You're hopeless, you know that?"

Cort slapped Sawyer on the back as they walked out into the bright desert sun. "Yeah, and you're deaf, dumb and blind. *Not.*"

Sawyer shoved his sunglasses on his face, covering the "busted" look in his eyes he knew his brother would see in a heartbeat. "Just find the car and get us out of here, will you?"

Maya had brought her own car and so followed Cort and Sawyer to the north end of town, where the homes were located in a gated community and set on expansive lots. They followed a narrow winding drive to another private gate. She waited while Cort pressed a code into a security box, then led her to a parking area in front of Sawyer's sprawling hacienda. One glance at the huge Mexican carved double doors and the elegant desert landscaping and she knew the place was everything she'd imagined…and feared.

Why did she feel so uncertain coming here? She knew she could help Sawyer if he would swallow his pride for half a second and let her. And she felt she owed him something because her parents' lifestyle was part of the reason he needed help in the first place.

But a lonely, sleepless night in a cold motel room had amplified her insecurities about coming into Sawyer Morente's world. It was a place that might as well be a foreign country to her. And she'd never felt more like an illegal alien.

Cort and Sawyer helped her haul her and Joey's things into the house. Cort started to carry her bag, but Sawyer grabbed it first with his good arm.

"I can see I'm no longer needed," he said. He dropped an armful of Joey's things into a bassinet that had been moved into the guest room. "I need to get back to the station anyhow. Got a big drug bust about to break."

Sawyer laid Maya's bag on the luggage rack. "My brother claims I'm the daredevil. But who's the one crashing in on guys with guns and knives who are a whole lot less than happy to see him?"

"At least I have the element of surprise on my side. What's on your side when you hang glide into a canyon with only a back-pack and a smile?"

Sawyer flashed him a cocky grin. "Luck, little bro."

"Yeah. Luck. That's why your shoulder's in a sling."

Despite her guilt over Sawyer's accident, Maya had to laugh, deciding they were good for each other. She was glad Cort was there to buffer her increasing discomfort about being in Sawyer's house. She looked around her lavishly appointed room and felt like a whore in church, not realizing Sawyer saw the disconcerted look on her face and mistook it for disapproval.

"Is everything okay?" he asked. "The room can be changed if you don't like it. Or if you need anything, I'll have it brought in. Regina, my housekeeper, has a bunch of kids. She said she found everything Joey needed."

"Oh, no, it's perfect," Maya said, trying to sound apprecia-tive. "We have more than we could want or need. Thank you. And please thank Regina, too."

"Why am I getting the impression something's wrong?"

Maya glanced at Cort, who was leaning in the doorway, watching them.

"Weren't you leaving?" Sawyer didn't hide the irritated edge in his voice. His shoulder and head were throbbing, and his pa-tience with the whole situation was wearing thin. "You have bad guys to surprise, remember?"

"I'm going already." Cort straightened and nodded to Maya. "Nice to see you again. Good luck." He cocked his head toward Sawyer. "Living with him, you're going to need it."

"Finally," Sawyer muttered.

Maya smiled. "You two seem to understand each other well enough." She turned her back to him, unzipped her suitcase and began pulling clothing out.

"I understand him a lot better than I understand you." Sawyer came up behind her and gently took her by the shoulder with his good hand, coaxing her to face him. "What's the matter? And don't say 'nothing,' it's all there in your face."

She sighed. "Everything is perfect, amazing really. This room, the bassinet, your house… Too perfect, I guess. You know how I grew up. I feel strange here. Out of place." Shaking her head, she gave a rueful little laugh. "I guess I sound pretty silly."

"Not silly at all." Sawyer could have fallen into the depths of her eyes, so full of an almost painful honesty. "Want to know a secret?" he asked, lifting his hand to stroke her cheek with the backs of his knuckles. His touch earned him a smile from her and he smiled back. "Most of the time I feel out of place here, too. It's a long story, but I bought this house from my mother. She intended to move here, but then she got sick and it never happened. The only thing that's really mine is that ratty old leather chair in the living room. As far as the house goes, that chair is pretty much where I live when I'm here, which is not often."

"But the house is fabulous, all of it. You must have liked it enough that you bought it."

Sawyer shrugged, the motion knifing his shoulder. He winced. "It's comfortable enough, I guess. But to me it's just a place to eat and sleep."

"You're in pain." Maya laid her hand on his forearm. "Why don't you rest while I make us something to eat?"

The warmth of her light touch distracted him, and Sawyer found himself studying the smooth curve of her cheek and the way the sunlight painted gold into her coppery hair. "Yeah, food sounds good. I don't have much around here to cook, though. We could order Chinese."

"Mmm…show me the kitchen and I'll see what I can put together first." She slid her hand around his good arm and encouraged him with a smile to lead on.

"I'd offer to help," Sawyer said on the way, "but my idea of cooking is opening a can of chili and beans, wrapping them up in a tortilla and zapping it in the microwave. Regina left some tamales, but they're long gone. Let's see...." He opened the pantry and peered inside. "We have beans, beans and more beans. Oh, and one can of tomatoes."

Maya, inspecting the fridge, bent to look in the vegetable drawer. "Do you have an onion?"

Sawyer turned around in time to see her blue-jeaned backside in an all too tempting pose. He quickly tore his eyes away. After reprimanding Cort only an hour earlier, he was now suddenly hit with all kinds of images of Maya—with and without her jeans— he had no business imagining.

"Other than beer, I have no idea what's in there. Whatever Reggie left."

"Ah, here!" She triumphantly held up an onion like a trophy. "And here's garlic." She bent over again and Sawyer inwardly groaned. "I see a couple of peppers. Perfect. I'll make chili."

Sawyer eyed the vegetables suspiciously. "How can you make chili out of that?"

"Have a little faith," she said with a wink.

Half an hour later the scent of roasted peppers and garlic lured Sawyer from where he sat in his favorite chair halfheartedly sorting through his mail. His stomach churned and growled as he walked into the kitchen. "That smells great."

Maya turned from the stove, a simple grace in her movement. He'd never seen a woman, except for Reggie, at his stove. The few women he'd dated didn't cook, claiming they had better things to do with their time. But the sight of Maya, all curves and femininity, looking so at home in his kitchen, contented even, moved him somewhere deep inside. Seeing her happy and smiling satisfied some primal protective urge he couldn't ever recall feeling before.

She turned, a satisfied curve to her lips. "Even without the meat?" she teased. "Never mind. If you point me to the dishes, I'll set the table."

"I think I can manage at least that."

They ate hungrily, downing the pot of chili and several tortillas in record time.

"My appetite is huge since Joey was born," Maya said with a repentant smile a little while later as she looked at her empty dish. "It's the breast-feeding. I'm ravenous 24-7. Although I admit, sometimes I eat just to stay awake."

Sawyer didn't quite know how to respond. She was so casual about it all. To her, everything about taking care of a baby was all so natural. To him, it seemed a complete mystery, along the same lines as trying to perform brain surgery blindfolded.

"I have to admit," he said, after weighing possible responses and choosing to avoid the subject, "that chili was delicious. For weed-lover's fare, that is."

"You didn't even miss the meat," Maya chided him. "I'll bet I could convert you, given enough time."

"Neither of us is going to live long enough for that," Sawyer told her flatly.

Laughing, she said, "Careful, that sounded like a dare to me." Then she shook her head when he stood up and started reaching for the empty dishes. "Don't worry about these. There aren't many. Why don't you go lie down and rest for a while?"

"You're the one who needs the rest," Sawyer said, but he let her take the dishes from him. He wouldn't admit it to her, but the pain in his shoulder made even a simple thing like clearing the table a big chore. And feeling awkward and useless wasn't helping his headache.

"Did they give you pain meds at the hospital?" Maya asked him as she put the dishes in the dishwasher.

"They gave me a prescription, but I forgot and didn't fill it."

"Well, I am glad to hear that."

"So, what, you want to watch me to suffer?"

"No, I want to help you," she said softly. Leaving the rest of the cleaning up for later, she came up to him and lightly touched his arm. "If you'll let me try."

Sawyer considered what she said and, uncertain of what she meant, his imagination darted in a variety of directions, most of them connected to those sinful fantasies he was trying not to have.

"Help how?" he asked finally, drawing reason to the foreground, ruthlessly burying the other images beneath his weakening good sense. "Don't tell me you're going to make me drink some herbal witches' brew?"

"I can try that, too, but for now I was thinking more along the lines of massage therapy."

"Massage?" Sawyer smiled and she blushed. "That sounds a whole lot better than a pill."

"It helps to relieve tension," Maya said, her cool voice a contrast to her hot cheeks.

"Yeah," he drawled, "I'll bet it does."

"Stop that. Relaxation is a very effective pain remedy."

"So I've heard. But relaxing isn't exactly my specialty."

"I know. Your body language screams tension."

"My body language?"

Maya moved closer to him. "Let me show you," she said, touching her fingertips to his neck and good shoulder. Gently but firmly she pressed her thumbs into pressure points she knew would make him smart.

"Hey," Sawyer yelped, pulling away from her. "That's not relieving pain, that's causing it."

"That's because you're so tense. If you'll just lie down and let me work on the knots in your back a while, you'll feel a lot less pain all over. I'll bring an ice pack for your shoulder, too."

Sawyer imagined having Maya bent over him, her wildflower scent surrounding him, her silky hair falling on his skin, her hands touching his shoulders, his back. Oh, yeah, massage therapy was sounding better all the time. "I suppose I could give it a try," he said, trying to sound casual about the whole thing. "Where do you want me?"

Maya looked him up and down, considering. "Well, if you lie on a bed, I can put pillows under your shoulder so you can lie on your stomach."

"A bed," he echoed the only word he'd heard. "Sure, I can do that. My bedroom is down the hall."

Maya put together an ice pack and followed him down a corridor on the opposite side of the house from where she was sleeping. He moved in long, even strides, his body taut, his muscles hard. Her fingers itched to take on the challenge of rubbing the stress out of them. The thought of massaging him, manipulating his beautiful muscles with her fingers, sent a warm buzz of awareness through her body, nowhere near her hands. Silently she reminded herself this was purely professional, an impersonal massage. *Remember that, Maya, when he takes off his shirt.*

Sawyer led her into a large room that looked as if it doubled as a bedroom and home office. As soon as she stepped into the room, his scent—a musky aroma of soap and old leather—filled her with a heady essence that was definitely all male. She glanced around, surprised to find that, unlike the rest of the house, his room was a mess. Jeans, boots, T-shirts and a leather duster were tossed over chairs and on the floor. Papers, scattered and piled high, cluttered his desk.

Maya couldn't help smiling. "I gather your room is off limits to Regina?"

"You got it," he said without a hint of apology.

"For the first time since coming here I feel at home," Maya said with a laugh.

His gaze lingered on her, suggesting all sorts of things that had nothing to do with therapeutic massage. "At home in my bedroom. Interesting."

Realizing too late she'd set herself up for that one, Maya rolled her eyes. "You know that's not what I meant. Now take off your shirt, please."

He cocked an eyebrow at her and Maya knew her face had to be flaming by now. She was digging herself in deeper and Sawyer obviously wasn't about to help her out.

"Anything you want." Awkwardly he began unbuttoning his denim shirt.

Watching him, Maya decided this might not have been one of her brighter ideas. She took a deep breath and walked over to him. "Here, let me do that."

"I could get used to this," he murmured as her fingers moved the buttons aside one by one.

"I haven't done anything yet," she said as she helped him ease the sling away long enough to slide the shirt off. As she helped him readjust his sling, her body brushed against his bare chest and his breath hitched. For an instant they both stood still, gazes locked.

"Didn't you say this was supposed to *relieve* tension?" Sawyer muttered.

"I, um, haven't gotten to that part yet." Inwardly she groaned at how breathless she sounded. *Professional, remember this is strictly business.* But it was hard to remember business with him this close, looking like *that.* She'd already seen how built his arms were, but his back, stomach and chest were just as magnificent—cut, buff, gorgeous.

Snatching her eyes from him, Maya moved to his bed and grabbed a pillow. "Mind if I rearrange this?"

"Be my guest. You can't make it any worse."

Maya fluffed a couple of pillows to cradle his shoulder, set the ice pack on them and motioned him to lie down. As he complied, she asked, "Do you have any lotion?"

Sawyer shifted and looked back over his shoulder. "Not in my bathroom, but in the guest bath next door there's probably some."

"Okay. Stay put. I'll be right back."

"I'll be waiting," Sawyer said, his voice deliberately low and suggestive. He angled himself to see her walk out of the room— watching the sway of her hips was becoming an expected pleasure. A low hum of hot expectancy gathered in his loins. "Don't go there," he admonished himself. Maya wasn't anywhere near even thinking about sex yet.

And he had no business thinking about it either. The situation they'd found themselves in was purely out of mutual need and convenience. This massage would simply be an unexpected bonus. Nothing more.

Right. Nothing more. He was going to try to believe that.

Moments later Maya returned with the lotion. She moved next to the bed and poured some lotion onto her hands, rubbing them together to warm it. "This is nice. Sandalwood. One of my favorites." Her palms comfortably warm, gently she laid them on his back. "Now close your eyes and think good thoughts," she said, her voice soft and soothing as she began searching with expert fingers to find and release the knots of tension.

"Good thoughts," Sawyer repeated. Nice, relaxing thoughts. Not thoughts of her skilled fingers working their way down his back and then lower. This could be either pure heaven or pure hell. Because right now she was torturing him by creating an odd combination of sensations: a warm easing of painful stiffness and a growing ache between his thighs.

Maya bent closer, her silken hair brushing the small of his back. She rolled the heels of her palms in a mesmerizing pattern there, stopping to press harder where his muscles bunched tightly. "How does this feel?"

"Um, great." It was partly true. Where she was touching him felt great. Where she wasn't was another story. "Where'd you learn all this stuff?"

"I went to school. I'm a certified masseuse."

"You must have graduated at the top of your class," he murmured. Had her voice shifted from soothing to sexy? Or was he hearing what he wanted to hear?

Maya laughed, low and easy. "Actually I did."

The breath from her soft laughter brushed his skin. If she kept this up, he'd have to sprain the other shoulder to keep from reaching for her.

"In case you're interested, I'm a certified acupuncturist, too." She punctuated her words with a deep pummeling motion down his spine.

"Not interested. No one's going to stick pins in me like some voodoo doll."

"They're needles and you hardly even feel them." She slowed her hands, rubbing inch by inch from the base of his back upward to where his dark hair curled in soft waves at his nape. Sliding her fingers into the heavy mass to massage his scalp, she tried to ignore the feel of it trailing over her hands.

He moaned in pleasure. "That's amazing. My head has been killing me since I woke up in the hospital. But now my headache is nearly gone."

"Wait until you see what the needles can do for you," she teased.

"There's nothing you could do that would convince me to try that," he said, his voice low and graveled, relaxed.

"Nothing?" She slowly slid her fingers down his spine and back up again.   "Nothing." He paused. "Just out of curiosity, what did you have in mind?"

"Ah, so you're not as confident as you pretend," she said, working her hands down his back again to just inside the edge of his jeans. She smiled with satisfaction as she felt the stiffness ease in his body, tight muscles releasing. Reluctantly she took her hands away from his bare skin and leaned back. She'd been enjoying this way too much, and that wasn't supposed to happen. She was a professional and she'd just had a baby. As a new mother, sex wasn't supposed to even cross her mind for another three weeks. As a professional giving therapy, sex wasn't supposed to cross her mind at all.

Sawyer rolled to his side to look at her. "You're a miracle worker."

"Well, I just hope it helped," she said and quickly got to her feet before she embarrassed herself.

Levering himself up, Sawyer swung himself off the bed. "I'd

like to return the favor, but at the moment I'm a little short-handed." He glanced at his immobilized shoulder and arm. "So to speak."

Maya found her eyes wandering over him and hastily looked away, taking a step back. "Knowing you feel better is all the thanks I need."

"What about needing something besides thanks?" With a single motion he used his good arm to pull her against him. "I can't touch you the way you touched me, but I can do this."

Before she could tell herself being held this close to him was a bad idea, Sawyer kissed her soundly, parting her lips with his tongue, refusing to take no for an answer. It took Maya all of a heartbeat to quit thinking and return his kiss. His lips seared hers, hot and tender at the same time. She felt that in a single kiss he'd branded her, spoiling her for the taste of any other man.

She felt herself falling into him, but in the next moment he caught her and drew back, breaking the spell. Sawyer put a safe distance between them, running an unsteady hand through his hair. "Maya, you need to leave now, for both our sakes."

Maya's throat went tight. "I—" What? She could hardly say she didn't want him, didn't like the way he touched and kissed her. "I didn't expect to feel…this," she said at last.

Sawyer looked at her, lingering desire mixed with confusion in his eyes, as if he'd just been hit with something that didn't make any sense to him. With a touch of disbelief in his voice he said, "Neither did I."

Chapter Eight

Maya pushed the up button on the elevator for the third time, wondering if the darned thing was stuck.

"You're gonna break it if you keep punching it like that," Sawyer said, laughing at her when she glared at him.

"I knew you should have stayed at home," she grumbled. She'd suggested that several times, sure he shouldn't be up and around just two days after taking that fall. But Sawyer had insisted on coming with her to the hospital to get Joey and finally bring him home. And Maya, impatient to get to her baby, had given up trying to stop him.

It felt a little strange having him here, almost in the role of Joey's father. Yet it felt right, too, because he'd been there for Joey from the start and he so obviously shared her happiness in being able to bring Joey home.

"Want to take the stairs?" Sawyer asked when she hit the elevator button again. "I don't mind the hike to the fifth floor if you don't."

"Don't tempt me. Finally!" The elevator door slid open and Maya, with Joey's diaper bag on her shoulder and car seat under her arm, maneuvered inside, Sawyer following to stand beside her.

"Just a few more minutes and then he's all yours." His right shoulder still in a sling, he took her hand in his left hand, squeezing lightly. "Excited?"

Maya nodded, swallowing hard. "And scared. I mean, what do I know about being a mother? My parents weren't exactly the best role models. I could really screw this up."

"Your parents did the one most important thing really well, though," Sawyer said as the elevator stopped at the fifth floor and the door opened. When Maya glanced up at him questioningly as they stepped out, he smiled. "They loved you. And you love Joey. I figure the rest of it is just learn as you go."

Maya looked at him a moment before raising up on tiptoe to brush a kiss over his cheek. "You know, Sawyer Morente, sometimes you're pretty amazing."

"Does that mean I get another massage?"

"Maybe…" Memories of yesterday sent a warm rush through her, and Maya cursed her telltale fair skin. "If you're good."

"Sweetheart, I'm always good," he said, flashing her that wicked grin. "Come on, let's go get your baby."

Cat was in the nursery, finishing changing Joey's diaper, and she smiled when she saw Maya and Sawyer come in. "I'll bet you're ready to take this little guy home," she said. "I'm going to miss him, though. He's such a sweetie. You'll have to bring him back for a visit."

"I will," Maya said, bending over to give her son a kiss and caress. "But not soon. Nothing personal, but I've had my share of hospitals for a while."

Setting down her load, she dug in the diaper bag for the clothes she'd brought for Joey and started getting him dressed as Cat turned to Sawyer.

"Paul told me about you falling through the floor at Maya's parents' house. You're supposed to be home resting," she said.

"That's what I told him," Maya agreed, bent over Joey.

"Resting is overrated." Sawyer moved to stand by Maya, watching her and Joey with an intent expression. "I had better things to do."

Maya glanced up and their eyes met, and Maya, knowing he understood her jumble of crazy, happy, mixed-up feelings exactly, felt a rush of emotion that twisted her heart and made her throat tight.

Sawyer reached out and gently touched her face, brushing away the tear that slid down her cheek. "It'll be fine, trust me. You're already a great mom. Joey's a lucky kid."

"He certainly is." Maya and Sawyer both turned as Lia came into the room smiling. "And he's a lucky boy that's ready to go home. I checked him this morning and he's doing great. So, Mom, he's all yours. Cat's got some paperwork for you and then, unless you have any questions, I won't be seeing you again for a couple of weeks. You, on the other hand, I shouldn't be seeing at all right now." She looked pointedly at Sawyer. "Aren't you supposed to be—"

"Resting, yeah, so everyone keeps telling me," Sawyer said, still looking at Maya and Joey. "I don't do resting real well."

Maya smiled a little and went back to finishing dressing Joey. "He'll rest once we get home, I'll make sure of it," she said before thinking how revealing her words were.

She wanted to kick herself when she glanced at Lia and Cat and saw their expressions. Lia was taken aback and Cat was smiling broadly. Expecting Sawyer to be annoyed by her practically broadcasting that they were living together, she was surprised to see his satisfied smile. She doubted anyone now would believe theirs was only an arrangement of convenience and nothing more.

To cover the awkward moment, she finished with Joey, asked Cat for the paperwork and began scribbling in answers as quickly as she could. Sawyer stood by Joey's crib until she finished, Joey's hand wrapped around his index finger, her little boy gazing up at the big man, making little gurgles of contentment.

Seeing them together eased some of Maya's uncertainty about whether or not she was doing the right thing by bringing Joey home to Sawyer's house. The feeling stayed with her during the trip back and even after she'd settled on the couch to feed Joey.

Sawyer tactfully found something to do elsewhere in the house when she started, coming back a little while later when Joey was close to finishing.

"It's okay," Maya told him when he hesitated in the archway. She'd draped a light receiving blanket over her shoulder, shielding herself from view. She smiled down at her son, lightly caressing his cheek. "He's getting to be quite an eater."

"He's a growing boy," Sawyer said, settling in his favorite chair. He winced as pain stabbed his shoulder, reminding him that he probably should have taken everyone's advice and taken it slow for a day or two. "Don't say it," he said when Maya gave him that look and opened her mouth. "I'm being punished enough."

In more ways than one, Sawyer thought, as she turned her focus back to Joey, her face softening into a loving expression that hit him hard in the vicinity of his heart. He tried to remember if all the new mothers he'd seen had been as beautiful as she looked with her whole face alight with the pleasure of finally having her son with her. But the only face he saw was hers.

"Maybe you and Joey should take a nap together," she said, and Sawyer realized he'd been daydreaming. Joey had finished, and she'd rebuttoned her shirt and was looking at him with an amused smile.

"I don't think that crib is big enough for the both of us," Sawyer returned lightly as she gently patted Joey's back. He resisted the temptation to offer to take a nap with *her.*

Maya looked at him, and for a moment he had the uncomfortable feeling she was reading his thoughts. Then she came over to him and surprised him by asking, "Would you like to hold him? I don't think you've had the chance, except for when you delivered him."

Not trusting himself to speak, Sawyer nodded, and with a soft smile Maya laid Joey in the cradle of his left arm. Joey looked up at him, seemingly trying to focus on Sawyer's face, his tiny hands flailing gently.

Sawyer didn't know what he'd expected to feel, but he wasn't prepared for the rush of emotion that tightened his throat and filled him with a sense of awe.

"It's amazing, isn't it?" Maya said quietly.

"I don't understand how anyone could just walk away from this," Sawyer said, echoing Maya's words about her ex-boyfriend the night Joey was born but thinking of his own father. Maybe Cort was right—maybe he did need to talk to Jed Garrett, if for no other reason than to make Garrett tell him what other thing could have possibly had the power to make him completely despise a gift like this.

Sawyer couldn't imagine any stronger bond, and if Joey were his son, he knew there wouldn't be anything on earth powerful enough to ever hurt Joey or make Sawyer turn his back on him.

Even though he had no right to feel this way, he knew it was going to be damned hard when Maya moved out to step aside and pretend that not being a part of Joey's life was okay with him. Damned hard.

"I'm glad we came," Maya said, and when he looked up at her, she sat on the arm of his chair and leaned a little toward him and Joey, her hand resting on his good shoulder.

"Me, too." Sawyer looked back at Joey, now sleeping peacefully. "I think we're all going to be just fine."

Three days later Maya was starting to question whether anything would ever be fine again.

She'd been warned that babies consumed every waking moment—and a good many of the sleeping ones, as well—and the sensible part of her had been ready for it. But in the back of her mind, a tiny part of her had stubbornly refused to believe that such a little person could require that much intensive care.

That tiny part quickly learned otherwise after three nights of interrupted sleep and trying to settle into a routine with Joey while at the same time worrying endlessly about whether or not she was doing the right things for her baby.

And although she appreciated having a comfortable, clean place for Joey, it was hard to remember that with Sawyer prowling the house like a caged tiger looking for an opportunity to escape. He growled like a tiger, too, obviously unused to going for more than an hour without something to keep him occupied.

Maya, despite her promise to help him out, didn't have the time or the energy to keep him entertained. She'd nearly kissed Cort this morning when he'd come by earlier to drag Sawyer out for coffee, saying he figured Maya needed a break from his brother's grumbling. She couldn't get used to this feeling of being overwhelmed by her new responsibilities taking care of Joey, her determination to help Sawyer recuperate and her worries about finding a job. She also needed to find a permanent place to live and care for Joey. The last two worried her most of all. She'd just brought her little boy home and now she was forced to think about leaving him again.

Sitting at the kitchen table with a cup of herbal tea and Joey's baby monitor the fourth morning, having just put Joey down for his midmorning nap, she began to wonder if she'd ever get it right.

The doorbell rang and Maya sighed. It was probably Paul or another of Sawyer's buddies who, obviously not used to him playing host to a month-old baby, dropped by at odd times to see how he was recuperating. She started up to answer it when Regina, carrying two loaded canvas shopping bags, pushed into the kitchen.

"*Buenos dias.* I just let myself in. No, sit, sit," Regina said. "I can do this. I know how it is with a little one. You should sit whenever you have the chance. I brought you some enchiladas, but no meat, I remembered."

"Thank you," Maya said, returning Regina's smile. "I'm going to get fat with all your wonderful cooking. But you don't have to come by every day. I promise I won't let Sawyer starve."

"Sawyer, I don't worry about. Ever since he was a little boy, he's been good at taking care of himself, even with all the trouble he gets into. But you—" Regina clicked her tongue as she surveyed Maya. "You need someone to look after you. It's too much, everything you're trying to do all by yourself."

Part of Maya—the very tired, worried part—wanted to agree. The stronger, sensible part, though, wouldn't allow her to wallow in self-pity and cry on Regina's shoulders. Besides, even though Regina had been a godsend, coming nearly every day to clean up, bringing enough food to feed a large family and offering to care for Joey if Maya needed to shop or start job hunting, Maya knew she had an ulterior motive.

From the very start it had been obvious that Regina thought having Maya and Joey here was just what Sawyer needed. More than once both Maya and Sawyer had been put into an uncomfortable spot with Regina's obvious attempts at matchmaking.

"Oh, I'll get used to it," she said, getting up to make Regina a cup of tea. "It's just going to take me a little time to learn how to do everything at once."

Regina laughed, settling herself in a chair opposite Maya. "When you figure that out, you teach it to me. Sawyer is the only person I know who has ever been able to do everything well."

"I remember that about him from school." While she had never been involved in anything at school beyond her regular classes, Sawyer had, as Val had put it, been Mr. Captain of Everything and had graduated the top of his class. "Was he always like that?" she asked Regina.

"Mmm…yes. That father of his, *ay,* such a terrible man." The older woman looked thoughtful as she sipped her tea. "I think Sawyer always felt like he had to prove he was good enough by being good at everything. And he still does that, no?"

Maya nodded, thinking of Joey. Would her own son be like that, feeling he wasn't good enough to have the love of a father, always trying to prove himself to someone who never wanted him? And what about Sawyer? Was he still trying to prove himself? Tears pricked her eyes and she hastily took a sip of tea to hide them from Regina.

Regina, though, looked at her knowingly. Before she could say anything, they heard the rumble of masculine voices outside and then Sawyer and Cort were coming in the door. When the pair of them came into the kitchen, Regina got up to hug Cort and Maya pasted on a smile for Sawyer. "Did you get enough coffee?" she teased him, knowing her attempts at making it had been less than successful.

To her surprise, he didn't respond in kind. "Yeah, for a couple of hours." From the tense set of his jaw and shoulders, Maya guessed either the coffee had been worse than hers or he and Cort had argued. "How about you? Did you get any rest?"

"Oh, we've just been talking about you," Regina said. She winked at Maya and then started gathering up her empty bags. "And now I'm going so you can get some real rest."

"I'll walk out with you. I need to get going myself," Cort said. He glanced at Sawyer. "Talk to you soon."

"Yeah, I'll count on that."

Maya said her own goodbyes and then let Sawyer walk his brother and Regina to the door while she went to check on Joey. When she finished assuring herself her baby was still sleeping soundly, she went back to the living room to find Sawyer there staring moodily out the window.

"Joey okay?" he asked, turning to her.

She nodded. "He's still sleeping. How about you?"

"Great, just great."

"Really." She walked up to him and lightly massaged the juncture between his shoulder and neck. He winced and she shook her head. "Oh, yeah, relaxed and loose as usual. Is your headache back?"

"You mean the one that never went away?"

"That's the one. Come on," she said, beckoning him to the couch. "You sit. I'll be right back." She left him slouching in a corner of the couch, looking disgruntled, and came back a few minutes later with a cup of tea and a small bottle. "Here," she said, handing him the steaming cup. "Drink it."

He sniffed at it, took a sip and then made a face. "It smells foul and tastes worse. What is it?"

"Mouse dung and turpentine," Maya said with a straight expression, then laughed when he looked at her in alarm. "Chamomile and honey, mostly. It'll help your headache, I promise."

"What, it tastes so bad I forget the headache, is that it?" he grumbled. "Couldn't I just have some good old-fashioned pain pills?

"This is better for you." She waited until he'd finished gulping the rest down in a few swallows before sprinkling a few drops of oil from the bottle on her hands and rubbing them together until the warmed woodsy scent surrounded them both. "This will help, too. Just try and relax, although I know that word isn't one of your favorites." She began to massage the tight muscles at the back of his neck, moving in slow, easy circles.

Sawyer tried as her hands worked their magic. Although he didn't put much stock in her voodoo cures, he had to admit the combination of the soothing smell and her rhythmic massage did begin to ease some of the tight stiffness making his head hurt more than usual.

"So what kind of stories has Reggie been telling you?" asked Sawyer after a few minutes, more to distract himself from how good she was making him feel than because he really wanted to know.

"Oh, the usual." Her breath brushed his ear as she leaned in a little closer, slipping her hand under his collar to start on his shoulder muscles. "You know, about how wonderful you are and how every woman in Luna Hermosa would like to be where I am right now. Although I suppose you've probably dated half of them already."

Sawyer turned his head in time to see her blush at his amused grin. "You think so?"

"Well, I just supposed, I mean, you're…I mean, you've done everything and you're—"

"Don't stop, this is just getting interesting."

She shot him a glare. "I could hurt you, you know."

"Who'd have thought you were that kind of girl."

"Who'd have thought you had such a talent for driving people crazy," Maya said and focused rather intently on the spot on his shoulder she was massaging.

"Just for the record," he said, still smiling, "I haven't. And the ones I have, it wasn't for that long."

"Mmm…" She sounded as if she didn't believe him. "And why's that?"

He shrugged, then cursed under his breath because he'd forgotten again how much it still hurt. "I'm not good at relationships. You get attached, you make a mistake, you don't get everything right and then someone walks out on you."

Sawyer didn't add that he'd long ago gotten tired of trying to live down his hero image. With all the women he'd known, he'd felt as if he had to live up to some standard he'd never be able to meet. But Maya was different. She was the one woman he'd met who'd made it clear that though she might reluctantly accept help in a desperate moment, she was determined to make it on her own. Her independence was one of the traits that made her more intriguing to him than any woman he'd ever known.

That, and the way she could drive him crazy with the slow rhythm of her hands.

"What about you?" Sawyer asked. "I'll bet you had your share of admirers along the way."

Sawyer felt her tense and he could sense her frowning even though he couldn't see her face.

"I wouldn't exactly call them 'admirers.'" She hesitated before letting out a breath and saying, "You know how my parents are. In school, boys thought I was part of their free-love movement. So I didn't date much. Of course, that worried my parents.

They thought I was missing out on an important life experience, as they put it. So they tried to help."

"Help how?" Sawyer asked, not sure he wanted to know.

Maya's hands slid off his shoulders. With a sigh she leaned back, and when he shifted to look at her, she made a little sound somewhere between laughter and pain.

"It's funny now, I guess. They thought I was unhappy because I'd never had a steady boyfriend. No *experience*. They had this friend, a young guy, early twenties, good-looking and really sweet, and I was seventeen and had hardly been kissed." She glanced at him as if she was trying to decide whether or not he really wanted to hear all this.

Sawyer took her hand and gave it an encouraging squeeze, hoping it was the right thing and that telling her story was what she needed.

"Well, it was a unique graduation present," she said with a small smile. "Although at the time I figured free love was seriously overrated."

When he didn't say anything—not sure what he could say—she squeezed his hand in return before pulling hers free and leaning her head back against the couch. "That's probably why I ended up with Joey's father later. He seemed so responsible. Nothing messy or free-spirited about him. I think I was looking for an antidote to my parents' lifestyle. And you see how well that worked out," she ended with a twisted smile.

"He's not worth wasting any more time or emotion on," Sawyer said. He didn't realize he'd clenched his hand into a fist until he felt the muscles in his neck and shoulder tighten again. "Trust me."

"Who are we talking about here?" Maya asked. She straightened, studying him for a moment before asking, "Did something happen while you were out with Cort today?"

Sawyer almost lied and told her no. He didn't really want to rehash his weeks-long argument with Cort that had started with that damned letter.

But on the other hand, she of all people might understand why he kept refusing to meet with Garrett.

"It's our father," he said shortly. "He wants a reunion."

Maya stared. "A reunion? How did he find you?"

"He didn't have to find us," Sawyer said, not bothering to hide the bitterness welling up inside him. "He's been here all along. My father is Jed Garrett. He owns Rancho Pintada, that big cattle ranch about fifteen miles south of here."

"Then Josh and Rafe Garrett are your brothers. Josh came to a few of my parents' parties when we were both still in school." Maya didn't know Josh well and she wouldn't have recognized his brother Rafe if she ran into him. But she'd never guessed there was any connection between them and Sawyer.

"We have the same father, if that's what you mean," Sawyer said. "But that's as close to calling them my 'brothers' as I get."

Letting that go for the moment, Maya asked, "Why does your father want to see you and Cort now, after all these years?"

"Hell if I know. Cort figures it's because he's sick and wants to clear his conscience. I have no idea and I don't care."

"Maybe Cort is right," Maya offered tentatively. "Maybe he does regret abandoning you both."

Sawyer shook his head and got up from the couch with a jerk. He paced to the window, staring outside. "That was probably the best thing he ever did."

Maya stared at him, confused. "But, I thought—"

"I lived with Garrett until I was seven. It was obvious, even to a kid, he never wanted a family. He adopted Rafe after Rafe's parents were killed in a car crash, but I think that's only because he figured he was getting a ranch hand he didn't have to pay." He didn't look at her, and Maya could tell every word was painful for him. There were echoes here, underneath his anger and bitterness, and she began, with a growing sense of dread, to understand.

"You remember me telling you I've broken my fair share of bones?" Sawyer went on, his voice hard and brittle. "The first time I was five. Garrett pushed me down the stairs because I didn't lock the barn door one night. I'd closed it but forgotten to turn the padlock. He spent a lot of time telling me how I'd never measure up at anything and then beating it into me that he still expected me to try."

Maya started to feel sick. "I don't understand how anyone could…" She wiped at the tears on her cheeks, thinking of Joey.

"Garrett drank and he never wanted us. I guess that was reason enough for him."

"But why did your mother stay with him so long when he was hurting her children like that? Didn't she ever try to stop him?"

"My mother…sometimes I think she would have preferred dying to admitting she'd made a mistake," Sawyer said. "It's pretty obvious she never told anyone, or the court would never have approved Rafe's adoption. In the beginning maybe she convinced herself Garrett was telling the truth when he said I was accident-prone. Hell, I don't know what she believed. Later she tried to keep us apart but…"

"When he finally kicked us out, I believed my mother when she said it was because Garrett's only love was his ranch." Now that he'd started, Sawyer seemed unable to stop. "But then Garrett started over. New family, new son, apparently gave up the bottle. And for a long time I believed it was my fault he never wanted us."

"Oh, Sawyer, how could it have been?" Maya said. She desperately wanted to go to him. But something about the way he held himself—stiffly, as if moving would break him—held her back. "You and Cort were just boys."

"He never touched Cort. I made sure of it," Sawyer said fiercely. "And now he wants to see us. But it's a little too late for regrets, don't you think?"

Maya struggled for the right words to say. Before she could say anything, Sawyer twisted back to face her so abruptly, she started. "How would you feel if twenty-six years from now Joey's father suddenly wanted back in his life? Would you be willing to just forgive and forget and pretend he'd never walked out on the both of you when you needed him most?"

"I…I don't know."

"Don't you? Well, I do. I know that it's too late for him to pretend he gives a damn. And unlike Cort, I don't want to hear his reasons for handing out abuse and then acting like we didn't exist all those years."

Maya desperately wanted to say something comforting, something that would ease the ache and the bitterness in him. But she didn't have any therapy to treat a heart wound.

And what he'd said about Joey troubled her. How would she feel if one day Evan decided he wanted to meet his son? And even if Evan never reappeared, what was it going to be like for Joey growing up like Sawyer and realizing that his father never wanted him? How could she ever tell Joey that? She couldn't. But what would she tell him when inevitably he asked?

"It doesn't matter what you tell him," Sawyer said, and she looked up at him, uncomfortable that he had read her thoughts so easily and stricken at the harshness in him, at how deeply Jed Garrett had cut him. "He'll wonder, and one day, even if you don't tell him, he'll figure it out. I can't understand how anyone could do that to a kid and I sure as hell don't think if I were you I could ever forgive him."

Right now, seeing Sawyer like this, Maya didn't think she could either. Knowing he was hurting and imagining Joey standing there, years from now, feeling the same things, roused a fierce determination in her to protect them both from ever being hurt again.

She wished with everything in her it could be that way, that she could do just that. And her heart hurt to know that it would never happen.

Chapter Nine

Maya walked back and forth across the bedroom for what seemed like the hundredth time. Joey lay against her shoulder, and she gently rubbed his back, humming softly to him as she tried to soothe him into sleep. It wasn't working, but then nothing had worked in the last hour. Joey had awakened just after midnight, content after feeding and changing until she'd tried to put him back in his crib. Then he'd gone from content to fussy in seconds.

Usually she could cope and usually she could find ways to lull him back to sleep. Right now, though, it seemed as if the mental and physical exhaustion caught up to her all at once and she felt like sitting down and fussing with him.

She was seriously considering it when the door pushed open and Sawyer, his hair ruffled and wearing only a low-slung pair of sleep pants, looked in. Seeing her standing in the middle of the floor with Joey, he came over to them. "Sounds like somebody doesn't want to go back to bed."

Maya didn't want to admit she couldn't quiet one small boy

without help, although it was difficult to appear competent at two in the morning in an oversized Winnie the Pooh T-shirt with bags under her eyes. "Oh, he's just in one of his moods," she said. "I'm sure he'll settle down soon. I'm sorry he woke you."

"It's okay, I've been missing those middle-of-the-night alarms. Here—" sitting down in the rocking chair, he beckoned with his good arm "—let me try for a while."

"Sawyer, you don't need to—"

"I want to. Come on, you look like you could use a break."

She couldn't deny that, even if she did feel guilty about letting Sawyer take over for her. Of course, it was only for a few minutes, not a lifetime, she told herself as she laid Joey in the cradle of his arm.

Joey, his face scrunched up, squirmed until Sawyer murmured, "Hey, guy." Blinking up at him, Joey stopped wriggling, seemingly caught off guard to find himself in somebody besides Maya's arms.

"The power of surprise. Works every time," Sawyer said, flashing Maya a grin.

"We'll see how long it lasts," Maya muttered. She sat down on the bed, curling up against the pillows as she watched Sawyer begin to rock Joey.

"You know, my mom told me I didn't like sleeping either," he said to the baby as Joey waved and kicked.

"Now there's a surprise," Maya said, but Sawyer ignored her and continued his conversation with Joey.

"Regina used to tell me a story when I wouldn't go to bed. Do you want to hear it?" Joey made a gurgling sound that Sawyer evidently took to mean yes. "Good, I think you'll like it."

Switching to Spanish, he started talking to Joey while continuing his slow, easy rocking. Her Spanish passable at best, Maya only caught about half the words, but it didn't matter. She'd thought that first night, when Sawyer delivered Joey, that his voice was the perfect distraction to any troubles. And now, listening to him, she decided she'd been right. Lulled by the low, gentle cadence and the almost lyrical-sounding words, she let herself sink a little further into the pillows.

The room suddenly seemed warmer with Sawyer in it, a sanctuary lit by the dim glow of the single lamp, wrapped around the edges in a comforting darkness. After a little while Sawyer's voice trailed off, and Maya could see that Joey, snuggled securely against Sawyer's chest, had fallen asleep.

Maya got up and carefully lifted up the sleeping baby and gently laid him in his crib and tucked his blanket around him. Sawyer moved to stand beside her, and they both stood looking down on Joey for a moment before very quietly leaving the room.

"Thank you," Maya said once they were in the hallway. "That's another thing you seem to do well." Jealousy stabbed at her at how easily he'd been able to soothe Joey when she couldn't. What a joke—she who made a living helping others relax couldn't get one tiny baby to fall asleep, yet the man who couldn't sit still for five minutes did it effortlessly.

"I told you, it was the power of surprise," he said. Slipping his hand under her chin, he tipped her face up so she had to look at him. "You're doing a great job with Joey. Everybody needs a little help sometimes, especially when they're only getting two hours' sleep every night."

"Everybody but you," she grumbled. "This was supposed to be a mutual favor, Joey and I living here. But it's you who's helping, not the other way around."

"That's not true. You've been a big help. And think of all the worry you've saved me. If you and Joey weren't here, I'd have had to wonder night and day how you were. Besides," he said and flashed her his killer smile, "right now I've got my own live-in masseuse. What else could a guy want?"

"Am I supposed to answer that? Never mind," she said hastily when it looked as if he was about to tell her. "You should go back to bed."

"And you shouldn't?" His hand lingered, lightly tracing along her neck, making warm patterns and turning what was left of her brain to mush.

"I should and I will. Just as soon as I get, um, something chocolate. From the kitchen."

"Chocolate sounds good," he said, making it sound positively wicked in that deep, exotic voice. "Let's go." Before she could protest, he took her hand and led her through the darkened house to the kitchen.

He didn't bother to turn on any lights there, just opened the freezer and used the small light inside to find what he was looking for. "Double-chocolate brownie," he said, holding up an ice cream carton. "You do like ice cream, don't you? I don't think it has any animal parts in it." He suddenly eyed her suspiciously. "When you said chocolate, you meant the real thing, didn't you? You weren't talking about some kind of weird healthy chocolate substitute, were you?"

Maya set Joey's monitor on the table while he rummaged in the cupboards for bowls and spoons, then she went to help scoop. "No weird substitutes tonight, I promise. And I love ice cream. I usually have the soy version, but once in a while I treat myself to the real thing."

"They make ice cream out of soybeans? That should be illegal."

Laughing at his affronted expression, Maya finished filling the bowls. "You know, I would never have guessed double-chocolate brownie was one of your vices."

"I never would have guessed we'd actually agree on a vice." Sawyer gestured her to the table, and setting the generous bowlful in front of her, he used a long wand lighter to one-handedly light two of the table candles before sitting down opposite her with his own portion. "Are you sure you aren't going to have an allergic reaction to all this sugar and caffeine?"

"Mmm…maybe. But right now sugar and caffeine are sounding pretty good," Maya said. "Of course, after all this I'm going to need a three-hour workout."

Sawyer answered her with a long, appraising look that slid over her body and brought the cursed blush to her face. She concentrated on her ice cream, all the while very aware he watched her.

Slowly Maya felt her frustration over her inability to get Joey to sleep ease. Sitting here with Sawyer in the darkened room, the flicker of candlelight casting a golden haze against the shadows, it felt as if they'd shut out reality for a few stolen minutes. And it was so like Sawyer, arousing every nerve in her body while at the same time making her feel as if she never wanted to leave the warm, intimate place he'd created with candlelight and ice cream.

When she slowly licked the last of her ice cream from her spoon, he abruptly got up and dumped his bowl in the sink. Standing at the counter with his back to her, Maya could see the tense set of his shoulders. She brought over her empty dish. "Thanks," she said lightly. "That's the first time I've ever had ice cream by candlelight. And thanks, too, for helping with Joey. He really likes you."

She expected a smile but he faced her with an intent expression. "How about Joey's mom?" he asked, a dangerous softness in his voice. "What does she like?"

Maya's pulse jumped a notch. "She likes you, too."

"Oh, yeah?"

"Oh, yeah," Maya whispered, and not waiting for him to make the decision, she went up on tiptoe and kissed him.

He responded instantly, sliding his free arm around her and pulling her against him while from one heartbeat to the next their kiss went from tender to hot.

Maya slid her hands up his chest, exploring smooth skin over hard muscle. An electric excitement surged through her when he groaned and pulled her even closer. She shamelessly pressed herself against him, forgetting he was half-dressed and she shouldn't be tempting either of them like this. All that mattered was the decadent, sinful way he made her feel, as no other man had and right now, with him touching her, kissing her, she felt sure no man ever would again.

From the urgency in his touch and kiss she was certain he felt the same. Until her hip brushed against the hard ridge of his arousal and he let her go so suddenly, she swayed and almost stumbled. Breathing hard, Sawyer took a few jerky steps away from her so he stood by the table, gripping the back of a chair so tightly, Maya wondered if he might break it.

"You're not ready for this," he rasped.

Maya wanted to argue with him. Even more humiliating, she wanted to beg him not to stop. Except she knew he was right. Still, she couldn't stop the rush of disappointment that he'd been able to stop so easily when even now her whole body felt sensitized and she felt restless, unsettled, aching for something only he could give.

"That wasn't easy for you either, was it?"

"Stop that," she told him. "How do you do that, read my thoughts?"

"They're right here." He stepped close again, slowly tracing a finger down her cheek.

She caught her breath. "Sawyer…"

He muttered a curse and dropped his hand as if he'd been burned. "You're sure making it hard for me to be the good guy."

"Oh, yeah, I'm really seductive here—a cranky, sleep-deprived new mom in a Pooh shirt. I dressed especially for you, knowing what a turn-on cartoon characters are."

"So—" Sawyer raised his hand again to follow the line of her collar "—you think you know what turns me on?"

Danger signs flashed in Maya's brain but she ignored them. "I have a few ideas."

"Any you care to share?"

"Maybe," she said, at the same time thinking maybe it wasn't such a great idea to be giving herself visions of what they could be doing. "But like you said, not now."

"I said that? What kind of idiot am I? Maya—" He stopped, then reached for her and brought them close again. "Damn it, you're killing me here," he said against her mouth and then kissed her again, hard, fast and hot, before letting her go. "You're making me crazy, and if I don't walk away now, we're both going to regret it."

Before she could respond, he turned and stalked out of the kitchen. Alone, Maya slowly sank down into a chair. What was she doing, so soon after her debacle with Evan, when she'd promised herself she'd never get that close to a man again?

Sawyer said they'd both have regrets. And she did, only he wasn't one of hers.

"Hold on, little guy. Just let me get your weight here."

Sawyer watched as Lia bent over Joey, who squirmed and started to scrunch up his face. Not that Sawyer could blame him. How could anyone like being dumped on a slab of cold metal and told to sit still? Maya hovered nearby, looking as if she'd love to snatch up her son and walk straight out of the pediatrician's office. And if Lia didn't finish up soon, Sawyer swore he'd beat her to it.

Sawyer had been surprised when she'd agreed to him coming along with her as she took Joey for his checkup. Since two nights ago, when he'd nearly forgotten she'd given birth only a month ago, she'd been skittish, not quite looking him in the eye and finding excuses to avoid spending time alone with him.

When he'd offered to come with her to Joey's appointment, saying he had a few errands he needed to run in town, as well, he'd expected her to give him a list of reasons why not. Instead, after hesitating briefly, she'd agreed, although she still wouldn't quite meet his eye and she deliberately avoided any conversation that remotely resembled something personal.

Sawyer wondered if she was regretting kissing him. It sure didn't feel like it that night, when she'd been as eager for it to go further and just as frustrated as he'd been when it couldn't.

But in two weeks neither of them would have that handy excuse for stopping. And then what? Would she be as willing then? Or would her determination never to depend on a man again for anything stop her from getting too intimate?

Sawyer guessed the attraction between them probably scared her. He knew it scared the hell out of him. As he'd told her, he wasn't good at relationships. But at the same time he didn't want her to walk out of his life.

He couldn't deny he liked having her and Joey around, even though he knew getting more attached to Joey wasn't a good idea. Secretly, though, he was pleased Joey was responding so well to him. Joey needed a father who cared and wanted him in his life, Sawyer knew that better than anyone. And more often, the thought crept into his mind that he could fill that role better than most. On one level the idea made him uncomfortable—he had no real ties to Joey, and Maya was determined to run out on him the first chance she got.

Besides, what did he know about being a father? It wasn't as if he had a good example from either of his parents. He didn't know the first thing about long-term commitments and the warm, fuzzy family thing.

But deeper, in a place he didn't want to explore too closely, he recognized the strengthening bond between him and the little boy he'd delivered, a tie that wasn't going to be easy to break even now.

"...do you think, Sawyer?" Lia was saying to him, snapping him out of his thoughts.

"Uh, sorry, I missed it. What was the question?"

"I was telling Maya that Dr. Gonzales recently started a holistic wellness clinic here and she could use an assistant. Maya would be perfect for the job, don't you think?"

Sawyer knew what he wanted to say and that was no, she needed to be with her son. But he didn't want to get into an argument in front of Lia. So instead he gritted his teeth and said, "I'm sure she would be."

Maya raised a brow at him and Sawyer figured she knew he was less than pleased. She confirmed it a half hour later when they were waiting for the elevator outside Lia's office.

"So what do you really think—about the job, I mean?" she asked.

"Great," Sawyer said, keeping his eyes fixed on the changing floor numbers. "Just great. Really. I'm sure Dr. Gonzales will appreciate your skills with weeds and that stuff you do with the incense and candles."

"You forgot the needles," she said, and he could hear the smile in her voice even though he didn't turn to look at her.

"Those, too. Of course, you're going to have to leave Joey with someone during the day and it'll most likely have to be a stranger. And let me tell you, working a full schedule on two hours' sleep isn't easy. After a while it starts to mess with your head, believe me."

The elevator door opened and Sawyer followed Maya inside, all the while trying to come up with an argument that she'd find reasonable.

"Don't say it," Maya told him as soon as the elevator doors closed behind them. "I know it's not going to be easy, but you know I don't have a better choice. Unless you think living with my parents once they get back is better. And before you start, I can't keep living at your house either."

The elevator opened and when they walked out, Maya put her hand on his arm, stopping him. "Please, let's not get into a fight about this. Not now."

"I don't want to fight either," Sawyer said. "I just—"

"I know. But it's a beautiful day, Joey's doing well and Lia said it would be fine if I took him to the park for a little while. It's only a few blocks' walk from here, and I brought Joey's stroller." Her hand slipped down his arm and she put her hand in his. "So will you come with us? Please?"

With her hand warmly in his and her gazing so hopefully at him with those beautiful green eyes, Sawyer didn't think he could have told her no even if he'd wanted to. And he didn't want to.

"I guess we can always fight later," he said with a smile.

Her whole face lit up as she smiled back. "You're on. Just remember, I hate losing."

"That's supposed to be my line."

Sawyer relieved her of the diaper bag and they went back to the car to get the stroller and, after settling Joey in, started down the sidewalk to the park.

They were nearly there when a man in faded jeans and a black cowboy hat abruptly pushed out the door of the pharmacy and almost collided with Joey's carriage.

"Sorry," the man said, looking first at Maya with an apologetic smile, "I wasn't paying attention and—" He abruptly stopped when he shifted his focus to Sawyer, and the smile went to a scowl in an instant. "And here I was thinking this day couldn't get much worse."

"Don't start with me," Sawyer said through gritted teeth. He stepped closer to Maya and put a protective hand at the small of her back, ready to nudge her forward. "Now if you'll get out of our way, I'll leave you to your misery."

The man smiled, but it was a cold gesture, completely without humor, that never reached his eyes. "You never had any manners, Morente. Aren't you going to introduce us—brother?"

Maya looked between the two men, not quite sure how or if she should respond but certain of one thing: Sawyer very obviously would rather eat nails than continue a conversation with the other man.

She'd never seen Sawyer look so hard and it unsettled her. He stood tensely at her side, his hand on her back flexing as if he wanted nothing better than to take his best shot, arm in a sling or not.

And from the look of the other man, the feeling was mutual.

But—brother? This couldn't be Josh Garrett, because Josh was blond and nothing like this man whose Native American heritage was obvious. Easily as tall as Sawyer, he looked as if he'd been carved out of earth and rock, his raven hair tied back in a short tail. She supposed it must be Rafe Garrett. Hadn't Sawyer said Rafe had been adopted?

"I hadn't heard about the wife and kid," the man said, not bothering to wait for Sawyer's reply. He swept Maya in a glance.

"The old man will be glad. It'll fit right in with his plan for his happy family reunion." He nearly spit out the word *happy* as if it were poison.

"He better have a plan B," Sawyer said tightly, not bothering to correct the other man's impression that Maya was his wife. "Because I'll be damned if I'm going to sit down with you and him and pretend nothing ever happened."

"Well, there's something we finally agree on, because I'm not interested in getting cozy with you either."

"Then maybe you can get the message across to your *father*. Tell him he's about twenty-five years too late." Sawyer took a breath, as if he was trying to get his emotions under control. He sounded almost regretful, the edge of his anger blunted, when he added, "Too late for both of us. Brother." Not bothering to wait for an answer, Sawyer urged Maya forward and away from the other man.

"Who was that?" Maya asked as soon as they were out of earshot. "You called each other 'brother' but you acted like you're each other's worst enemy."

"We were brothers once, for about a year," Sawyer said shortly. "But now I'm a Morente and he's still a Garrett. We don't get along. And we never will."

"That much I got," Maya said, hoping to encourage him into saying more.

"We'll take that walk another day," he said flatly. As they reached the car, he didn't say a word while Maya settled Joey in the back and they both got into the front for the ride back to Sawyer's house.

Maya pulled away from the curb and Sawyer said abruptly, "That was Rafe."

"I guessed it might be." Maya kept her eyes on the road, frowning. "You said your—Garrett—adopted him after Rafe's parents were killed."

"Rafe was six. His father was Garrett's partner, and when he and his wife were killed by a drunk driver, Garrett and my mother adopted Rafe. And before you ask," Sawyer said, not looking at her but staring straight ahead, his free hand gripping the dashboard hard enough to leave a mark, "Rafe and I are the same age."

Which meant that Garrett had adopted Rafe before he'd abandoned Sawyer and Cort. Maya began to get an idea of why Sawyer resented Rafe. Jed had chosen Rafe, another man's son, over his own two sons and had apparently treated him better than his blood sons.

And Maya could imagine what it must have been like for Sawyer after he found out his father remarried and had yet another son, seeing Rafe and Josh at school and in town and believing that Garrett thought his new son and even someone else's son were more worthy of loving than his first two sons.

Although she'd been uncertain before over the issue of whether or not Sawyer should answer his father's request to meet, Maya's dislike of Jed Garrett was rapidly becoming full-blown loathing.

"I'm sorry," she said, aware of how inadequate that sounded. But she didn't know any remedies for a lifelong wound that had never healed. "I can only guess how hard it must be for you to see him."

"Yeah, well…" Sawyer rubbed at his temple. Maya could feel the tension radiating from him and she wanted to get him home so she could do something to ease it. "Cort says I'm being unreasonable because it's hardly Rafe's fault his parents were killed and Garrett kept him. And maybe I am. Part of me knows how he feels, because my mother left him behind when Garrett kicked us out. I didn't understand why she did it because by then I'd started thinking of him as my brother…."

A spasm crossed his face, as if the thought hurt him. In the next moment he shook it off. "But Rafe's got a chip on his shoulder the size of the Pecos Mountains and he's never made it easy to remember that he didn't choose to be Garrett's son."

Maya stayed silent as she turned into Sawyer's driveway. She felt close to tears thinking of how many lives Jed Garrett had marred. Mixed up with that was fear for her own son—who one day would have to settle with his own father's abandonment and who would ask questions she had no answers to—and hurt for Sawyer, who still hadn't found a way to reconcile with it.

"Maya?"

She turned to find Sawyer watching her and realized she'd probably been parked in the driveway for several moments lost in thought. "Sorry, I got sidetracked for a minute." Not giving him time to question her, she gathered up Joey's stuff and went around to the passenger door to lift out his car seat and carry him inside.

She'd hoped for a few more minutes to talk with Sawyer alone. But Joey started waking up from the nap he'd taken in the car and by the time she'd gotten him inside, he was howling for his lunch.

An hour later Sawyer came into the living room, where Maya, finished with feeding and changing her son, had Joey in her lap and was showing him a brightly colored stuffed-elephant rattle.

Sawyer sat down next to her on the couch and watched them for a few moments. "I think he's doubled in size in the last few weeks," he said, reaching out to touch Joey's tiny fist. Joey latched onto his fingertip, kicking and waving his hands, and Sawyer smiled.

"Well, there's nothing wrong with his appetite. Or his lungs. I don't think he's going to be shy about speaking his mind."

"Good for him."

Maya hesitated, then, moved by the shadows in his eyes and the tension she could still see in his neck and shoulders, asked, "Are you okay?"

"Why wouldn't I be?" he answered, keeping his eyes on Joey. A muscle twitched along his jawline.

"I just thought after running into Rafe today and everything..."

His expression hardened. "I don't need a counseling session. It's over. Let's just forget about it."

Maya knew a warning sign when she saw one, so she gave up and went back to playing with Joey. But no matter how determined Sawyer was to push the Garretts out of his life and mind, she knew it was far from over.

Chapter Ten

Maya couldn't wait to tell Sawyer she'd gotten a great job.

Sancia Gonzales had been impressed by her credentials and said Maya was just what she'd been looking for in an assistant at the wellness clinic. She was an internist, a friend of Lia's, who had also begun to use alternative-medicine approaches to pain management. But her practice and surgery schedule were so packed that she needed another person qualified to administer acupuncture, massage, aromatherapy, herbal medicines and other alternative therapies. It was exactly what Maya had been looking for.

Maya felt even better about taking the job because Dr. Gonzales was five months pregnant and needed the help all the more.

But most of all Maya was relieved she wouldn't have to impose on Sawyer much longer. She and Joey had practically taken over his house. She'd never realized how much space one little baby could take up or how much noise he could generate. Sawyer had been extraordinarily patient—and other things she couldn't even begin to let herself think about. Still, it had been a temporary arrangement from the beginning. They both knew that.

At least, that's what they'd both agreed to. She remembered Sawyer's reaction the day Lia had told her about the possible job at the clinic. To say he was less than enthusiastic was generous. They hadn't actually argued about it—yet—but doubts about what he would say now that she had the job dampened her eagerness to tell him.

"Guess what?" she said, deliberately keeping her tone light and teasing as she tapped at his bedroom door, then crossed over to where Sawyer sat working. He looked up, his solemn face and furrowed brows not exactly welcoming. "I got the job!" She found herself mentally holding her breath, and when he didn't say anything right away, she added, "Isn't it great? Now I can start looking for a place of my own."

His frown deepened. "I guess. If that's what you want to do."

Her doubts solidified into full-grown concerns. He was not going to take this well. "It's what I need to do."

"I just don't see what the big rush is," Sawyer said. He turned back to his desk as he shuffled papers. "It's not as though I'm going to throw you out on the street tomorrow. Don't women usually get maternity leave for a month or six weeks?"

"Sure, if they have a job," Maya retorted, trying to bank her irritation. "Unfortunately I don't have that luxury."

Sawyer abandoned his papers and stood up, facing her eye to eye. "You could if you wanted to. I thought you liked staying here. I'll be back to work soon and you and Joey will have the place to yourselves most of the time."

Maya struggled for the right response. He was taking this far too personally, as if she were walking out on him. And maybe, in a way, that was how he felt. It was obvious he had an attachment to Joey. Knowing what she did about his childhood, she had the feeling he had made it his business to save Joey from the same hurt of abandonment. And he'd also made it clear he was attracted to her. Neither of them could deny the spark between them.

To someone like Sawyer, starved of warmth, love and acceptance by most of his family, sharing her and Joey's lives might be like a feast.

But they couldn't have a relationship built on sexual attraction and his determination to rescue Joey.

And she couldn't risk another failure like she'd had with Evan, not with Joey to consider.

"Of course I like—we like—staying here," she said at last, carefully choosing her words. "But you've already done way too much for us. I need to start taking care of myself and get Joey settled in one place."

Sawyer's jaw tightened. "Joey is fine in this place. He just got out of the hospital. Moving him so soon could be disruptive to him."

"He's very young," Maya pointed out. "I hardly think he'll know the difference as long as I'm there for him."

"And you're the only person that can be there for him? He seems to know the difference when I'm holding him. Ask Reggie who he quieted down for this morning when you left him with us to go job hunting. And what about the other night? You didn't seem so quick to turn down my help then."

An unfamiliar emotion jabbed Maya and it took her a moment to realize it was jealousy. Joey did seem content when he was with Sawyer. But she wasn't ready to share Joey with anyone. He was hers. If Evan didn't want him, no one else was going to be responsible for him. A fierce possessiveness swept through her, making her blurt out the first thing that came to her without thinking. "I'm the only one that's always going to be there for him."

He jerked back as if she'd slapped him. Maya instantly regretted opening her mouth, and more, letting her insecurities speak for her. "Sawyer, I'm—"

"Forget it," he said shortly.

"No, I shouldn't have—"

"I said, forget it." He turned back to his desk and started re-stacking papers again, although Maya was sure he wasn't seeing anything in front of him.

She had hurt him. She knew it. She also knew it was completely unjustifiable given all that Sawyer had done for them, all he wanted to do.

But the idea of Joey getting attached to Sawyer—and vice versa—scared the hell out of her.

She couldn't allow herself to go from the frying pan to the fire, not with her precious baby to think of. Less than a year ago Evan had seemed so perfect. She'd trusted him. And look how that had ended. She had to get out on her own with her baby. That was the right choice, the only choice she could make right now.

Maybe afterward, she and Sawyer could take it slowly, decide then if what they had was real and worth nurturing. Maybe.

Chewing at her lower lip, she tried to think of something to say to him now, hating to leave things so badly. "Thank you for watching Joey," she finally settled on. "I hope he wasn't too much trouble. I know he can really belt it out when he's tired or hungry."

"No problem." He didn't look at her. "Reggie did most of the work."

The distance he was putting between them felt like a chasm. Maya didn't know what to say to him, how to explain what she was feeling without sounding lame. And obviously he wasn't going to share his feelings with her other than to make it clear he was putting up a wall between them.

Still, she felt compelled to try to ease the tension between them. "Sawyer, I— Maybe we should talk about this more."

He spun around in his chair to look at her. "Why?"

"Because, I…you…you're unhappy with the idea of us moving out and I feel—" Maya stopped, not sure what to call the mixed-up emotions inside her.

"I'm fine with it," Sawyer said. He got to his feet. "I shouldn't have started an argument about it. It's got nothing to do with me. It's your decision. Go ahead and find your own place. Like you said, Joey won't know the difference as long as you're there. Now if you don't mind, I've got some things to get finished up."

It was a clear invitation for her to leave. Maya held herself stiffly, determined not to cry in front of him again. "I should go and check on Joey," she said and headed out the door.

Sawyer pressed a towel to his wet head. The afternoon had been a total waste as far as catching up on any of the paperwork his grandfather's lawyers had dumped on him, and though he'd intended to finish it today, after his confrontation with Maya, he couldn't focus. So instead he'd gone to burn off some steam at the poolside gymnasium he'd built off the back patio.

It was a real pain in the backside to workout—and to shower, for that matter—with a sling and the elastic bandage on his shoulder. So he'd yanked both of them off and spent over an hour pushing his body to the limit on the weight machines. Now, free of the binding on his shoulder and after a hot shower, his earlier foul mood was beginning to turn.

He'd behaved like a jerk, and for what? he wondered, toweling off his chest, torso and legs, then casting the towel aside. Getting all bent out of shape over someone else's baby and a woman who didn't want his help was a waste of time. They'd been doing each other a favor with this live-in arrangement and now it was about to be over.

Sawyer stood in front of his bathroom mirror. Jaw lathered, with his good arm he elbowed away the steam from a spot, took his razor out of the chrome stand on his black-tiled counter and swiped the dark stubble on his cheek.

"You're making a fool of yourself, Morente," he told the face staring back at him. "You don't need the complications. It's definitely over."

Unimpressed with his rationale, a set of all too familiar coffee-colored eyes stared back at him, reminding him just who he was talking to. He swiped his jaw again and when he looked back, his face melted away in the steam, replaced by another face—softer, more fair, with a pair of sensuous, intelligent jade eyes that could flash with fire or ice from one moment to the next, just as they had earlier today.

For an instant he saw Maya at his bedside, her eyes smoldering dark green, like a lake at midnight, looking down at him. He closed his eyes and felt her hands on his shoulders soothing and exciting him, her soft breath on his skin, her husky voice an invitation to more. His body stirred. His mind drifted to his bed, where he had so nearly taken advantage of her.

Again his vision shifted and he saw Joey's big, innocent blue eyes looking so trustingly at him the way they had when he had held him today.

He opened his eyes and looked at his reflection. The eyes staring back now, his own, held a mocking, *gotcha* glint.

So much for the workout and the pep talk. He was totally screwed and he knew it.

He finished shaving in a blur, threw on a black shirt, jeans and black boots and grudgingly headed down the hall to find the two people who seemed determined to make him crazy.

He found Maya's room door open. Joey lay kicking and cooing happily on her bed while Maya bustled around the room ticking off a list for her diaper bag for the new babysitter. "Diapers, wipes, bottle, powder…"

"Need some help?" he asked, hanging back, leaning against the door.

Maya flinched, startled. She looked up from the pile on the bed, first noticing how utterly gorgeous he looked, his dark hair still damp and softly curling against the collar of his soft cotton shirt, jeans hugging lean hips and muscled thighs, no sling or bandage.

"Where's your bandage and sling?" She didn't have time to check the surprise and chiding note in her voice.

"They were annoying me. I tore them off."

Despite the fact that he looked delicious enough to eat, Maya felt like wringing his neck for pulling such a stupid stunt. The healer in her had a lecture on the tip of her tongue, but the steel set of his jaw and the rigid line of his shoulders shut her down before she started. "Are you sure that was smart?"

He shrugged her off, then walked in the room, a rebellious swagger to his gait. "I couldn't stand the damned things another minute. They were supposed to come off later this week anyhow."

"Mmm, right. Well, you have a physical therapy appointment, don't you?"

He stepped up behind her and peered over her shoulder into Joey's bag, so close she could feel his breath on her neck. "Didn't get around to making that yet."

The air between them vanished and all she felt was the heat of his body inches from hers. "Um, well, I know some therapy that could help."

"Massage therapy, I hope."

"Something like that." He was nearly pressed against her. What was he trying to do? How could he go from the cold distance of a few hours ago to this wicked warmth so easily? It wasn't fair he could do this to her. Even without looking at him, the sheer power of him made her dizzy. Her knees went liquid and she struggled to focus on the task at hand. "I hope I have everything."

"Looks like taking a baby out is like packing for a three-week vacation," he said, moving around the bed to where he could tickle Joey's bare toes.

Maya breathed for the first time in what seemed like minutes. "No kidding." She zipped the bag and slung it over her shoulder, stealing a sideways glance at him as she did. "Shouldn't you at least be wearing the sling?"

He shrugged. "I guess, if you're going to insist." He reached into his back pocket and pulled out a crumpled ball that Maya guessed used to resemble a sling.

"Here, let me," Maya said when he started to put it on himself. Checking to make certain Joey was safe, she set down the diaper bag and came over to Sawyer. Ever so gently she reached for the sling and reset it on his shoulder, her fingers working delicately, with absolute tenderness. "There, that's better," she said softly, distracted by his fresh, masculine scent, a now-familiar blend of earthy soap and leather that dizzied her senses. When she'd finished, she let her hands slide down his chest.

"Thanks," Sawyer murmured back, looking down at her with an expression that made Maya hot all over. "Maya, about today…"

"Don't. I shouldn't have said what I did. You had a right to be upset."

He bent, his mouth a breath from hers. "I don't know what I have a right to or not, but right or wrong, I want this now."

Her lips were ready, aching for his kiss when he lowered his mouth to hers. She parted them willingly, drinking the kiss he offered.

He took her lips, her tongue, in his, tasting, plundering, longing for more, pulling her closer, pressing them chest to breasts.

Joey let out an annoyed yelp, and simultaneously they started like guilty teenagers, automatically pulling apart.

Maya laughed. "I think he's used to being in the center of attention."

"Late was feeling pretty good," Sawyer said. He looked at Joey and shook his head. "Great timing, kid. Just great."

Chapter Eleven

For one frozen moment Maya just stared, so caught off guard to see her parents inside Sawyer's house that she could only stand there with her mouth open. Sawyer apparently shared her surprise, because apart from his hands tightening on her, he didn't react, as if he didn't know what to do either.

Before Maya had a chance to pull herself together, her parents came and gathered her into a group hug that Sawyer just managed to avoid. He hastily stepped back, retrieving his shirt and pulling it on while Maya extricated herself enough to look at a beaming Shem and Azure. They looked the same as they always had, albeit older: Shem big, burly, in his threadbare jeans, tie-dye T-shirt and bandanna headband, his graying hair long and tied in a ponytail; Azure still curvy but thin, in her peasant blouse and braids, wearing her lucky quartz-stone necklace, with colorful peace signs and hearts embroidered on her ragged jeans.

"I can't believe you're here," Maya said with a weak smile. And if that wasn't an understatement, nothing was. Although it was just like her parents to waltz right into someone else's house, figuring everyone else in the universe had the same never-close-the-door policy as they did. "How did you find me? I tried to reach you, but—"

Azure held fast to Maya's hands. "Well, we thought we'd find you at the house, but when we you weren't there, we went to Val's and she told us about your accident—I hope you didn't spend too much time in the hospital, because you know how unhealthy that is—and Val said you and your baby were living here. Joey, now that's *nice,* I guess, but maybe you could have been just a bit more creative," Azure mused. She eyed Maya intently. "Are you sure it's *balanced?* That's so important, you know."

Maya stopped a sigh and she could just imagine Sawyer rolling his eyes behind her. Shem, though, just draped a papa-bear arm around her shoulders and laughed. "I'm sure our girl's done just fine," he said. "It's really good to see you, honey. We were worried when Val told us about everything, but I can see you've been taking care of yourself. We're looking forward to meeting that baby. Where is he?"

"Ready to go to sleep," Sawyer said from behind Maya, so close to her she started.

She twisted to look at him, and the tense set of his jaw and his almost grim expression didn't surprise her. Even before they'd shown up, Maya knew that Sawyer and her parents would be like day and night. Then she realized she'd forgotten to introduce her parents to him. She started to remedy that when Azure turned to Sawyer and threw her arms around him, hugging him tightly before Sawyer had time to react.

He stiffened but Azure didn't seem to notice. "We're happy to meet you, too. I can tell Maya is happy, and that's all that matters to us," she told him. "And I'm sure you must be a good daddy. When Val told me your name, I was afraid you were going to be one of those uptight, stuffy men and not the right lover for our Maya at all. But you aren't anything like that, I can tell. You have a very passionate aura, you know. Are you an Aries?"

Sawyer now looked as if he'd rather be doomed to the Sahara with no water than stay here. "I'm not—" he started.

"Mom, you know Evan is Joey's—" Maya began at the same time.

"There's my grandson," Shem interrupted.

"Oh, yes! Maya—" Azure rushed to the crib. "He's adorable!"

Maya was beginning to feel the way Sawyer looked. "I want you to get acquainted with Joey, too, but he had a busy day and I was just getting him to sleep. I'll bring him to play with you first thing tomorrow, I promise." A sudden thought occurred to her. "Where are you staying?" she asked, not sure she wanted to hear the answer. Knowing her parents, they could as easily invite themselves to stay at Sawyer's house as they invited themselves inside.

"At our place, where else?" Shem answered.

"But—you've been there. There was a fire and—"

Shem waved off the fire. "Eh, it's not that bad. Kind of a mess, but we've got the camping gear. We don't need much, and the old place probably needed a cleaning out anyway. Besides, Spring and Tai and Diego are with us and we were thinking of calling up a few others to let them know we're back so we can have us a little get-together. I'm sure you remember Diego," he said with a knowing grin and a wink.

Maya felt her face grow hot, and Sawyer's sharp, questioning glance at her only made it worse. How could she forget Diego, the man who'd delivered her parents' graduation gift to her? This was getting better all the time.

"Staying there isn't a good idea." Sawyer spoke up. "That house isn't the safest place. The fire did a lot of damage and no one's had a chance to get by there to do anything with it."

"Oh, stop worrying," Azure said, already cuddling Joey in her arms. "It's bad for you. We couldn't think of staying anywhere else. That house has always had the best vibrations."

Thank goodness, Maya breathed to herself, a little ashamed at herself for the thought but relieved she didn't have to find a tactful way of talking her parents out of Sawyer's house. Besides, once her parents' minds were made up there wasn't any way she was going to change them. "Then I'll bring Joey by in the morning and we can have a long visit," she told them. "Right now he has to go to bed."

"Sure, come on by, all of you. We're all friends and family," Shem said, clapping a meaty hand to Sawyer's bad shoulder so Sawyer winced. "Tai and Diego have been working on some new tunes, and we've been talking about maybe starting an organic herb farm. You can give us your ideas."

Maya doubted that, but she smiled and returned their hugs and taking Joey from Azure walked them outside to where they'd left their van in Sawyer's front drive. After promising again to bring Joey in the morning and waving them off, she heaved a sigh and slowly walked back up to the house to face Sawyer.

He met her at the front door and they walked together back inside. Maya fed Joey then tucked him in for the night. She returned to the living room to find Sawyer waiting.

Unsure of his reaction from his unreadable expression, she didn't know what to say to him. Apart from the unwelcome surprise of her parents just showing up in his house and catching them in each other's arms, she guessed her parents deciding he might as well be Joey's father and her lover had made him uncomfortable. It had bothered her—and probably Sawyer, too—having them even inadvertently comparing Sawyer to Evan. As far as she was concerned, there wasn't any comparison—not in the way Sawyer cared for Joey and certainly not in the flare of attraction between them, so much sweeter, hotter and uncontrolled than anything she'd ever felt with Evan.

But she didn't know how to bring up any of that without making it worse.

"Well, that was…interesting," Sawyer said finally.

"Look, I'm sorry—" Maya began but Sawyer cut short her apology.

"It's not your fault. You didn't know they were back in town."

"No, but I should have warned you they don't bother with normal rules of life, like knocking before you walk in someone else's house." She hesitated, then said, "I know it must have been uncomfortable, them labeling you as Joey's father and you and I as…well, I'll try and set things straight tomorrow."

Sawyer's shoulders shifted in a semblance of a shrug. "It's okay."

"No, it isn't."

"I said it's okay," Sawyer said shortly. Turning away from her, he paced to the window, flicking at the shades, and then to the front door to turn off the porch light and check the lock. He came back to prowl the room, adjusting a cushion, clicking off one of the lamps, fidgeting with a book that was slightly askew on an end table.

Maya recognized his inability to sit still as a sign he was unsettled and she obviously wasn't helping. "Okay, then, I think I'll go check on Joey once more and then get to bed myself," she said, moving to pick up Joey's baby monitor. "Good night."

"You aren't thinking of moving back with them, are you?" Sawyer asked abruptly as she started to leave him.

"With my parents?" She stared at him, surprised he'd think she'd even consider it. "Definitely not. I know the vibrations are good," she said with a slight smile, hoping to earn one in return from him. Fat chance, she decided when his scowl deepened. "But I'm not into camping amid the ruins. The only move I'm making is to my own place."

He nodded his expression shuttered again. "Good night then."

"Sawyer—"

"Yes?"

"I… Nothing, never mind. Good night," she said and hurriedly left, leaving him standing alone in the middle of the room, looking after her.

What had she started to say? Hours later Sawyer, stretched out on one of the patio lounge chairs, thought about that one and

decided that if he hadn't acted as if she was personally responsible for everything that happened, she might have told him. As
it was, he was the one who needed to be apologizing to her.

For some reason, her parents had knocked him off balance.
The Rainbows had shown up with their auras and good vibra-
tions and clueless comments about him being Joey's father and
Maya's lover and knocked him for a loop.

He didn't know why it should bother him. Probably at least
half of Luna Hermosa believed the same thing and the other half
figured it was inevitable. He'd thought many times about it himself.

If he was honest, he'd admit what bothered him were the
Rainbows themselves. It wasn't their retro clothes or their de-
votion to astrology and organic herb farming. It was how they
ignored personal barriers and hugged everyone in sight, accepting strangers as friends and openly showing their love for Maya
and the grandson they'd yet to meet.

Part of him wanted that with Maya and Joey—all the complications and the rewards of a real family.

Part of him had no idea what that kind of commitment meant.
He'd never had that growing up, never wanted to risk it with anyone later. Even if he was willing to take the chance, how could
he expect Maya, with Joey depending on her, to take that risk?
She'd trusted Joey's father and he'd let her down hard.

How could either of them be sure he wouldn't do the same?

"You don't have to go." Maya, finishing packing up Joey's
things for the trip to her parents' house, looked over her shoulder at Sawyer leaning in the doorway of her bedroom. Unshaven,
his hair rumpled and in nothing but well-worn jeans, he was a
distraction she didn't need right now. And from the glint in his
eye and his lazy half smile, she figured he knew it.

"What, and miss the discussion on organic herb farming?"
he drawled.

"Yeah, right," she said, shaking her head. She was getting dizzy trying to decipher Sawyer's shifts in mood—one time distant and cool and the next flashing that killer smile and acting as if the three of them really were a family. Last night he'd been restless and withdrawn, but this morning she'd gotten the smile that never failed to kick her pulse up a notch. Then he'd surprised her by telling her he intended to accept Shem's invitation and go with her and Joey.

"I mean it, Sawyer," Maya told him. She glanced over to where Joey, in his crib, was seriously examining his fingers, before zipping up the diaper bag and turning to face Sawyer. "I'll explain about everything. You probably had enough of the group hugs and aura readings last night."

"Oh, I don't know. Maybe I'll learn something about your aura." Straightening, he sauntered over to her. He fingered her loose braid of hair hanging over one shoulder, pulling free the tie at the end and threading his hand through her hair until it slid loosely through his fingers. "Tell me, are you an Aries?"

"Sagittarius, and you're not helping," Maya muttered, her words belying the frisson of excitement his touch created.

"Who says?" He moved closer until their bodies just brushed against each other. Leaning even nearer, he nuzzled her ear and murmured, "By the way, who's Diego?"

Uh-oh. She should have known he hadn't missed Shem's not-so-subtle innuendo last night. Maya briefly considered fudging on the whole truth. But chances were Sawyer would hear it from either her parents or Diego himself anyway.

"You remember I told you about the, um, graduation gift my parents arranged?" she said, her face getting warm. "Well, that was Diego."

"Really." Sawyer's hand moved down her back, bringing her up fully against him. "What's he doing here now?"

Irritation stabbed her, warring with the coiling heat he'd started inside her. "How should I know? He and my parents stayed friends, but this will be the first I've seen him since I moved out."

"I'll look forward to meeting him."

"Don't go all primitive on me," Maya warned. She nearly told him they didn't have any claims on each other, so he had no reason to get possessive at the idea of meeting her former lover. But the words wouldn't come because she didn't quite believe that, especially at this moment, with his hands on her and the fire in his eyes burning just for her. "If that's the only reason you're going, then—"

Sawyer cut short her sentence by bending and kissing her, a hard, intimate, openmouthed kiss that made her go weak in the knees and left no doubt he was staking his claim. He broke it off just as abruptly and stepped away from her, breathing quickly, his eyes hot. "I'll be ready to go in five minutes."

He quickly left the room, and Maya leaned back against the changing table trying to gather her scattered senses.

Joey gurgled and Maya automatically turned to pick him up and, cuddling him close, breathed in his comforting baby smell. "It's going to be a long day, sweet stuff," she murmured to her son. "A very long day."

He wasn't sure what he'd expected, but after an hour at the Rainbows' Sawyer decided that at least the company wasn't too bad. He'd already made up his mind that the house was past redemption, and neither the fire nor the Rainbows moving back had improved it.

Shem and Azure had accepted him showing up as easily as they welcomed their new grandson. They'd rushed to see Joey even before Maya had come to a complete stop in the driveway and had snatched him from her on sight.

Joey now lay in his pumpkin seat on the floor, studying the brightly colored fabric birds, bees and butterflies Azure had strung on a wooden frame to form a sort of standing mobile. She sat next to him on several fat cushions, propped against Shem, including Joey in the conversation with the odd group scattered around the living room as if the baby understood, then getting Shem to accompany her on guitar while she sang to Joey.

The Rainbows' idea of cleaning up the house had apparently

consisted of shoving all the debris in the living room out the front door, haphazardly mopping up the floor and throwing questionably clean pillows and sleeping bags down for seats. Sawyer managed to avoid the communal floor seats and grab a corner of the couch next to Maya and Joey.

The first chance he got, he leaned close and asked in a low voice, "Are you sure this is a good idea?" He nodded to Joey.

"He's fine," Maya said, glancing at her son. She reached out and caressed Joey's cheek. "It's not the first time I've put him in his seat while I'm doing something else."

"It's not the seat I'm worried about, it's this floor. Even the air in this place still smells like smoke and something I'm not sure *I* want to be breathing, let alone a new baby. Joey's not been out of the hospital all that long."

Irritation flicked across her face before she made an effort to banish it. "Do you honestly think I'd have brought Joey if I thought it would hurt him?"

"I wasn't implying you're a bad mother, because you're far from it," Sawyer said, trying to soothe the feelings he'd inadvertently ruffled. "But you know how I've always felt about Joey being here."

"You worry too much. Azure's right, it's bad for you. And give me some credit, it's not like I'm letting him touch the floor, and all the windows are open. Now, if they start smoking the home-grown weed, I'll probably have to move him. I'm just kidding," she said, holding up her hands to ward off his protest. "They aren't going to do that around a baby."

"That probably explains the smell," Sawyer grumbled. "And I wouldn't put it past some in this crowd."

Apart from Spring and Tai—a short, thin woman with long black hair and an Asian man with equally long hair wearing some sort of robe, both of whom looked to be about the age of Maya's parents—several other people seemed to have shown up for the impromptu gathering. Including the infamous Diego.

Tall and lean, with spiky dark hair, he smiled too much, had too many piercings and tattoos and looked to Sawyer like the kind of guy he wouldn't trust with his dog, let alone his daughter.

"He's not as bad as you're thinking," Maya murmured. She leaned against his leg, one hand gently caressing Joey's tiny fist.

"How do you know what I'm thinking?"

She laughed up at him. "That's pretty obvious from the way you keep glaring at him." She reached up and took his hand in hers. "Forget about him. It was a long time ago and I was over him in about a week. I hadn't even thought about him in years until yesterday. Besides—" her smile turned provocative "—you're all the distraction I can handle."

"Maya, you remember this, don't you? I'll bet Joey will love it as much as you did," Shem broke in before Sawyer could get a comeback out. Shem started to play and sing a song about a magical unicorn, and Sawyer had to settle for giving Maya a look that let her know he considered her just as much of a distraction.

During the next several hours he looked at her a lot, watching her laugh and sing and talk with the rest. She looked happier and more relaxed than she had in weeks, and Sawyer began to understand a little better why, despite her parents' oddities and complete lack of responsibility and decorum, Maya remembered her childhood as happy and loving. While the laid-back, easy-going idleness would have driven him crazy in a day, Sawyer conceded there was something peaceful and satisfying about the way the Rainbows lived.

At the same time, watching her so at ease, feeling the camaraderie among everyone else there, made him feel more the outsider.

"Could you hold Joey for a minute?" Maya interrupted his thoughts. "He's done eating and I need to take a quick break. I think he'd like you better than the pumpkin seat."

"Of course he would," Azure said as Maya put Joey in Sawyer's arms. Joey gave a contented sigh as Sawyer automatically began rocking him. "He'd much rather be with his daddy."

Maya shot a worried glance at Sawyer and then gave her

mother a warning look. "Mom, you know perfectly well Sawyer isn't—"

Azure waved her away. "Oh, please, none of that matters. Being a daddy is about love. Can't you see they belong together? They're the *same*." For a moment Azure's expression sobered as she included both Sawyer and Maya in her gaze. "That's what's important. You have to trust it and not let your head mess things all up." She stared pointedly at Sawyer. "That's you, you think too much. When were you born?"

The question caught Sawyer off guard after Azure's brief serious moment and he answered without thinking, "July twenty-third."

"Leo, not Aries. I should have known. That's why you're so restless. Of course, you're cusp born, so you're influenced by Cancer, and depending on the moon…" She trailed off, apparently musing on the various aspects of Sawyer's astrological positioning.

Sawyer looked back at Maya and found her watching him cautiously, as if she wasn't sure what to expect. He wasn't sure what to expect either. He looked down at Joey, now sleeping soundly in his arms, and heard Azure's assertion: *They belong together.*

Did they? Or would he turn out to be Maya's worst fear—just another man who let Joey down?

Coming back from the bathroom, Maya paused in the arched doorway leading into the living room to look at Sawyer holding her son. Amid the clutter and the buzz of conversation and occasional music, he looked like sanctuary, and not for the first time she felt a tug of yearning that urged her to let him be that for her and Joey.

Impossible but tempting. Always tempting.

Sawyer shifted Joey across his shoulder, against his heart, and Joey curled up a little, looking content. Sawyer stroked his back and his expression softened as he cradled Joey close.

Maya's throat tightened and she blinked away sudden tears.

At the same time a completely unwelcome emotion stabbed her, and it took her a moment before she realized it was envy. How ridiculous, to be envious of her own son, and yet she couldn't help but wonder what it would be like if Sawyer ever looked at her that way.

Dangerous, it would be dangerous. She knew he wanted her as much as she wanted him, but that was different. That was passion, desire. If he looked at her with that plus the love and tenderness she saw now, the combination would be positively lethal.

Dangerous because she didn't know if he could ever wholly commit himself to her and Joey. He obviously cared for Joey, all the more because she knew he wanted to spare Joey the same heartache he'd had growing up without a father. But equally obviously Sawyer never had the example of a close family. She couldn't risk getting any more involved with him than she already had until she could be sure he was ready for that kind of commitment, if he ever was. His past was a monster that she didn't know if he could ever fully confront and defeat, especially since he seemed determined never to acknowledge his father again.

It was becoming more and more difficult to stick to her guns, though. A touch, a heated glance, and she nearly forgot her good intentions where Joey was concerned. And she couldn't ever afford to forget.

Up until now Joey's birth had given both of them an easy reason to stop before things had gotten out of hand. Except now it had been almost two months since Joey was born. She hadn't told Sawyer yet, but she'd finally made an appointment to see the doctor this week for a checkup. After that she fully expected the doctor to say it was now okay when Sawyer kissed her to kiss him back. And that she didn't have to stop there. She didn't have to stop at all.

He looked up and caught her eye, and Maya caught her breath. She wanted to be with him, but she also needed to protect Joey—

and her heart. She couldn't afford to make another mistake she'd be regretting for a long time afterward.

That meant it was time to leave.

Because the longer she stayed with Sawyer, living as if it were forever, the harder it would be to keep her promises to her son and herself and the more risk there was that they'd all three be hurt.

"You know, I have it on good authority that all that thinking's bad for you," Sawyer said softly when she came over to sit next to him and Joey.

She smiled, hoping the shadows still haunting her didn't show. "I thought that was worrying."

"You looked like you were doing both." He studied her for a moment, then said, "What's wrong?"

"Nothing. Everything's fine," Maya said and the lie made her want to cry. "Just fine."

Chapter Twelve

Two mornings later Maya wondered if her first day at her new job could have gotten off to a worse start.

First, she'd tossed and turned all night, worried about everything that could go wrong. She felt apprehensive and unsettled about having to leave Joey with a sitter for the first time and anxious to do her best work for Dr. Gonzales. Added to that was the friction between her and Sawyer over her going back to work in the first place and her making plans to move out.

She'd awakened with a throbbing headache, too much to do and too little time to do it all.

Yawning and rubbing her eyes, she staggered into the kitchen to make some tea. At least she'd had the foresight to pack Joey's bag the night before, she thought, rummaging through Sawyer's pantry for her basket of herbal teas. When she didn't find it, annoyed, she closed the pantry and searched the countertops. Her eyes stopped at a white sheet of notepaper balanced against her tea basket. Her stomach clenched. Had Sawyer left early to avoid seeing her this morning? He'd made it abundantly clear that he wasn't happy about her new job or her moving out. So had he decided simply to avoid her until she and Joey left?

Reluctantly she picked up the note, which looked as if Sawyer had scrawled it on the run.

Sorry to have to leave so early on your first day of work. Rafting accident, they're shorthanded, I decided to go.

Maya groaned. His shoulder wasn't ready for this. What if he had to lift? Or swim or who knew what. Shaking her head, she turned back to the note, irritated. And worried.

Stop frowning. I can see the worry lines from across town. The doctor cleared me.

Maya felt the frown lines melt. Did he know her that well already? Although she knew very well he was only cleared for "light" duty—as if he would ever make that distinction. If he went back, he'd plunge in feetfirst. It wasn't in him to give any less.

I heated the water and left your favorite morning herbal weed in the pot to steep—not that it'll jump-start you, but it's made. By the way, that stuff really stinks.

Maya turned to the beautiful copper teapot Sawyer had bought especially for her. Before she'd brought her thirty or so various teas into his house, he'd had no use for anything but a coffee/espresso/cappuccino maker. Her heart twisted at his thoughtfulness. He was so good about the little things.

I asked Regina to come over to help so you won't be late to work. I know, you don't need help. But just this once accept it, please, since I can't be there. Good luck. You'll be great. You could feed bat dung to a patient and he'd think it was the nectar of the gods….

Ever,

Sawyer

"Ever. Oh, Sawyer," she whispered on a deep sigh, rubbing her fingers over the note, "if only it could be."

* * *

Somehow with Regina's invaluable help she managed to pull herself and Joey together to drive to the sitter's house, then to the clinic. Dropping off her son was the hardest thing she'd ever done. Even though she was leaving him with someone Val knew and trusted, nonetheless she could barely stand the moment of separation. Her stomach knotted, her heart swelled and she couldn't hold back the tears as she gave up her precious baby to another woman.

The home-based childcare Val had recommended couldn't have been more ideal, complete with a degreed and certified caregiver who was the sister of an old friend of Val's. Her home was immaculate, with rooms specially designed for her business. She obviously didn't really need the money and therefore had taken on only three small children and Joey, who no doubt would be hopelessly spoiled.

Still, leaving him, watching him look at her and imagining the reproach in his eyes as she walked away from him and opened the door, nearly did her in. The temptation to change every plan, quit her job, take Joey, run back to Sawyer's and beg him to let them stay forever in his care nearly overwhelmed her. Never more had she needed every ounce of willpower she possessed. Grabbing that doorknob, turning her back on her son, had to be the most anguished thing she had ever forced herself to do.

On the way to the clinic she'd told herself she was being melodramatic, silly even. Yet her heart didn't listen to her head. Rational or not, she couldn't help her feelings.

Once she'd gotten to work, she'd called the sitter every chance she'd gotten all morning, and thankfully the woman never seemed irritated or chided her for the numerous calls. Instead she cheerfully reassured her each time that Joey was fine, eating, laughing, enjoying the other children. By ten o'clock, Maya could almost breathe.

Doctor Gonzales had been very patient, showing her the clinic, the acupuncture room, the massage room, various herbs and aromatherapy bottles and outlining Maya's duties. Her new employer had also been extremely empathetic to Maya's distraction over Joey.

"Don't worry," she'd said, her dark eyes sympathetic. "It gets easier every day. I have two of my own, so I know what you're going through. You will live, honestly. Look at me—" she patted her gently rounded belly "—I'm going to have my third and I still get sick to my stomach when I think about having to leave him or her when I go back to work. That's why I'm so glad you're here now."

After Dr. Gonzales had hugged her, Maya had almost broken down and bawled, but managed to keep all but a few tears in check. Now, again, standing alone in the linen closet, for no apparent reason the tears were back and she was swallowing hard to keep them at bay.

"Enough already," she muttered, swiping her eyes for the thousandth time and reprimanding herself as she grabbed some fresh hand towels and hurried down the hallway to greet a patient in the front office. There, instead of the one person she expected, she saw five.

One of which was a soaking wet Sawyer, his T-shirt gashed in several places as if he'd had a fight with an angry cat. He and Paul—who also looked as if he'd spent the last hour standing in a heavy rain—stood propping up a teenage girl between them. The girl, in a swimsuit top and shorts, looked half-drowned and seemed to be favoring her right leg. Two younger boys hovering in back, wet, wide-eyed and shivering, appeared scared but otherwise unhurt.

"Rico and Tonio are bringing the parents," Sawyer said, easing the girl into a chair. "They should be right behind us. I think Cathy here sprained an ankle, and her dad may have broken a couple of fingers. Other than that, everyone seems okay."

Just then Dr. Gonzales rushed out of a patient room and into the lobby. "Bring these first three back," she said, motioning to Sawyer and Paul. "I have rooms ready. Mom and Dad will have to wait."

Maya looked from Sawyer to Dr. Gonzales, eyes questioning.

"I'm sorry, Maya," Dr. Gonzales said. "I didn't have time to warn you. I was in the middle of a treatment when my beeper went off. Sawyer called to tell me the Romero family was in a rafting accident. They're all patients of mine. Have been since I delivered their first child. They refused to go to the hospital."

Maya waved off her apology. "What can I do?"

"For starters, help Sawyer take Cathy into Room Two. Paul can help me get the boys settled and then we'll bring in the others when they get here."

"You're pregnant. Why don't I wait and bring in the others?" Maya asked.

Dr. Gonzales laughed. "Don't fret, *mamasita*. I'm not lifting anybody. I've got all these men to do that. I just want to take a quick look first." She turned to Sawyer. "And I don't want you lifting anyone either. If you didn't do it out on the river playing superman, I won't have you messing up that shoulder again in my office. You already look like you added a few more scars to your collection out there," she said, nodding toward his ripped shirt. She looked at Maya. "Your drenched friend here dived into the rapids to pull Cathy and her brothers out of the river."

"Yeah, he was awesome!" Cathy spoke up for the first time. "He got me out, then went back in for Mark and Matthew."

Paul snorted. "And he ought to be fired for breaking white-water protocol."

"Tell that to the river," Sawyer said, scowling at his friend.

"Okay, I'm ready," Maya said, leading the way to the examination room. They helped the thin, shivering girl inside and onto the table, and Maya arranged a pillow for her ankle, then gave her a gown, instructing her to undress down to her underclothes and promising to check on her in a few minutes.

Outside in the hallway, Maya rounded on Sawyer, about to

insist he let her take at look at the damage under his shirt, when Rico and another firefighter came in with the older Romeros.

She didn't have time to fuss over him for the next hour as she worked side by side with Dr. Gonzales treating the injured family members. Sawyer was right about Cathy's sprain, and in fact, Cathy, her cheeks pink with the thrill of a youthful crush, had eagerly invited him to watch as Maya and Dr. Gonzales applied an herbal poultice, then wrapped it.

Only one of the Romeros, the father, had broken bones. He'd broken two fingers on his left hand when a rush of rapid waters threw him up against a boulder and he'd tried to break the impact with his hands. Maya stood beside Dr. Gonzales now, prepping his fingers with an herbal gel before Dr. Gonzales set the bones.

Sawyer, with orders to get himself patched up and go home since he hadn't been officially on duty in the first place, stood nearby watching with open curiosity. "What does that green gunk do anyhow?"

Maya felt the power of his body shadowing her from behind, his deep voice resonating against her skin.

"Keep dissing my medicines, Morente, and your lesson is over," Dr. Gonzales warned.

"It helps to reduce swelling and numbs the pain so Mr. Romero can relax while Dr. Gonzales places the splints," Maya explained.

Dr. Gonzales smiled. "You do know your craft, young lady."

Maya said nothing, but a sense of pride filled her. She knew it was mainly because Sawyer was there. She found herself wanting him to respect her work instead of thinking of her the way he thought of her parents—alien visitors from a Martian moonbeam.

Beside her, Pepe Romero closed his eyes a moment while the salve did its work. "Much better. Thanks."

Sawyer watched the procedure but looked unconvinced it was doing any good. "Are you saying that's some kind of local anesthetic?"

"Only better," Dr. Gonzales said.

Maya nodded. "No needles and no side effects."

"Interesting." Despite his skepticism, Sawyer couldn't deny there seemed to be something to this natural-healing stuff. Dr. Gonzales's patients not only believed in her and in her treatments, but he had to admit the whole experience felt more humane, less hurried, far more personal than similar experiences he'd had taking patients to the E.R. And he himself could attest to the benefits of Maya's massages.

Whether or not he trusted in it, he could tell Maya was good at what she did and that Dr. Gonzales respected her skill. Although he hadn't reconciled himself to her moving out, he knew this job was the perfect opportunity for Maya to make use of her obvious skills. And he knew he should tell her that, even if it meant she took it as support for her determination to be completely independent of everyone, including him.

When Dr. Gonzales had finally finished and was giving the family last-minute instructions on their way out, Maya took the opportunity to practically drag him to the medical supply station down the hallway.

"You're bleeding," she said once they were inside the small room, critically eyeing him up and down. "Take off your shirt and let me have a look."

Sawyer obliged her by whipping off his T-shirt. "Anything else you'd like me to take off?"

As if on cue, warm color flooded her cheeks. "That smirk on your face," she muttered. Gently she examined the several shallow gashes and scratches on his chest and abdomen. "How did you manage to get all these?"

"Took a little swim with some unfriendly rocks and a few branches. It's just a couple of scrapes. They'll be gone by the weekend."

"What, you heal faster than mere mortals, too?" Maya said. Shaking her head, she turned and began searching the shelves. When she found what she was looking for, she used a swab to dab the grayish ointment on each wound. "Thank goodness it looks like you're right about these. But they're going to sting for a while unless I put this on."

"More stinky stuff," Sawyer said, wrinkling up his nose. "Doesn't anything *natural* smell decent?"

"You do." She didn't look up from her deft ministrations, but her soft, low voice held echoes of emotions beyond the concerns of a healer. "I could close my eyes and know it's you, even with all the river water."

Sawyer forgot the cold cling of his damp clothes, the smarting sting of various scrapes and cuts and everything else except Maya as his body reacted to her touch and the suggestion in her voice. "What is it about you that I can spend two hours in the river, drag in here feeling like I've been on the losing side of a fight and in thirty seconds you can have me ready to ravish you in the supply closet?"

"Maybe all the smelly stuff is going to your head," Maya said lightly.

But her hand trembled slightly where she touched him, betraying her attempt to appear unaffected. Sawyer smiled to himself. Taking the swab away from her, he brought her hand to his mouth and kissed her palm. "Your weeds have nothing to do with it."

"Don't be so quick to bad-talk my weeds. You'd be surprised what I can do with them." She smiled herself, a little secret curve of her lips guaranteed to give him several ideas. "For instance, someday I'll show you a thing or two about aromatherapy. I promise you'll enjoy that, especially when I combine it with reflexology."

"Are you sure that's legal?"

Maya laughed. "Probably. It's a fancy word for the best foot massage you'll ever get."

"Are you making me an offer?" Sawyer asked. "Because if you are, I accept."

"If you're lucky, I might give you the chance. But right now

I need to get back to work." Snagging his shirt from where he'd tossed it onto the sink, she held it up, eyeing it doubtfully. "Are you sure you want this?"

"Unless you've got a replacement around here somewhere." He took her hand as she made to give his shirt to him, his expression suddenly serious.

"Fresh out," she said lightly, wondering why the shift in his mood. "But I could offer you one of these sexy white clinic smocks." Her attempt at humor was lost on him and she laid her other hand atop their clasped hands. "Hey, what's the matter?"

"You'll think I've lost it, but I have to tell you that I've been worried all morning about Joey. I couldn't stop wondering if he's okay with the sitter."

Maya reached up, drew the back of her hand down his stubbled cheek and smiled. "Believe me, that makes two of us. But he's fine. Really."

"Good," he said with a nod. He pulled his damp shirt on, the motion drawing Maya's eyes to him. "Then do you mind if I see for myself and pick him up early?"

She looked up quickly, flushing, realizing he'd caught her staring at his chest. "Sure, of course. I'll call and tell her you're coming."

"You know," Sawyer drawled, deliberately moving closer to her, "if you like what you see from the waist up, there's a lot more I could show you. If you're interested." Bending to her, he kissed her, holding her only with his mouth for a few lingering moments. "Are you?"

A little breathless, she asked, "Are you being a tease or do you really need an answer?"

Sawyer kissed her again, this time making sure she'd remember it the rest of the day. "You just gave me my answer," he murmured as he forced himself to draw back. "But since this closet is too small for what I have in mind..." He trailed off deliberately.

"If you keep this up, I'm going to get fired my first day for illicit use of this closet." Maya glanced to the open door. "Dr. Gonzales is probably already wondering where I am."

Touching a finger to her lips, Sawyer smiled. "One look at all that pretty pink color in your face and that sparkle in your eyes and she won't be wondering long."

"Thanks for that," Maya muttered and gave him a push toward the hallway. "Go already, before I do something to embarrass myself even more."

"And what might that be?"

"Sawyer!"

"Okay, I'm gone," he said, grinning at her. Stealing another quick kiss, he left before she could make good on either the threat in her eyes to throw something at him or the promise that he'd made up his mind to hold her to later.

Maya came home exhausted but delighted with her first day at the clinic. It had been everything she'd hoped for and, with Dr. Gonzales as her guide, much more. Famished, she went to the kitchen, grabbed a bottle of carrot juice, then headed through the house in search of Joey and Sawyer. Sawyer's truck was in the garage, so she knew they were home. But a quick look around the house proved futile.

Then she noticed that the French door leading to the side patio hung open. She hurried outside, her heart pounding with anticipation, eager to hear all about Joey's day and more about Sawyer's river escapade. But when she found them, instead of bursting into questions, she stood still, watching.

The two of them lay sleeping in a gently swaying hammock, Sawyer's big body cradling her tiny son. A light sage-scented breeze caught at the dark wave of hair sweeping Sawyer's brow. His handsome face looked more content, more relaxed than Maya had ever seen before. And Joey, snuggled safe and warm against Sawyer's chest, looked as peaceful and secure as any baby possibly could be.

Moving quietly, she stepped closer, near enough to lightly

brush her hand over Joey's silken tufts of hair. She'd missed him so much today. Joey wriggled a little, yawned, but didn't open his eyes. But Sawyer did. He blinked a few times against the salmon blaze of setting sun, then smiled when he focused on her. "Hey," he said softly, "don't worry, he's fine. He had a great day."

Maya moved her hand from Joey's cheek to brush the errant wave of hair back from Sawyer's forehead. "Thanks. I can see that. You two look so—"

"Right?" Sawyer brushed a kiss over Joey's head. "At least, that's how it feels."

"That's how it looks. He fits perfectly into the crook of your arm."

"With his appetite he won't for long. He'll outgrow me cuddling him in no time."

An ache of sadness caught at Maya's throat and for a moment she couldn't speak. She sensed Sawyer preparing himself for their move, for the rejection, for the loss of Joey. "He'll always want you to cuddle him," she said. "Children never outgrow wanting to be loved."

Sawyer looked from her to Joey, and for a moment Maya glimpsed behind the defenses he'd built for himself and saw a tenderness for Joey that brought tears to her eyes coupled with an old longing for something he might never have. In the next moment he'd checked the emotion.

"Can you take him, please?" he said. "We've been crashed here for a while and I need to get up and move. Besides, you look like you won't be able to stand another minute of not holding him."

Gently Maya bent and picked up her sleeping baby. As she nestled him against her breast, back in her arms, all her anxiety seeped from her. "I knew he was okay," she said, "but touching him, holding him, I never imagined I'd miss him this much."

Sawyer rolled out of the hammock and folded them both in his arms. "Believe me, I know exactly how you feel. I was practically nuts by the time I got to the sitter's house. The way I rushed in and grabbed Joey, she probably thinks I'm a maniac."

Maya laughed at his rueful expression. "Don't feel bad. I would have done the same thing."

"Why don't you put him to bed while I rustle up some dinner?"

Joey gurgled and wriggled a little in Maya's arms but didn't awaken. "Dinner sounds great. I didn't have time for lunch. But I'll cook," she said.

Sawyer rolled his eyes. "Let me, would you? I won't poison you."

Maya considered him with mock suspicion. "You won't try to sneak any meat in, will you?"

"Scout's honor. Though you'd have more color in your cheeks if I did."

"The lack of color is from sleep deprivation, not a need for animal protein."

"Whatever. I won't serve you anything that used to breathe, okay?"

"I guess I'll have to trust you," she said, laughing at his pained look. "I'll put Joey down and then freshen up. I won't be long."

Ushering her ahead of him, Sawyer tugged at the band holding her braid, then combed his fingers through her hair until it fell in a wild cascade that captured the glow of the setting sun. "Feel free to slip into something a little more comfortable," he breathed against her neck. "I'll be waiting."

Maya hurried to freshen up, taking a quick shower, then bathing herself in rose water. Joey awoke just long enough to nurse and have his diaper changed, then he drifted back into a deep sleep. Maya took her time with him when he was awake, relishing his every sound, the powdery baby scent of him, his searching blue eyes, his contentment as he nestled against her.

After she tucked him in, she rifled through her wardrobe, tempted by Sawyer's invitation. Finding a casual sapphire-blue cotton skirt she'd forgotten she had, she slipped it on over her black thong, satisfied with the way the bright material clung to her hips before flaring out to float lightly around her ankles. She topped the skirt with a lighter blue snug-fitting spaghetti-strap camisole, daring to go braless for the first time in nearly a year.

Sawyer didn't have to know she had only one scrap of satin on underneath her long skirt, but it made her feel womanly, sexy again as she hadn't felt for a very long time, even if it was a secret she shared only with herself.

Dabbing a little blush and a little lipstick on, she tossed her head down and brushed out her wild hair. Flipping it back, she scrunched it a little, then decided that would have to do. This wasn't a date, after all. Even if it felt like one.

She found Sawyer on the patio, lounging in an oversize rattan chair next to a small wrought-iron table set for two—cloth napkins, candles and all. He'd lit the garden torches all around, so that the huge pots of pink, yellow, purple and orange bougainvilleas encircling the patio dining area swayed beneath the flames of a golden aura. In the corner, a small outdoor kiva fireplace puffed out sandalwood-scented smoke, adding a slightly sensuous scent to the air.

"Wow," she said, taking in the gorgeously romantic scene. "I feel like I'm at one of those elegant hotels in Santa Fe."

Sawyer stood up as soon as he heard her steps. He watched her walk toward him, her light steps gliding gracefully over the cool Spanish tiles, catching teasing glimpses of her slim ankles and slender calves beneath the diaphanous billows of her skirt. He traced the curve of her hips to her small waist and full breasts outlined by the thin sheath she wore with his eyes, wanting to take the same path with his hands. Coppery wisps of hair framed her face, catching a little in the moisture on the lips he ached to taste and brand with his own.

"You're so beautiful," he murmured as she came into his arms as if she had always belonged there.

Running her hands up his chest to rest on his shoulders, she smiled into his eyes. "You're not so bad yourself, cowboy."

Sawyer started to answer the invitation in her eyes when Maya's stomach growled loudly and she blushed.

"Sorry," she said, backing out of his embrace. "My stomach is being obnoxious. Kind of a mood killer, I guess."

"Oh, I don't know, I'm still hungry," Sawyer said as he pulled out a chair for her at the table. He moved close with the pretense of helping her closer to the table and instead pushed her mass of hair aside to kiss the bared curve of her neck.

He felt her tremble and knew they were thinking the same thing. And it didn't have anything to do with food. "I'd better eat something first," she said even as she leaned back into him.

"Yeah. Me, too," he said, tasting the tender curve of her throat.

"I meant food."

"Oh, that." Reluctantly Sawyer let her go. "Okay, your stomach wins. Here—" He poured her out a glass of the sparkling grape juice she'd been substituting for wine since she'd gotten pregnant and was nursing. "You sit and sip that and dinner will be served in a minute."

A few minutes later Sawyer returned with a platter bearing two steaming bowls of soup and two covered plates.

Maya looked at him in surprise. "What's all this?"

Sawyer gave her a lopsided smile. "I'm busted. It's Regina. She left tortilla soup, vegetarian of course—she caters more to your diet than to mine these days—and a veggie burrito for you and a meat burrito for me."

"Well, every great chef needs a great waiter," Maya said.

"I did make the jalapeño corn bread. It was a mix, but I say it still counts as cooking."

"Ten points for the corn bread. Fifty points for those jeans."

"Hey, no fraternizing with the hired help," he said, serving her the soup. "At least not until after dinner. So how was your first day—I mean the part I wasn't there for?"

Maya smiled happily. "Better than I could have wished for. Dr. Gonzales is great. We're right in sync with our treatment methods and philosophy."

"I could tell you were in your element. I was impressed," he said, reaching across the table for her hand, "genuinely, with you and with your weeds."

So he had noticed the compliment Dr. Gonzales had given her and even offered one of his own. Her heart warmed with pleasure. "I couldn't ask for a better boss. And something else happened today that—"

The ring of Sawyer's cell phone interrupted them. "Sorry," he said as he grabbed the phone from the low wall next to them. "I need to be sure this isn't business." He looked at the number display and cursed. "Damn. It's Cort. I'll keep it short."

"No problem, I'm a slow eater anyhow."

"Great timing as always," Sawyer answered the call tersely.

Maya couldn't hear Cort's side of the conversation, but from Sawyer's responses and his ominous scowl she guessed his brother was pressing him again about a meeting with Jed Garrett.

"I've already moved on," Sawyer was saying. "I told you I'd think about it and I did, for the approximately two seconds it took me to decide it was a waste of time." There was a pause, and then Sawyer snapped, "Never is looking better all the time. Later, Cort."

Maya waited a moment, then gathered the courage to say, "I don't think he's going to give up until you go and see your father."

"Can we please change the subject?" Sawyer said tightly as he downed the remains of his wine in one drink.

Maya bit her tongue and took a sip of her own drink. "Okay," she said, thinking the opposite. Although she knew it was the last thing Sawyer wanted, she was inclined to side with Cort. If Sawyer never faced his past and laid it to rest, Maya was beginning to believe he'd never be able to trust himself to commit to anyone else. And more and more, the idea of them being apart seemed harder to accept.

"So what were you telling me before the interruption?" he asked, obviously making an effort to recapture their earlier mood.

Maya's heart sank. Oh, no, the timing was all wrong now. This was the last thing she wanted to talk about after that phone call. "Oh, that." She let out a little nervous laugh she knew only made things worse. "Well, um, nothing. It can wait."

Sawyer's eyes narrowed. "Spit it out, Maya."

Maya fumbled with her napkin, then sighed and put it down. It might as well be now. Putting this off wouldn't make it any easier. "It's just that, well, I had mentioned to Dr. Gonzales when I took the job that I was looking for a place to live."

Sawyer went very still. "And?"

"And today she was talking to the Romeros about the rest of their family, you know, asking how they were and so on." Maya wet her lips, forcing herself to hold his gaze. "They have a cousin, actually cousin and cousin-in-law, a young couple who had built a little adobe *casita* at the back of their property for the wife's mother-in-law, but the mother-in-law died unexpectedly, leaving them with a mortgage they can't afford."

"Unless they rent the *casita*," Sawyer said flatly.

Even in semidarkness, Maya saw the light fade from his eyes. "Yes."

"So when do you and Joey leave?"

Chapter Thirteen

"Well, that's the last of it, I think." Maya stood on Sawyer's front walk, watching as he secured the last of her things in the back of his truck. She was taking all the baby furniture at his insistence. He refused to even talk about her paying for it, and she couldn't think of a way of insisting without wounding his pride or his feelings or both—something she suspected she'd already done with her announcement she was moving out.

He'd barely talked to her since she'd told him five days ago about the house she'd found except to say he'd help her move. In fact, she hadn't seen him at all until this morning. He'd worked straight through the week, getting home early this morning and going right to work loading the truck.

"Whenever you're ready," Sawyer said as he gave the last tie-down a final tug to make sure it was secure.

Maya tried to guess at his mood but she didn't have a clue, and with his eyes hidden behind sunglasses and his voice carefully expressionless, he wasn't giving her one. She wished she could get some reaction out of him; even anger would be better than this cool detachment. It left her feeling lost, more alone now than when she'd first come back home.

She supposed the distance he seemed to deliberately be putting between them should make it easier to leave. Yet it had just the opposite effect, and she fought the urge to run to him and tell him it had all been a mistake.

Instead she made herself sound casual, as if this was exactly what she wanted, and said, "Joey's still napping. As soon as he wakes up and I feed him, we'll be ready to go."

"Sure, okay. Then I'm going to grab a sandwich." He started inside, paused when he came even with her. "You want some lunch?"

Maya shook her head. Her stomach felt as if someone inside had a serious vendetta. Just the thought of eating made her slightly nauseous. "No, I'm not hungry. But I made some limeade. I'll sit with you and have some of that. If that's okay with you," she added uncertainly.

He shrugged. "Lead the way."

Following him inside, she got them each a glass of limeade, then sat down at the kitchen table while he fixed a sandwich. They sat in silence while he ate and she sipped her drink, looking everywhere but at him. Finally, when he got up to put his plate in the dishwasher, Maya couldn't stand it any longer.

"Are we not talking anymore?" she asked pointedly.

Sawyer leaned back against the counter with his arms crossed over his chest, meeting her eyes at last. "Why wouldn't we be?"

"I don't know, you tell me. We haven't had anything I can call a conversation in almost a week."

"I've been working. So have you."

"Well, neither of us is working now," she said.

Sawyer shook his head. "What do you want me to say?"

Maya wanted to shake him. "I want you to talk to me, tell me what you're feeling about all this. Obviously you're unhappy about our moving out. I'm not thrilled about it either. But this

was only temporary, right? We agreed to that at the beginning."
She started to feel a little desperate—to convince him or herself,
she didn't know. "I have a safe place to live, you're back to
work. We don't need each other anymore, do we?" Stopping, she
didn't know how she wanted him to answer that.

"Sure, right," he said. At first glance, he looked at ease standing there. But Maya recognized the tension in his shoulders, the
way he held himself stiffly. "It makes sense. You need to get settled permanently somewhere. I understand that."

"It's only a few miles away. And it's not as if you'll never see
Joey again or that we'll stop being…" What? What exactly were
they? "…friends," she settled on, although that didn't begin to
describe the way she felt about him.

"Of course not," he answered in that same maddeningly calm
voice. "You know you can call me anytime."

"We didn't make any commitments. I mean, you didn't want
that. Did you?"

"You didn't either. Did you?"

"I—no. I mean, I thought I had a commitment with Evan."
She stumbled over the words in her haste to get them out. "And
look what happened. I don't know if I can trust myself to try that
again now that I have Joey to consider."

Sawyer shifted, dropping his arms, and for a moment something flickered in his eyes, an emotion Maya couldn't read. "The
last thing I want is for Joey to get hurt."

"I know that," she said softly. "So…it's all for the best.
Right?"

"Yeah, right." He glanced away, then back at her again. "It's
the best thing for everyone."

They looked at each other for a long moment and suddenly
Maya couldn't pretend anymore.

"Oh, this is so frustrating." She pushed away from the table
and got to her feet so suddenly, the table rattled. Coming so close
they were almost touching, she laid a hand on his arm. "I know
you're not like Evan, but this has all happened so fast. You've

been so devoted to us. But one minute I think I know who you are and what you want and the next it's like you're a stranger. Especially when you won't talk to me!"

She had shaken him and she could almost see the change in him, from distant to looking uncertain, as if he didn't know how to respond. That more than anything else unnerved her, because Sawyer always seemed certain where he stood. Now he looked vulnerable, and she turned from wanting to vent on him to wanting to hold him.

"Maya, I—" He stopped, started again. "I just want what's best for Joey and you."

"And what if that's you?" Maya asked. It was probably a stupid thing to say, but wanting to push him past his detachment made her reckless.

Sawyer's expression hardened and he straightened, the tension in him so palatable, she could almost touch it. "Can you be sure of that? Because I sure as hell can't. And until I can be sure, I can't ask you to take that risk."

"I don't need you to make up my mind for me. It's not your decision to make, it's mine."

"But you're not the only one who gets hurt if you make the wrong decision again. Joey gets hurt, too."

"I don't need to be reminded of that," Maya snapped at him. She was close to shouting at him and didn't care. "Do you think I'd let that happen again?"

"*I* won't let that happen. He's already been abandoned once."

Maya's anger died as quickly as it had flared. "And you think you would... No, you wouldn't do that." She forced out the words around the constriction in her throat. "I know you wouldn't."

"I don't know I wouldn't," Sawyer said roughly. He jerked away from her, as if putting a shield of space between them made it easier to say the words. "I don't know how to be what you want, what you both need. I've never known anything about being a husband or father. But it never mattered before."

Maya came to him and put her hand against his face, both needing and wanting to give comfort in touching him. "Sawyer, just look how great you've been so far—"

He took her hand away, holding it for a moment before letting her go. "So far. Exactly. Joey is a baby. His needs are simple. What about later, when he needs discipline, emotional support, real parenting? My experience with discipline involves a fist or a belt. What if I—" He stopped cold. Taking a shaky breath, he went on, "You know I couldn't live with that. I'd have to get out of your lives."

"Don't say those things. You're nothing like Evan or Garrett," she said hoarsely.

"Maybe not. But you can't ignore my history any more than I can, can you?"

Maya wanted to deny him. Except, in a small, dark place in her heart, she was afraid—afraid Sawyer didn't believe in himself enough to carry through with their relationship. He was so afraid of failing, of not being as perfect at being a father and husband as he was at everything else. She had the sad sense, when it came to being Joey's father and her partner, he'd rather not try than fail.

"We can't build on that," Sawyer said softly. Very gently he brushed his fingertips over her face, collecting her tears. "So maybe this is best. Maybe it'll give us both time to back off and be honest about what we've gotten into here."

Maya shook her head. "It doesn't feel best. It feels like the worst thing I've ever done."

"No, the worst thing you've ever done is try to make me drink decaffeinated weed tea first thing in the morning," he teased her in a clear attempt to lighten the mood.

She tried to smile, failing miserably. Sawyer took her face in his hands and looked at her intently, searching her eyes for answers she didn't have, before bending and joining her mouth to his in a kiss so achingly tender it released Maya's tears again.

They slid down her face, wetting his shirt, as Sawyer held her against his heart until Joey began to stir and Maya knew it was time for her to go.

"There, much better," Maya said, coming back from the tiniest bedroom, where she'd been changing Joey. The baby bounced along contentedly, propped on her hip. She followed Sawyer's glance around the main room that was living and dining room together, the kitchen separated from them only by a low half wall. "Well, it's small, but I think we're going to be just fine here."

She echoed his thoughts and to Sawyer it sounded as if she was trying to believe it, too. "Will you stay for dinner? Unless you have somewhere else you need to be," she added hastily.

She was giving him an out but Sawyer didn't want it. She was also giving him a reason to put off the inevitable moment when he had to leave Joey and her here and go home alone. Not an appealing idea. Right now this tiny, half-empty house seemed more warm and inviting than his ever had.

"No, I don't have to be back at work until tomorrow morning," he said. "But how about I take you and Joey out? It's been a long day and we both could probably use a break." He came over to where she stood and put his arm around her shoulder, reaching out to rub Joey's cheek. "What do you say, big guy? How about a night out?"

Sawyer smiled as Joey grabbed his finger. Then Joey smiled back.

"Wow, that's the first time I've ever seen that," Maya cried, delighted. She nuzzled her son. "Hey, how come you haven't done that for me yet?"

Sawyer grinned. "It's a guy thing."

"Oh, I get it." She gave Joey a mock-serious look. "You're gonna be one of those guys who drives the girls crazy with that killer smile. Just like your fellow guy here."

"So," Sawyer said, "you're saying I drive you crazy."

Maya looked fully at him and smiled just for him. "Always. Now—" before he could react, Maya slipped out from under his

arm and handed him Joey "—I'll let you guys hang out together
for a minute while I change into something that's not covered
with dust and spit-up."

Joey made no protest at being shifted to Sawyer's arms, instead
wriggling and gurgling happily as Sawyer looked at him. Maya
was right—no matter what, he'd never deliberately do anything to
hurt Joey. His gut twisted as he forced himself to think about what
that meant. It meant he had no choice but to end their relationship
while Joey was an infant, before too much time passed. Before they
drifted into a situation that would only devastate Joey when Maya
realized the man she'd trusted her future to knew nothing about
real fathering. Before she was forced to end it for her son's sake.

"I hope your face doesn't freeze like that." Maya came out of
the bedroom next to Joey's, smiling, in a dress Sawyer had never
seen before. Sleeveless, the emerald-green cotton lightly shaped
her body to just above her knees. She'd unbraided her hair and
left it loose, tempting him to touch, to compare the texture of the
coppery ripples against bare skin.

She flushed a little. "You're staring."

The sight of her distracted him from his dark thoughts. "You
look great. I mean, you looked great before, but…"

"Mmm…better stop now," she murmured, coming close. She
reached up and quickly brushed her mouth against his so for a
moment he was caressed by her heat and a whisper of her scent,
warm and spicy and just a little sweet.

Then just as quickly she backed away, grabbing up Joey's bag.
"Ready when you guys are," she said.

"Ready for what?" he said close to her ear as he followed her
out the door to his truck.

He found himself falling under the spell she wove, the spell
that let him believe this could last. At the same time a feeling
just as strong told him it couldn't.

They drove the ten minutes back to his house so Sawyer
could change and then he took them to a small Mexican restau-

rant in the center of town. He'd known the owners, Josefina and Eduardo Pillero, for years and so they were all smiles as they came out personally to greet him and Maya, fuss delightedly over Joey and find them a table in a quiet corner.

"Maybe we'll see you more often now that you're not working so much," Josefina said with a nod toward Maya and Joey.

Sawyer smiled easily. He knew Josefina was hinting for his confirmation that Maya and Joey were a permanent fixture in his life and tonight he needed to pretend. "I don't know," he said, glancing at Maya and catching her smile, "it's amazing how much work one little baby can be."

"Try five of them," Eduardo said. "Some days, twelve hours at the restaurant seemed like a vacation." He laughed as his wife swatted his arm. "You wait," he said to Sawyer, "one, two more, you'll never sleep again."

They chatted a few minutes longer, the Pilleros asking about Cort and Sawyer's grandparents and then Josefina asked, "So we will see you at the picnic, of course?"

"I've been working on my recipe," Eduardo said with a wink. "This is the year I finally beat your grandfather."

Maya looked at Sawyer questioningly. He took her hand and smiled at Eduardo. "How could we miss that?"

"Okay, I guess I missed something. What picnic?" Maya asked when the Pilleros had left them to their dinner.

"The last Saturday of the month, the big fund-raiser for the firefighters' association. You probably remember, they've been doing it every summer for years. And Eduardo has never beat my grandfather in the chili cook-off." He rubbed the back of her hand in slow circles, liking the way she blushed at his touch. "I've been meaning to ask if you and Joey would like to come with me. We could spend the day together."

"We would love to come with you," Maya said. "Although I'll be rooting for Eduardo. They have five children?"

"All girls. They married the last one off in February, so now they're looking forward to spoiling their grandchildren."

Maya glanced to where Josefina was greeting another couple and their two small children. "I'll bet they will, too. Shamelessly."

She didn't say anything about his letting the Pilleros assume they were a couple, so Sawyer didn't bring it up. Maybe she felt the same—that for a little while they could pretend together and forget everything that kept that from being reality.

And for the next hour it worked. They talked and laughed, kept Joey entertained and lingered over dessert. Only when Joey started getting drowsy and a little fussy did Maya reluctantly say she needed to get home.

They didn't talk on the drive back to her house, and by silent agreement Sawyer followed her inside and waited in the living room, idly flipping through her CD collection, while Maya fed Joey and settled him for a nap.

When she came out, baby monitor in hand, easing the door closed behind her, she smiled at the soft, sultry Spanish ballad Sawyer had quietly playing on the stereo. "That's one of my favorites," she said.

"Dance with me and it'll be one of mine, too."

Sawyer held out his hand and she came into his arms without hesitation. He pretended it was dancing, but for him it was just an excuse to hold her. The feel of her, molded against him, soft to hard, started his blood pounding and his senses humming. Yet tonight holding her was all he wanted to do. Holding her, imprinting her scent and her shape on his skin, making memories for when he was alone again.

The music finally wound down slowly and when it ended, Maya pulled back a few inches to look up at him. He could see in her eyes all the things she didn't want to say.

"Thank you for everything," she said as she walked with him to the door.

Sawyer bent and kissed her, lingering, then gently breaking away before he couldn't. "Call me if you need anything. You know where I am."

"And you know where I am. I hope you won't suddenly become a stranger."

"You couldn't be so lucky," he said, giving her another quick kiss. "I'll call you soon, I promise."

Maya slid her hand to his face. "Promise you'll come back soon."

"Count on it."

"I am," she said and this time it was she who pulled his mouth down to hers and kissed him as if soon was right now.

Sawyer finally decided he'd better make his exit now before he embarrassed himself by begging her to let him stay. She stayed in the doorway while he pulled out of the driveway, and he watched her there until he turned the corner and her house was out of sight.

A week later, alone in what still seemed like a strange house, Maya wondered for what had to be the hundredth time if she'd ever feel at home here. Even though she'd told herself from the beginning that living with Sawyer was temporary, she only now fully realized how at ease she'd been there and how totally unsettled she felt now without him around.

She hadn't seen him at all and only talked to him once in the last week, when he'd called her from the station to see how she and Joey were settling in. Then they'd been interrupted by an alarm, which only intensified Maya's loneliness.

Even Joey seemed listless and inclined to fuss more now that Sawyer wasn't there, although maybe he was just reacting to her own moodiness or the change in his schedule. Joey's sitter had remarked on it a few times, adding guilt at having to leave Joey to the whole messy mix of emotions.

She sat and rocked him now, trying to soothe him after he'd quit halfway through his evening feeding. She worried about him, but he didn't have a fever or any congestion, nor did he seem to be having any tummy troubles, although she checked him again after getting him settled in his crib. Maybe the move itself had been more disruptive for him than she'd thought.

"We're going to see Dr. Lia if you aren't any better by tomorrow," she told him, although Lia would probably tell her it was nothing but new-mom panic and not to worry so much.

After Joey fell asleep, Maya went around the rest of the house picking up the few toys and dishes left out and making sure the doors were locked and the outside lights on. She told herself she ought to work on finishing unpacking her boxes. But there wasn't much left to do and she felt too restless to settle down to any task. Sleep would be better. Although Joey was now sleeping longer at night—sometimes as long as seven hours at a stretch—since their move, Maya had been sleeping less.

She made herself go through the motions, though. And then, like the last weeks of nights, lay there staring at the ceiling, tossing and turning. Finally, after half an hour, she gave up. She checked on Joey, then went into the kitchen, opened the refrigerator and stared unseeingly at the contents and closed it again. Wandering into the living room, she picked up a book and tried to get interested in it but tossed it aside after reading the same sentence four times without knowing what it said.

It was nearly eleven. She glanced at the phone. "I can't call him now," she said aloud to the empty room.

Why not? temptation whispered back.

He probably wasn't even home. And besides, what would she say?

Hi, just thought I'd call and see if you were missing me as much as I'm missing you? How desperate did that sound? Only a week on her own and already she was aching to hear his voice.

She couldn't do it.

She kept telling herself that, even as she picked up the phone and dialed his number.

Sawyer answered so quickly, she briefly wondered if he'd been waiting for her call. "Maya?"

"Hi. I'm, um, sorry for calling so late." She tried to think of a rational explanation for why she was calling him in the middle of the night, but nothing came to her. "I hope I didn't wake you up."

"No," he said. "Is something wrong?"

"No, no, everything is fine. How about you?" Maya winced at her words. How lame could she get?

"Fine. Only it's been much too quiet here. I miss the noise."

"I miss your ice cream. There's nothing to tempt me here." Sawyer was silent for a moment. "I could fix that."

Maya's pulse quickened. "I know." She chewed at her lower lip, then said in a rush, "I miss you." It probably wasn't wise but it was the truth and she was tired of pretending.

"Is Joey asleep?"

"Yes," she said, not sure why he'd asked. "Why?"

"You want me to come over?"

Maya didn't hesitate. "Yes. But only if you want to."

"You might as well ask me if I want to keep breathing, *querida.*" The endearment caught her by surprise. The way he'd said it resurrected the first fantasies she'd had of him—of midnight seduction whispered against her skin in that dark voice of his.

"I'll be there in ten minutes," he said and hung up.

Maya stared at the phone in her hand for a full twenty seconds before the realization kicked in that she'd just invited Sawyer into her bed. She waited for the rational part of her to seriously backpedal and come up with twenty different reasons why that was a bad idea. It didn't happen.

That was probably because the crazy part of her had decided it was in charge. And the crazy part had corrupted her body with wicked fantasies and convinced her heart she cared for Sawyer more than she feared the consequences of falling in love with him.

She liked him. She wanted him. She'd wanted him ever since the first time he'd kissed her and melted her insides that day in his office. It was hormones and those wild, lightning, needy feelings he'd discovered in her. Only him.

Maya suddenly put down the phone and hurried to check on Joey. She found him sleeping peacefully. Making certain the monitor was working properly and finally satisfied he was fine, Maya left him to his dreams.

She went to the bathroom to run her hands through her hair and caught sight of her Pooh nightshirt in the mirror. No way she'd let Sawyer see her in that again. Peeling it off on her way to her bedroom, she couldn't decide what to replace it with that didn't look obvious or calculating. After pawing through her drawer, she at last settled on a black spaghetti strap dress in a soft, clingy T-shirt material she sometimes wore around the house on hot summer evenings.

She'd barely dropped it over her head when she heard Sawyer's truck pull up in the driveway. A shiver raced over her as she went to the door and flipped the lock. Before she could turn the doorknob, Sawyer pushed the door open and stepped inside, pulled her into his arms and covered her mouth with his for one of those bone-melting kisses.

"I missed you, too," he whispered in her ear when they both needed air. Without letting her go, he reached behind him and shoved the door closed. He slid his hand over her bare arm to the curve of her hip, bringing her body into intimate contact with his. "I lied when I said I didn't need you. You're all I can think about. I need you. I need this."

Maya didn't bother with words. She didn't have any for how he made her feel. Instead she let her kiss and her touch tell him how much she needed him, too.

Tugging his T-shirt free of his jeans, she pushed it up and he finished the job, yanking it over his head as she ran her hands over his chest. Sawyer let her stroke and explore. At the same time he teased her by brushing close but never quite touching the places she most wanted his hands and mouth to touch.

He made her wild, rushing headlong toward completely losing control. She'd never been like this with anyone else, and it was both exhilarating and frightening. Yet it felt as though she'd been waiting forever to feel like this and now she didn't want to wait any longer.

Slipping her fingers around the edge of his jeans, she worked free the button. Sawyer's hand caught hers and dragged it up so he could press an openmouthed kiss against her palm.

"*Lentamente, mi amor,*" he murmured. "I want this to last." He smiled slowly when she made a frustrated sound. "Tell me what you want, *querida.* Anything you want, any way."

"You," she said. Stepping back, she pulled her dress up over her head and let it drop. His control cracked, and she smiled to herself at the naked desire on his face as he raked her body with a look so hot it scorched her skin. "I want you. Now."

In one swift motion he reached for her and scooped her into his arms, his mouth slanting against hers. Carrying her to her bed, Sawyer gently laid her down, his hands now hot and hurried on her, burning a path from her throat to her breasts, before he followed the same path with his mouth.

Maya gasped and arched up, greedy for every sensation. When his hand slid to her thigh, touching her through the flimsy barrier of her panties, she grasped his shoulders, wanting more of him, wanting everything.

Instead Sawyer stilled. "Maya…" The urgency in his voice compelled her to look into his eyes. "Are you sure you're ready?" he asked hoarsely. "I don't want to hurt you. If it's too soon—"

"I'm way past ready, Sawyer."

He kissed her and as he hooked the edge of her panties, she fumbled at the zipper of his jeans.

A small mewling cry sounded over the baby monitor and Maya froze.

His breath coming quick and hard, Sawyer kissed her neck and whispered, "Give it a few minutes. You know Lia said not to run the instant you hear a noise."

Maya knew he was right, tried to kiss him back, but the spell was broken.

Sawyer felt it immediately. Yet all the weeks of waiting, of sleepless nights and pent up desire had caught up with him, and right now he was having a devil of a time banking his aching needs. Hoping to hold on to the moment he'd dreamed of for so long at least for another minute or two, he tried to claim her lips, her breasts again.

But the sound coming from the monitor this time doused his passion. This time it was a weak raspy sound, as if Joey were hurting.

This time they both reacted.

Sawyer levered himself off the bed, pulling Maya with him. She followed him out of the bedroom and grabbed up the first piece of clothing she saw on the way to Joey's room—Sawyer's shirt. Yanking it over her head, she rushed to Joey's side just as Sawyer bent over him.

There was nothing of the passionate lover of moments before left in him now as he deftly examined Joey, then looked back at Maya. "Call Lia's emergency number," he said. "He's burning up."

Maya didn't question. After one terrified glance at her son, she turned and ran for the phone.

Chapter Fourteen

Maya stood in the emergency-room cubicle holding tightly to Sawyer's hand as they both watched Lia examine Joey. Seeing her baby lying there, whimpering and trembling with fever, Maya wanted to snatch him up and hold him close. She knew without asking Sawyer felt the same way, but all either of them could do was wait for what seemed like forever while Lia worked.

She kept telling herself it would be okay, but it didn't stop the sick shakiness inside or the guilty feeling she should have known Joey was sick and done something before he ended up in the emergency room with a one-hundred-and-four-degree temperature.

"Well, this guy's got a nasty ear infection," Lia said, looking over at them. "We'll need to give him something to get the fever down and then he'll need antibiotics to knock out that infection."

Sawyer nodded, giving Maya's hand a squeeze. "Sounds good."

"No, it doesn't." Both Sawyer and Lia stared at Maya. She held her ground. "I'm sorry, I want Joey well again but I'm not too excited about giving him antibiotics, especially this young.

If you just treat the pain and fever, isn't there a good chance he'll get over the infection without them?"

Before Lia could answer, Sawyer swung to face Maya, his expression incredulous. "I can't believe you're talking about this now. It's obvious Joey needs medication. You're taking this chanting-and-meditation thing of yours a little too far this time."

Maya stiffened. For a moment she was back in Taos, with Evan ranting and raving about her stupidity in getting herself pregnant, his belittling her for being such a freak about taking medication. He'd made her doubt herself, and Sawyer's criticism brought it all back, intensified because of the guilt eating at her already.

"You're not Joey's parent, I am!" she snapped. "I want to do what's best for him. And that means thinking about the consequences of giving him drugs that might do more harm than good."

Sawyer looked as if she'd hit him hard. "Maybe you should think about the consequences of not giving him drugs," he said tightly. "His temperature is too high and it's not going to come down unless he gets medication. It's dangerous to let this infection go when it can easily be treated."

He glanced to Lia and she nodded. "I understand your concerns," she said slowly. It was apparent she was choosing her words carefully. "But I wouldn't have recommended an antibiotic if I didn't think it was necessary. I'm not a fan of using antibiotics with babies this young either, but in Joey's case, he's still a little behind physically and his temperature needs to come down."

Joey whimpered a little and Lia put a hand out to soothe him before looking back at Maya. "I'll respect your choice, Maya, but you need to decide now. We need to do something now for this fever."

Maya wanted to tell them all to go away so she could calm the turmoil of emotions pounding in her head and twisting her stomach and think. But then she looked at Joey, so small and in obvious distress, and she couldn't wait any longer. "Go ahead," she told Lia. "Whatever you think he needs."

She didn't look at Sawyer, and he said nothing as he followed

Lia out of the cubicle when she went to get what she needed to treat Joey.

After Joey had been given medication for the fever and infection, Lia asked Maya to wait to take him home until Lia was sure Joey's fever would go down. So Maya sat holding her son, gently rocking him until he finally drifted off to sleep again.

Alone, with the crisis passed, Maya had time to regret her confrontation with Sawyer. She was still angry with him for what he'd said, especially because it wasn't the first time he'd accused her of putting her own interests above Joey's well-being. But he'd reacted out of his caring and worry for Joey, and she'd let her past with Evan provoke her into lashing out at him in a way certain to hurt. She'd reminded him he didn't have any right to make decisions where Joey was concerned and implied he didn't have Joey's best interests at heart.

From the beginning there had been a bond between Sawyer and Joey, and she believed Sawyer would do anything for her son. Even risk hurting her, it seemed, resurrecting all her doubts about whether she and Sawyer would ever be able to put aside their pasts and their differences enough to have any kind of a future.

When, an hour later, Lia, satisfied Joey's temperature had dropped, said she could take him home, Maya was too tired to feel anything but relief that Joey was better.

She found Sawyer waiting for them. "Ready?" he asked and, at her nod, turned and ushered her out to the parking lot before she could think of anything to say to him.

He stayed silent on the way back while Maya sat next to Joey and tried to keep from falling asleep herself. At the house, Sawyer helped her get Joey inside and Maya left him in the living room while she settled her baby in his crib.

When she came back, Sawyer was gone.

Maya awoke the next morning to someone pounding at the inside of her head. It took her a few moments to realize the pounding was at the door and even longer to drag herself off the couch, where she'd dozed off after checking Joey for the umpteenth time.

"This better involve death or dismemberment," she muttered as she went to answer it.

Sawyer stood there holding a paper shopping bag. He wore the same clothes he'd had on the night before and he hadn't bothered to shave or do much more than run a hand through his hair. Maya wondered if he'd bothered to sleep at all.

"Hi. I brought a peace offering," he said, holding up the bag. "Unless you've decided to kick me out for good."

"Like I ever would," she said, standing back to let him inside. She didn't feel up to arguing with him again, but she also couldn't send him away when he was making a serious effort to patch things up between them.

"How's Joey?" he asked as he went straight to her kitchen and began unloading the bag.

Maya picked up a carton of organic yogurt and realized he'd been to the natural-food market. Definitely a peace offering. "He's still a little warm but he's been sleeping quietly. He woke up about five and ate a little and then went right back to sleep." Glancing at the kitchen clock, she saw it was now about seven-thirty. She looked pointedly at Sawyer. "I'll go and get the rest of his antibiotic today. Happy?"

Sawyer stopped and faced her squarely. "I'm happy Joey is better." He stopped and then said slowly, measuring his words, "I'm sorrier than you know about last night. I shouldn't have questioned you like that, especially in front of Lia." He held up a hand when she would have broken in. "You're Joey's mom, you know what's best for him. I admit I have a hard time with your idea of healing, but I also admit I'm no kind of parent and have no business pretending to be one. I'd say last night proves that since I was more interested in what I wanted than in checking on him."

"Oh, Sawyer, don't say that. I wanted it, too. And I should have known something was wrong earlier. At the hospital…I understand why you reacted the way you did and I'm sorry I lashed out at you the way I did. But I can't afford to make snap decisions where Joey is concerned. This time I'll go ahead with the antibiotics, but I'm going to do a lot of research and talk to Lia and Dr. Gonzales so next time Joey's sick I can be sure of my decision."

"Like I said, you know what's best for him. And despite last night, please believe I only want what's best for Joey, too."

"I know you do. Anyone can see that. It's just when you said what you did…" Maya let out a long breath. "It just brought back a lot of bad memories. Evan was embarrassed by my work and he was always criticizing me for what he called my 'fetish' about not taking medication. He blamed that for my getting pregnant. He never respected my beliefs or my work, and it hurt thinking you felt the same way."

Being compared to Joey's father doubled Sawyer's guilt about his selfish lapse last night. From the beginning he'd wanted to wring this Evan's neck for abandoning Maya and Joey, but last night he hadn't treated Maya any better than her ex.

Sawyer ached to take her in his arms. He wanted to wipe out the memories that put the shadows in her eyes and stole her smile. But he held back, knowing he was partly responsible for that. "I don't feel like that. I don't always agree with you when it comes to your work, but I've seen how good you are and how much good you do. I never meant to hurt you. I hope you believe that, too."

Maya took his hand and made nonsense of his attempt to keep some space between them. "I believe you're nothing like Evan or your father, no matter what you're thinking. You've always been there for Joey and I know you care deeply for him. Sawyer, you have to believe that I understand how difficult it's been for you to take on this fatherlike role and I couldn't have asked for a better…friend. And we can still be friends, right?"

Sawyer shook his head. "No."

Maya's smile turned to a look of dismay.

He smiled a little and pulled her close. "We're way past friends. I think we skipped that part and went straight to something else."

"Something like this?" she asked as she slid her arms around his neck.

He accepted the invitation in her eyes and kissed her, taking his time, then gently pulled back before he lost control of the situation again. "I came to make you breakfast, so why don't you grab a shower while I get it ready. Leave Joey's monitor—I'll keep an ear out for him while I'm cooking. And I promise I'll make sticks and twigs, just the way you like it."

She gave him a suspicious look. "I didn't think you could cook."

"All I need for this is a blender. Trust me." He put his hands on her shoulders and turned her toward the bathroom. "I got a quick lesson from that dandelion-tea girl at your favorite market. I think I can handle it."

She shook her head but went off willingly enough, first to Joey's room to check on him and then to the bathroom, where after a few minutes Sawyer heard the water running.

He found her blender and got to work on breakfast. He'd messed up big-time last night, but something in him wouldn't let him give up trying to be what Maya and Joey needed. He didn't know how not to give it his all. If that turned out not to be enough, though, he would do what had to be done.

He would end it.

For the next two days it seemed to Maya as if she and Sawyer were still living together, only at her house now instead of his.

He'd been there nearly the whole time, even one night when he'd ended up on her couch after she'd fallen asleep exhausted from too many sleepless nights worrying about Joey. Only because Joey had steadily improved and was fever-free did Maya reluctantly decide to go to work on Monday. She hated having to leave him, but Dr. Gonzales had been good about letting her work a flexible four-day week and Maya didn't want to mess up a good thing by taking advantage of her generous nature.

When Sawyer offered to stay with Joey instead of the sitter, Maya agreed with little hesitation. Joey seemed much more content with Sawyer around, and a happy Joey was more likely to recuperate even faster.

So when Sawyer had to go back to work on Tuesday, Maya couldn't help a pang of regret. It was easier with him around. Yet it unsettled her to realize how much she'd come to rely on him being there. What had happened to her determination to be strong and independent?

She was still asking herself that on Friday. She'd been hurrying around the house getting Joey ready for his checkup with Lia as Joey lay on his quilt in front of the fireplace batting at the mobile Azure had made him, when the phone rang. She juggled the diapers and baby T-shirts she was holding to grab it up, thinking it was Sawyer calling again to check on Joey and her.

"Well, I can tell it wasn't me you were expecting to hear," Val's laughing voice said in her ear.

"No, hi, I'm glad you called. I just thought it was Sawyer," Maya said, then flushed, realizing she was giving herself away, glad Val couldn't see her face.

"I knew that. I just called to see how Joey was doing. And to see if you guys were still planning on being at the picnic tomorrow." Maya sat down on the floor next to Joey and caught Val up and they chatted for a few minutes. Then Val threw her by saying, "Why don't you and Sawyer just make it official? It seems pretty obvious how you feel about each other."

"Where did that come from?" Maya asked.

"Oh, come on. I don't know why you bothered moving out of his place. Now he just spends all his time there."

Maya squirmed a little at Val's direct questions. She wasn't sure if she was ready to look that closely at her feelings for Sawyer. "Maybe everything is obvious to you. But I'm not so sure."

"You could have fooled me," Val said. "I can tell you two are crazy about each other."

"He makes me crazy. I'm not sure if that's the same thing."

Val laughed. "Sure it is. Paul still drives me crazy. That's one of the reasons I love him."

Love him? Maya stared at the phone after she hung up with Val. That couldn't have happened—could it?

The phone rang again and it took her a moment to realize this time it was Sawyer asking her if something was wrong. "No, everything's fine," she said quickly. "I'm just distracted. I'm trying to get Joey ready for his checkup."

"Are you sure? You sound strange."

Big surprise. Right now she felt strange, as if she'd been slammed off her feet by something she should have seen coming but didn't recognize until it was too late. "I'm sure." She stopped, ran her tongue over suddenly dry lips. How could she explain to him what she couldn't explain to herself? And what if he didn't want to hear it? "Sawyer…"

"What's bothering you?" Sawyer said and Maya could hear the tension in his voice. "Tell me what's wrong."

"Nothing. I just need to talk to you. In person. I can't do this over the phone."

He let out a frustrated breath. "I'm here until tomorrow morning. I was planning to come by then anyway, as soon as I'm off, unless you've changed your mind about the picnic. Can it wait?"

"No, but it'll have to." Maya decided she'd better give up this conversation before she confused Sawyer any worse. "It can wait, really. And no, I haven't changed my mind about the picnic. We'll talk tomorrow. And Sawyer, I miss you."

"Yeah, I miss you, too," Sawyer said to his phone, since Maya had abruptly hung up.

He had no idea what all that had been about. Obviously something had upset her but she didn't feel comfortable telling him what it was. He didn't know what bothered him more—that Maya was worried or that she didn't trust him enough to confide in him.

"Here's that report you were looking for." Paul came in and threw a stack of papers on Sawyer's desk. He gestured at the phone still in Sawyer's hand. "What, is Cort hounding you again?"

Sawyer tossed his cell phone aside. "Not today. It's nothing," he said as Paul continued to look at him questioningly.

"Yeah, I can tell that by the scowl. Are things okay with you and Maya?"

"Why wouldn't they be?" Sawyer picked up the report and pretended to read it, hoping Paul would get the hint and go away. Even if he wanted to confide in Paul, he didn't have the first idea what was wrong with Maya.

"Because I figure this is a totally new experience for you," Paul said, as usual ignoring the hint. "I mean, what's it been, three months now? My guess is you have no idea what you're doing with Maya and it's frustrating the hell out of you."

Sawyer said nothing, largely because he didn't want to admit Paul was right. He didn't have any idea what he was doing and it was messing with his head and making him question everything he did and wanted.

It was also messing with his body. He'd been tortured by the memory of her stripping off that scrap of a dress, of her lying under him, wild and willing, the smell of her skin and the taste of her body. Sawyer ruthlessly cut off the vision. He'd been in the workout room and under a cold shower enough this week.

He transferred his scowl to Paul. "Don't you have something to do?"

Paul laughed. "I knew I was right. It's okay, buddy. You'll figure it out. Eventually."

Her cell phone rang again just as Maya, wrestling with Joey's carrier and a bag of groceries, got inside her front door and pushed it closed against a rush of wind and rain. She decided the phone must have it in for her today since it kept ringing at the most inopportune times.

She answered while setting Joey's carrier on the table and dumping the groceries, surprised to hear Sawyer's partner, Rico, on the other end. "Is something wrong with Sawyer?" she asked, her heart quickening.

"No, it's not that," Rico reassured her. "Paul's out on a call or he would have called you. He asked me to let you know because you'll probably be seeing it on the news and he didn't want you to hear about it that way."

Maya resisted the impulse to demand he get to the point. "Hear about what?"

"Sawyer's team got called out to Black Mountain Canyon. A couple of climbers got into trouble and are trapped about halfway down the gorge. They're gonna have to rappel in to get them out."

"In this wind?" Maya asked. She glanced to the window, now splattered with rain.

"Yeah, that'll make it tricky. But tricky is what Sawyer's team does best."

It wasn't very reassuring, and after Maya thanked Rico and hung up, her concern for Sawyer turned to fear. Joey kicked and babbled at her and Maya automatically picked him up, carrying him to the kitchen window to stare outside at the rain being blown in gusts by the wind.

People kept telling her about how Sawyer was known for this kind of risky heroics, but it hadn't seemed real until now. He'd told her he had trouble understanding her work and now she felt the same way. Why did he insist on willingly putting himself into situations where he might not be able to come back? He seemed driven to demonstrate over and over he could rescue anyone, fix everything, as if he needed to prove to himself and everyone else he could do it.

But she didn't need him to be everything. He was a hero to her because he loved Joey and he wanted to make things right for him. She only wished she could make him believe that.

For the first time Maya also wished she had a television or even a radio because right now she hated not knowing more details about what was going on.

Then she thought about Mrs. Garcia. Sawyer knew the elderly woman from the numerous calls he'd made to her house, and Mrs. Garcia had been delighted when she figured out Sawyer was a frequent visitor to her new neighbor's home. Sawyer had introduced them, and since then Maya had made it a point to make friends, especially after Sawyer told her Mrs. Garcia's calls for the paramedics were prompted by loneliness.

"Of course you can come, both of you," Mrs. Garcia told her when Maya called to ask if she could come over and watch a few minutes of the noon newscast while feeding Joey. "I'll make us some of that tea you brought me last week."

A few minutes later Maya sat in Mrs. Garcia's ancient rocker giving Joey his lunch and waiting anxiously for twelve o'clock.

Mrs. Garcia had settled herself on the couch next to her and pointed as the news finally started and the picture switched from the studio newsroom to a live remote from Black Mountain. "That must be where Sawyer is," she said. "*Ay,* that does look dangerous."

Dangerous described it pretty well. The reporter obviously couldn't get close to the rescue scene, but behind him Maya could see the sheer, craggy walls of the canyon, dark clouds hunched over them. Apparently one of the climbers was injured and two rescue-team members were getting ready to rappel down to bring both of the climbers up. Maya would have bet her last dollar Sawyer was one of them.

The report was frustratingly short. Maya stayed long enough to let Joey finish and to drink a cup of tea with Mrs. Garcia before getting up to take her now-sleepy baby back home.

She thanked Mrs. Garcia but the older woman waved her off. "You come back later if you want. Maybe they'll have more news about your man."

Maya accepted the offer, though she preferred having the

man back, whether she could call him hers or not. At home, she put Joey down for a nap and then tried to keep herself busy while she waited.

Paul called, not able to tell her much more than she already knew. She also talked to Val and then her parents, who'd initially called to ask about Joey and check on her plans for Saturday's picnic but then wanted to hear all about Sawyer. When Cort called late in the afternoon, Maya's stomach clenched, praying he wasn't the bearer of bad news.

"I just wanted to see how you were doing since this is probably the first time you've had a real taste of my big brother's talent for throwing himself headfirst into trouble," Cort said. "Don't worry, Sawyer's always doing this kind of thing and somehow he manages to land on his feet."

Maya was thinking of the time he'd landed on his head rescuing the kid who'd set her parents' house on fire. "I just hope he hasn't used up his nine lives," she told Cort.

At five, Maya couldn't stand waiting any longer and she took Joey over to Mrs. Garcia's to watch the early-evening news. She went weak with relief when the camera panned to a group of men and emergency equipment and she saw Sawyer, muddy and wet, still in his helmet and climbing harness, helping to load a stretcher into a waiting medical helicopter.

"…nearly five hours to reach the stranded climbers and bring them to safety," the reporter was saying. "Team leader Captain Sawyer Morente, of the Luna Hermosa Fire District, and Lieutenant Luis Sanchez, of Rio Vista Fire and Rescue, rappelled down to the two men, who had become trapped midway down the canyon after…"

Maya didn't hear any more. She smiled and agreed with Mrs. Garcia that Sawyer was wonderful, thanked her and took Joey back home without really knowing what she'd said.

All she could think was that Sawyer was all right.

It was later that night, as she sat rocking Joey to sleep in the quiet sanctuary of his room, that it hit her. All day she'd been worried and upset, telling herself it was because Sawyer was risking his life and she didn't know if she could accept the dangerous part of his work.

But that was an excuse to keep her from admitting the real reason why she'd been so unsettled. It wasn't about his job or his penchant for risk-taking. She loved him. And that scared her.

If he hadn't come back, she never would have had the chance to tell him. And now that she had the chance, she didn't know if she should take it.

Their problems hadn't disappeared because she'd lost her heart to him. If anything, they seemed magnified now because the stakes were so much higher for her. She didn't even know how he felt, if he cared enough for her to want to be more than just her lover.

The only thing she knew for certain was that she wanted that and everything else from him. And what frightened her most was that she didn't know if she was willing to risk everything to have it.

Sawyer showed up at her door just after ten looking tired but happy to see her as Maya greeted him with a hug. He held her close for a few moments, then moved to slump in a corner of the couch, pulling her to sit next to him.

"The chief let me off early," he said, draping his arm around her shoulders as he leaned his head back against the cushions and closed his eyes. "I think he was afraid I was going to sleep through the next alarm."

Maya stroked the hair back from his forehead. Her hand shook a little and Sawyer reached up and captured it in his. Kissing her fingertips, he smiled. "Hey, it's okay. I came back."

"I was worried about you," she admitted. "I saw part of it on the news and…"

"It wasn't as bad as it probably looked," he said lightly. "The worst part was dodging all the cameras afterward. I hate having my picture taken. Don't television cameras add ten pounds or something?"

Maya gave a shaky laugh. "I thought you looked pretty good." She ran her fingers over his face. "You look pretty good now."

"You look pretty good yourself," Sawyer said softly. He shifted so he could gather her close and draw her into a long, slow kiss.

Sliding her arms around his neck, Maya tangled her fingers in his hair to hold him even closer. She didn't pretend she hadn't been thinking about this, hadn't been hoping he would come here tonight. She needed this, to feel him hard and warm and strong against her softness. To have him inside her, filling the empty places in both body and heart that ached for him alone.

He deepened his kiss, his tongue stroking hers, feeding the fire between them. His hand caressed her face, her throat, slid over her shoulder, brushing aside the skinny strap of her dress.

It was the same dress she'd worn the night they'd almost made love, Sawyer realized. That little bit of soft black that slipped so easily down her body. The memory of her stripping it off hit him again—hard. If he didn't cool things down now, in a few more minutes he'd be past the point of no return. Maybe she would, too, but he wanted to be sure it was what she wanted.

"Maya—" He straightened up so he could look into her eyes. She made a throaty little sound of protest and Sawyer nearly said to hell with his good intentions.

He forgot he'd ever had any good intentions when she moved in close and began unbuttoning his shirt while she murmured in his ear, "If you ask me again if this is what I want, I'm going to scream."

"Then I won't ask. I can think of a lot better ways to make you scream." He punctuated his words with a slow slide of his hand up her thigh that bunched up the soft material of her dress to her hip. Leaning in to kiss her, he stopped.

She looked at him. "What's wrong?"

"Maybe you better check on Joey," Sawyer said with a significant glance at the baby monitor.

Maya couldn't help it. She laughed and kissed him and said, "Maybe I'd better."

She came back a few minutes later to the low sound of her favorite Spanish ballad. Sawyer, wearing only his jeans, was finishing lighting the two fat candles she'd set on the fireplace mantel. When he saw her, he walked over and flicked off the lamp and then held out his hand to her.

"Dance with me, *querida*."

She came into his arms on a breath of longing.

And then she was lost.

Chapter Fifteen

He held her close to the sway of the soft, sensual music and she melted against him, ready to let him lead. Ready at last to let go.

As the passion in the music rose, so did the fire between them. His body made love to hers in a rhythm that joined them soft to hard, in a slow caress of bare skin and heat. The ballad finally ended on an achingly tender climax to a long breath of silence and then flamed into a hot, pulsing salsa. Sawyer didn't miss a beat.

"Oh! I don't—" Maya stumbled along several steps until the press of his hips to hers let her find the soul of the music along with him.

"Don't think about it. *Sientes el ritmo,*" Sawyer urged, his voice low and husky with the passion echoed in the music. "Feel the rhythm." He spun her in his arms, bringing them close enough for her mouth to brush his.

If their first song had been a slow dance of love, this was a wild, wicked coupling. "What I'm feeling is probably illegal," Maya said breathlessly as his hips thrust against hers.

"Nothing between us is forbidden anymore." Dipping her low, laying her back in his arms, he gave her a smile that said he promised to fulfill her every fantasy. "This is only the beginning. Tonight I'm yours. For whatever you want."

"Then I want everything." She caught her breath as he suddenly brought her up hard against his chest in one dramatic sweep. "You can dance, you can *really* dance."

"My grandparents insisted I take flamenco, and later I learned to salsa in Puerto Vallarta. It all seemed a complete waste of time—until tonight."

"Wow. Cool," she said, then inwardly groaned. How lame. Had she really said that? Growing up with Shem and Azure had permanently kept some of her English locked in 1965. She always fell back on her roots whenever she got nervous.

And tonight Sawyer had definitely unsettled her.

He knew it, too, and laughed, then spun her away from him and back again.

Maya tried again. "I mean, I've never danced like this. You're amazing."

"Ah, *querida mio,* I haven't shown you amazing yet," he said. He pulled her close against him as the salsa beat ended with a flourish and another, slower rhythm began. Holding her gaze with his, he teased the strap of her dress from one shoulder and then the other. "There's another dance I'd much rather be doing now."

"Yes," she whispered. "Now."

That was all Sawyer needed to sweep her up in his arms and carry her to bed.

Maya clung to him, feeling the same tension in him that clutched at her, a tight, hot anticipation that wanted to hurry her into ecstasy. And yet, as Sawyer, in the midst of a long, soul-reaching kiss, laid her slowly, gently on her simple white cotton comforter, she knew he wouldn't rush. They'd waited so long, she sensed he didn't want this night to end.

He began to undress her ever so slowly, and when she tried

to help, he took her hands in his, kissed them, then laid them aside with enough firmness to make it clear he didn't want or need her help.

"I want to savor you," he murmured. "Just relax and let me enjoy you, inch by beautiful inch."

"I've never…I mean no one ever—"

"I'm glad. I want to make you forget there ever was anyone else."

When he touched her like this, Maya had trouble remembering her name, let alone any other lover. There was only him, filling her with the taste of his kiss, the scent of him, whispering Spanish in that dark voice that could have convinced her to say yes to anything. His touch was fire, sweet and hot, and she wanted to burn. Her eyes drifted closed as she let the feelings sweep over her.

How could he imagine she would ever compare him to any other man? If only he had any idea of how far this was from anything in her limited sexual experience. The only other two men she'd been with had been happy to get to the point. Fast. They had obviously never learned the art of this lingering seduction.

Sawyer, on the other hand, was a master. And she was more than ready to surrender to his skill.

Brushing butterfly kisses over every inch of her bared skin, he drew her sheath of a dress over her shoulders. She trembled as the heat coiled low and tight inside her, awakening needs and desires she scarcely recognized. For the first time in a long while she felt wholly feminine again, a woman apart from the child she loved, and it felt good; it felt right.

Sawyer slid her dress downward from her breasts, over her now-flat belly, her thong, her thighs, her calves, following its path with hot trailing kisses, finally shoving it aside.

"*Te quiero, mi amor.* I want you," he breathed against her skin. "I need you."

Maya's breath left her in a rush. *Mi amor*…my love. Had he said it in the heat of passion or was he echoing what was in her heart? It was on her lips to tell him, but Sawyer, in one swift motion, pulled off her thong and ran his hands up her thighs, opening her to his touch, blanking her mind so she could only feel.

"Sawyer." She said his name on a gasp and a plea, arching up, encouraging him to take more, give more.

Sawyer nearly lost it then. She turned him inside out, made him crazy with everything he wanted. But he forced himself to take his time. It had been so long for her, he needed to be careful so all she felt was pleasure, the same mind-stealing pleasure she incited in him.

Lacing his fingers with hers, he held her lightly and pulled back enough to look at her. The moonlight showed him what he'd been imagining for so long—Maya stretched out beneath him, all smooth creamy skin and soft curves, her hair a wild tangle, the desire in her eyes just for him.

Glancing away from him, Maya looked uncertain and Sawyer could tell even in the dim light she was blushing. "I know… It's not been that long since I had Joey and—"

"And you're beautiful," Sawyer told her. "I've always thought so, from the moment I saw you."

He put everything he felt into his kiss, knowing he'd wanted this, wanted her, from the first time he'd touched her. Since then, he'd been waiting for her even as he'd tried to tell himself it couldn't happen, shouldn't happen. None of that mattered because she'd gotten under his skin and into his heart, and now his body was long past listening to anything his head had to say.

He tasted and touched, indulging some of the fantasies that had kept him awake so many nights while keeping them both balanced on the edge of falling. Until she made a frustrated sound and fumbled open the button and zipper of his jeans to slide her hands inside.

At her intimate caress, he rocked against her. His kiss was wild as he rose up long enough to shove off his jeans.

"Wait," he muttered when she reached to pull him back into her arms. He moved away from her long enough to dig in his jeans pocket for the protection he'd brought—last-minute wishful thinking on his part that one night she'd want to share all those fantasies of his.

Maya looked up at him, thinking her fantasies were never this good. Sawyer stood over her, all power, all male, tall, chiseled and obviously ready to take everything she was more than eager to give. "My God, you're every inch as gorgeous as I've been dreaming you would be all these weeks."

Sawyer smiled slowly, his eyes smoldering with anticipation as they raked over her body. "I want to make all your dreams come true."

"You can. Sawyer, please—"

Her plea went unfinished as he quickly covered her body with his, drawing them together, kissing her deeply, his tongue parting her lips as she opened herself to him.

Having her pressed against him so wet and willing and not plunging into her was pure torture. But gritting his teeth, Sawyer held back. "Maya, are you sure? I don't want to—"

"Don't think," she demanded. "Feel." Then she wrapped her legs around his hips and took him inside her, moaning her pleasure as he gave up any pretense of being in control and thrust deep.

Knowing she wanted him as fiercely as he did her made it all the sweeter, all the more exciting. He forgot to care about any of his questions or doubts. Nothing mattered but Maya and this feeling they'd made together.

Maya felt swept away by a flash flood of sensations. She wanted to capture each feeling and hold it to savor. But it was like trying to catch a shower of falling stars, each one hotter and brighter than the last.

And in the end she gave up, crying out his name as Sawyer took her with him to heaven.

Rays of watermelon sunrise slanted through Maya's bedroom window, warming her face, gently waking her. Her eyes fluttered open. Had last night been a perfect dream?

Then she felt the very real sensation of Sawyer's chest pillowing her cheek and she smiled. No, definitely not a dream.

Gazing in a sleepy state of awe out her window as the sun rose over jade and turquoise mountains, she traced her fingers lightly over his chest and arm, memorizing again the texture of his skin, the shape of his body. He slept soundly, holding her close to him. She lay there, listening to his slow, even breathing and the steady beat of his heart, as she relived their passionate night together.

Making love with Sawyer had been everything and far more than she'd fantasized about all those long weeks of waiting, wondering if it would, if it could, ever happen. How had he known exactly how to charm her, how to excite her? That she loved to be kissed on the neck, for one thing? Or that nibbling her ear or drawing circles on her lower back drove her wild? Either he had the lovemaking instincts of Don Juan, or he'd been picking up little signals from her all along, saving them for one special night. Even now, thinking about all of the ways he had teased, tempted and finally carried her all the way to paradise, her body began to hum again with anticipation.

Sawyer shifted and groaned softly when her leg slid against his thigh. Maya decided she'd better get up or she'd be waking him and demanding a repeat performance—for the fourth time. Besides, any minute now Joey, the human alarm clock, would be jolting them both into action with a hungry howl.

Reluctantly she eased out of his arms and out of the bed they had shared. The idea of it as *their* bed crossed her thoughts, but she didn't allow herself to dwell on it. For now, it was enough to watch him sleeping there, her white sheet grazing his lean hips, a stark contrast to his dark skin, his hair sexy and disheveled.

Exerting no small effort, Maya managed to pry her eyes from him. She hesitated over something to wear and then gave into temptation and got Sawyer's shirt from the living room. It smelled like him, and she smiled as she slipped it on before heading for Joey's room. Surprisingly she found her baby boy awake, happily cooing and staring up at the mobile Azure had made for him.

"Good morning, sweet stuff," Maya whispered as she bent over his crib.

Joey answered with a wide smile and an excited squeal, his little feet kicking wildly out from under his baby pajamas.

"Thank you for not waking Sawyer," she said, lifting Joey out of the crib and moving to the rocking chair to nurse him. "You must have known he needed some rest." Or maybe he was just happier with Sawyer here, with them all together. Just as his mama was.

The better part of an hour later, with Joey fed, changed and perched on her hip, Maya stood at the stove scrambling eggs and green chili. She didn't hear Sawyer move up behind her until he wrapped an arm around her waist and pulled her back against his body.

Brushing her hair aside, he greeted her with a kiss on her nape. "Morning," he murmured, his voice raspy with sleep.

"Morning, yourself." She turned to smile up at him. He'd pulled on his jeans but hadn't bothered to button them, and with his hair rumpled and the shadow of a beard, he looked wicked enough to make her wish for breakfast in bed. Without the breakfast. Then Joey babbled and flapped his hands, wriggling in her grasp so Maya laughed. "I think he feels ignored."

"Then why don't you let me hold him while you finish?" Sawyer lifted Joey from her arms and up over his head playfully. "Morning to you, too, little guy. I didn't hear you wake up today."

"I think somehow he knew you needed your sleep." Maya smiled, a little catlike twist to her lips. "You earned it, after all."

Sawyer lowered Joey and bent to kiss her lingeringly. "I was hoping I'd earned more than that."

"Mmm…well, maybe later. Definitely later," she amended as he slid his hand up her thigh, flashing that killer smile when he realized his shirt was all she wore. "Stop that or I'm going to burn your eggs."

"What eggs?"

"You have a one-track mind." She waved him toward the cof-
feemaker she'd bought just in case he spent the night. "I made
your poison. We need to get dressed and start packing for the picnic, remember?"

Sawyer let her go. "Oh, that."

The sudden flat tone in his voice confused Maya. "I thought
you'd be looking forward to it. All the guys from the station will
be there, won't they?"

"The whole town will be there," he said, turning to pace the
kitchen floor.

"And?" Maya turned off the stove and set the pan aside. "Is
that a bad thing?"

"Maya—" He turned toward her, started to say something, apparently thought better of it, and turned away, patting Joey's back
with a nervous, almost hypnotic rhythm. "It'll be fine."

Baffled and increasingly apprehensive, Maya walked up to
him and laid her hands on his shoulders, making him face her.
"What's going on? What's the problem? I thought this would be
a fun day. I've been looking forward to it. I even got salami so
you wouldn't be stuck with weed sandwiches today."

Sawyer handed Joey to Maya and pushed his hands through
his hair, rubbing at the back of his neck. "The problem is all in
my head. It's nothing." He attempted a half smile. "I'll look forward to the salami. Thanks." Bending to touch his lips to hers,
he added, "I know what that cost your vegetarian soul. I'm going
to hop in the shower."

"Um, okay." As he strode out of the kitchen, she asked, "What
about breakfast?"

"Sorry, I'm not hungry. Will you save me something for later?"

"Not hungry?" Maya asked a wide-eyed Joey. "What are we
getting into today?"

By noon the city park was absolutely mobbed as Maya and
Sawyer scouted the crowd for Val and Paul, both deciding it

wasn't going to be easy to spot them with what seemed like most of Luna Hermosa in one place.

"At least the weather cooperated," Maya said as they wove their way through the milling people. She carried Joey in a sling that wrapped over one shoulder, leaving Sawyer with Joey's bag, folded stroller and the picnic basket.

Sawyer couldn't argue with her. The New Mexico sun dazzled against a perfectly turquoise sky, with just the right number of clouds to punctuate the overall beauty. It was warm but not hot, and you could count on New Mexico to cool down by evening in time for the stars—or tonight, in time for the fireworks.

But he was having a hard time shaking the feeling this whole thing was a bad idea even though it had been his idea in the first place.

"Hey, you guys!" Val shouted from several yards away. "We have a spot over here." She stood on tiptoe, hands waving wildly at them.

"Great, we found them." Slipping her hand around his arm, Maya squeezed lightly, stopping him for a moment. "Are you sure you want to do this?"

Guilt pricked at Sawyer for making her suffer his lousy temper, especially after last night. "What I want to do would get us arrested here," he said lightly. He gave her a quick kiss. "We better get over there before Val hurts herself."

Maya eyed him, then shook her head before starting off toward Val.

Sawyer hoped everything that could go wrong today wouldn't, for Maya's sake. It was the possibility of running into other people he'd rather not claim as family that made him uneasy. Josh Garrett was a rising star on the rodeo circuit and there was a good chance he'd be here today, performing for the home crowd. That meant there was also a good chance Josh's father and brother would be here, too, and they were the last people Sawyer wanted to see.

When they got to where Paul and Val had set up under an ancient cottonwood tree, they were immediately caught up in greeting the group gathered there.

In addition to Paul, Val and their kids, Lia was there with Tonio Pena from Sawyer's station, and Sawyer was surprised to see Rico coupled with Paul's sister Cat.

"This is new," Sawyer said to his partner, nodding to Cat, who was fussing over Joey. "And when did Lia and Tonio hook up?"

Rico laughed. "It's not really new. And Tonio stepped in after Lia finally gave up on you. You've just been too busy to notice." He glanced significantly at Maya.

Sawyer looked over to where she was talking animatedly to Lia, Val and Cat. She'd dressed casually today in that full skirt and skinny little top he liked, her hair loose and wild. He didn't realize he was smiling until Rico prodded him in the arm.

"Man, you got it bad," Rico said with a knowing grin.

Before Sawyer could think of something to say to that, Val had drawn them into a group that was now discussing the day's activities.

After a few minutes, several of the members of the group went off in the direction of the horseshoe pits. Val and Paul began doling out food to their twins. Maya moved a little to the side so she could discreetly nurse Joey.

"I'll take him when he's done so you can eat," Sawyer offered.

"Thanks, I'll let you." Maya smiled at him, noticing a change in his tone. He looked more relaxed now, less edgy and withdrawn. Maybe whatever had been bothering him earlier had resolved itself. She hoped so. Today was working out to be the perfect follow-up to a perfect night. "What are you grinning at?" she asked, growing warm with his attention fixed on her. Sawyer in this mood was irresistible.

He bent close, speaking for her ears only. "I was just noticing that pretty pink blush in your cheeks and wondering if I should take credit for it."

Maya felt her face grow hotter. "Yes. And now you can take the blame for making me look like Rudolph."

"If I have that much power over you after one night, you'll be my slave after two."

"Hold on Casanova. I'm not that easy."

"But are you willing?"

He held her in his sexy, suggestive gaze, giving her vivid visions of the body beneath his T-shirt and jeans and all the ways he'd used it to drive her crazy. "I think I'm already your slave," she confessed. She caressed him with her eyes. "Just remember, lover, it works both ways."

"That sounded like a dare. And you know I can't resist a dare." Sawyer leaned over and took her mouth with his, kissing her too hard and too long, he knew, given their public situation. But in that moment he didn't give a damn who saw them together, who knew they were lovers.

The sound of someone loudly clearing his throat broke them apart. Sawyer looked up and inwardly groaned.

Skirting the edge of Maya's blanket, his grandparents stood staring down on the intimate scene, looking as if Sawyer was personally responsible for permanently blackening the Morente name.

The pair of them looked as if they belonged somewhere where there wasn't grass, trees, children or dust to mar the perfection of their classic summer-white linens. If he hadn't been anticipating a battle, Sawyer would have laughed at the irony of his grandparents, who prided themselves on their flawless social sense, looking totally out of place here.

Unfortunately Maya looked just as unsettled, but for different reasons. Joey's little head was still buried under the drape of his sling as he finished nursing, and Maya was caught in the awkward position of having to confront his grandparents while unable to stand up and with everyone knowing she was exposed under the sling.

Sawyer rescued her at once, standing in front of her to shield her from his grandparents' disapproving scrutiny. "I was beginning to think you weren't coming this year," he told them, though *hope* was the better term.

"We had a charity brunch for the opera this morning in Santa Fe," his grandmother said coolly.

His grandfather's hand tightened on the top of the silver-handled walking stick he was grinding into the dirt. "I've supported the fire department for thirty years, and we haven't missed this event yet." He eyed Sawyer up and down, then looked pointedly behind him to Maya. "But perhaps this year should have been our first absence."

Maya stood up beside him, Joey in her arms. Sawyer took Joey from her and took her hand. All the chatter from the rest of their group had given way to an uncomfortable silence, and Sawyer wished he could just whisk Maya and Joey away before things got worse.

But she gave his hand a squeeze, telling him she was with him and could handle it. "Maybe it should have been," he told his grandfather, matching his icy tone. "But since you're here, I'd like you to meet Maya Rainbow and her son Joey. Maya, this is Mr. and Mrs. Santiano Morente, otherwise known as my grandparents."

Maya put on a smile. "It's an honor to meet you both."

Neither of the Morentes so much as acknowledged her existence. Sawyer's grandfather looked past her as though she were invisible; his grandmother looked her up and down as though she were some sort of vermin that had gotten into her pristine house.

"And does this child have a last name?" his grandmother asked.

Maya's eyes narrowed. "*His* name is Joseph Lincoln Rainbow."

"I suppose you had no choice but to keep that ridiculous last name your parents invented. But then I suppose it's somewhat fitting for them, considering the way they choose to live. They never married, did they?"

"And why is that your business?" Sawyer asked. With Joey

in his arms, he was trying to keep a rein on his temper but losing it fast.

"It's our business because you've proven once again you can't make appropriate decisions," his grandmother snapped.

With that Paul nudged his way-too-curious twins. "Come on, girls, time to hit the horseshoe pits."

With a quick glance of concern at Sawyer and Maya, Val gathered up Johnnie and followed.

"You live with this girl and her son, flaunt your relationship in front of everyone, and now half the town is convinced the boy is yours."

Sawyer smiled tightly. "Then I'll have to work harder at convincing the other half."

His grandmother looked as if she wanted to slap him. "You don't know any more about being a parent than your father did."

Maya's hand gripped his hard, but Sawyer didn't trust himself to look at her, knowing she of anyone here would see how hard that blow had hit. He wasn't about to give his grandparents the satisfaction of knowing that. "And you sure as hell never provided an example," he gritted out.

"You've always been a disappointment, you and your brother," his grandfather said, glaring hard at him. "I warned your mother nothing good would come out of her marrying Garrett." He swung the glare to Maya. "And I'm warning you no Rainbow will ever touch a cent of the Morente inheritance. That I can promise you."

"Did we hear our name?"

Oh, God, not now. Maya prayed she was wrong, knowing she wasn't. This was already bad.

Now it was worse.

Shem appeared behind Mr. Morente and slapped a friendly hand on his white-linen shoulder. Against the pale, delicate fabric, Shem's scorpion tattoo practically jumped off his forearm. "Looks like you're having a little family reunion here," he said.

He reached out to hug Maya. "Hey, honey, how's that grandson of mine?"

"You didn't tell us they were going to be here," Azure said as she kissed Sawyer's cheek and nuzzled Joey. "It's so nice having family together."

"Please, don't even start," Maya begged her mother in a low voice. "Things are bad enough."

"Oh, Maya, don't be so stuffy," Azure chided. "I'm sure we can all be friends."

"I'm sure you're making this worse," Maya said under her breath. Right now the last thing they needed was her parents' live-and-ignore-it approach to uncomfortable situations. Looking at Sawyer, she could tell his temper was fraying fast.

"Don't worry, your money is safe from me," Sawyer said, his voice cold and hard. "I don't want anything from either of you and I couldn't care less what you think of me. But I'll be damned if I stand here and listen to you insult Maya or her parents." He took Maya's hand again, pulling her close. "Maya is strong and caring, she's a great mother and I've never met anyone I admire or respect more. She and Joey are part of my life and nothing you say is going to change that. You can either accept it and her or you can go to hell. And don't flatter yourselves to think I care which."

Maya stared at Sawyer, guessing she was probably gaping stupidly at him. Her heart swelled at Sawyer's support and all the wonderful things he'd said about her. But what stunned her was that he'd practically announced to the world they were a couple. Maybe he'd said it in the heat of anger, to spite his grandparents. Looking at the straightforward expression in his eyes and the determined set of his jaw, though, Maya believed he'd meant every word.

And that left her with a confusing mix of elation and fear. Right now she didn't know which was stronger.

He'd apparently shocked his grandparents into temporary silence. No such luck with her own parents as Shem clapped Sawyer on the back. "Thanks, man. That was a fine speech. We knew our girl was in good hands with you."

Azure patted his arm. "Of course she is." She winked at Sawyer's grandparents. "We're going to have to get along, you know. These three belong together, I've known it from the very first time I saw them."

"Az is right," said Shem. He looked from Sawyer to Maya. "You don't need a piece of paper to be a family. Just be together. It's worked for your mom and me," he added, grabbing Azure around the waist and planting a kiss on her cheek.

"This has obviously been a waste of my time," Sawyer's grandfather said. With a final disgusted look at Sawyer he took his wife's arm and turned away. "Sawyer has made his choice. It seems he'd rather be a Rainbow than a Morente."

For the fourth time in the last hour Maya asked Sawyer if he wanted to leave the picnic, and for the fourth time he firmly refused, assuring her he could handle his grandparents, her parents and anything or anyone else that happened to them today.

Nonetheless, while roaming around the corrals where the rodeo events were being held, pushing a sleeping Joey in his stroller, Maya was clearly worried about Sawyer's nasty encounter with his grandparents. The summer air was heavy with animal smells, horsehair and manure, and dust stirred and puffed into tiny clouds around their feet as they went.

Finally she blurted out her thoughts. "What if your grandparents disinherit you?"

Sawyer simply shrugged off her question. It wasn't the money he cared about; it never had been. He was angry with himself for letting his grandparents' barbed comments bother him. He'd been told so many times he was a disappointment, rejected for making what they considered the wrong decisions, that hearing it again shouldn't make any difference.

You don't know any more about being a parent than your father did.

Except that one hurt. Maybe because he knew it was true.

"Sawyer? Are you all right?"

Realizing he'd drifted, Sawyer shoved his feelings aside, focused on Maya and tossed her a crooked smile. He wasn't about to have her feeling guilty about any of this. "If they disinherit me? Then I'll have to bum money off of Cort."

Maya abruptly stopped. "You'd never do that. Would you?"

"It was a joke, Maya." He took the stroller handles from her and started pushing again. "Don't let my grandparents wreck your sense of humor. I've never cared about the legendary Morente inheritance. Cort and I inherited my mother's share of the restaurant business, but apart from having to constantly sign stacks of papers I'd rather not read, I never touch that money. I do well enough on my own."

"I didn't mean to suggest you didn't," Maya said. "It's just—"

"That I can't do it in the style my grandparents are accustomed to? Does it matter?"

Maya stared at him, incredulous. "You're kidding, right?"

"Yes. And no."

"What's that supposed to mean?"

"Only that a lot of women over the years seemed more interested in the Morente money than in me."

"Then they were idiots," Maya said firmly. "I just don't buy that any woman could be more interested in anything but you. Especially if she shared your bed."

Sawyer was stopping then to pull her into his arms. "Nobody like you ever shared my bed, Maya Rainbow, or ever will. You're something special," he said and kissed her deep and long to make her believe it.

Maya fell into him, eagerly returning his kiss, the feel of his hard body against her stirring her blood. "You're something special, too, Sawyer Morente," she told him when they finally pulled apart. "If I could just get you to believe it."

"Give me a couple of thousand more nights like last night and maybe I will," he said.

He bent to check on Joey and Maya couldn't resist coming up behind him and sliding her hand up his thigh. "Only a couple thousand?"

"Careful, woman," he warned, turning quickly and catching her up against him so she could feel what she'd started. "You're going to get us arrested yet. And wouldn't that make my grandparents proud?"

"I'm so sorry about all of that," Maya said. She put a hand to his face. "You won't say anything, but I know what they said had to hurt." He shook his head to deny her but she told him with a look she didn't believe him. "I want to thank you for saying what you did about me. No one else ever cared enough to do that for me. You made me feel special and very proud to be with you."

Before he could say anything, Maya reached up and kissed him, putting everything she felt for him into her touch, wanting to give him all the love he'd been denied for so long.

Sawyer held her tightly, and for a few moments the rest of the world receded and it was just the two of them. Until an amused voice from behind them broke the spell.

"You know, there are laws against that kind of thing in public."

"Aren't there laws against interrupting where you're not wanted?" Sawyer grumbled as he let go of Maya. "Do you practice being annoying, Cort, or is it just a natural talent?"

"Just trying to keep you out of trouble," Cort said with a grin.

Maya couldn't help laughing. "We were wondering if you were going to be here."

"No, we weren't," Sawyer muttered.

"Aw, come on, you know you would have missed me. Besides, I came to warn you. The grandparents are here."

Maya and Sawyer exchanged a look. "Too late," Sawyer said.

Cort sobered. "What happened?"

Before Sawyer could answer, the gate to the corral swung open and a tall, burly man with grizzled hair and what looked like a permanent snarl, clad in silver-tipped alligator cowboy boots, leather chaps and a ten-gallon hat, stepped out almost directly in front of them. When he saw Sawyer and Cort, he stopped so suddenly, the woman with him bumped into his back.

"Well, now," the man said, eyeing the pair of them with satisfaction. "Looks like I'm finally gettin' what I've been waiting for."

Chapter Sixteen

Sawyer's grip on her hand tightened so hard and fast, Maya sucked in a sharp breath. She looked from him to the couple facing them and finally to Cort, trying to get a clue.

Cort obviously didn't need one. He moved quickly forward, putting himself a step ahead of Sawyer. "This isn't the time or the place," he snapped with a hard stare at the man in front of them. It was clearly a warning.

The man didn't flinch, but the woman Maya guessed was his wife put a restraining hand on his arm. "He's right, Jed," she said. "Let's just go."

Maya's eyes widened. Jed Garrett. She turned to Sawyer, although she didn't need to see him to know he was angry. The tension in him was like a living thing, pulsing in the air around them.

She felt totally helpless. Neither Sawyer nor Cort would thank her for interfering, but she desperately wanted to do something to prevent a confrontation between Sawyer and Jed. Cort was right, this wasn't the place and, for Sawyer, it definitely wasn't the time. Not now, not so soon after the argument with his grandparents.

Jed had other ideas. "If I leave it up to your brother, it'll never be the time," he said. He looked directly at Sawyer. "I'm not asking for much, just an hour so you can hear me out."

"And what if I don't want to hear anything you've got to say?" Sawyer gritted out the words. "After everything, after all this time, what could you possibly have to say that would make any difference?"

"Maybe nothing, but I want the chance to tell my side of it." He looked from Sawyer to Cort and back again. "I doubt your mama told you everything."

Sawyer let go of Maya's hand and pushed past Cort so he stood a foot from Jed. Although Sawyer had the advantage in years and conditioning, Jed matched him in height and had the tough, canny look of a man who knew how to fight and win.

But if Garrett figured to back him off, Sawyer intended to show him he'd figured wrong. He wasn't a kid Garrett could knock around anymore. "She didn't have to. I didn't need her to remind me that you're the one who gave me my first black eye. Or that you're the one who decided his ranch was worth more than his wife and kids."

"Maybe that was true once and maybe it's different now," Jed said. "But I'm also your father, boy. And you can't change that no matter how much you might want to."

"Well, I can damn sure try and forget it."

"Let's finish this later," Cort said, putting a hand on Sawyer's shoulder.

Sawyer shook him off. "Later, hell. Isn't this what you wanted?"

"Not this way. And try to remember I'm on your side."

"I'm not choosy anymore about when and where," Jed said. "If we don't finish this now, there may not be a later." He took a step toward Sawyer. "I'm your father and sooner or later you're gonna have to square with that. I hope for your sake it's sooner."

"And I'm supposed to believe you give a damn one way or the other." Sawyer swung away from him, trying to get a handle on a lifetime of anger boiling up inside of him. Maya caught his eye and she gave a little start forward, then stopped, as if she wanted to reach out to him but knew she couldn't.

He had to settle this on his own, one way or the other, now or later. Maybe he and Garrett could agree on one thing—maybe it should be now.

He turned back. But before anyone could speak, Rafe came striding up to Jed, his face like thunder. "I told you this was a lost cause."

Jed glared at him. "And I told you I'm not interested in your opinion. Stay out of it."

"It's too late for that." Rafe spun on Sawyer. "Then again, maybe it's not a lost cause. You'll never turn down the money."

Sawyer stared at him, momentarily thrown off by the mention of money. "Am I supposed to know what you're talking about?"

"You figure it out. I'm betting you're not the Boy Scout everyone thinks you are." Rafe glanced behind Sawyer to where Maya stood by Joey. "I heard about her and the kid. You like playing house but you haven't claimed either of them. Like father, like son, right?"

Sawyer didn't think, he acted with all the pent-up anger and bitterness inside him. He lunged for Rafe, but Cort shoved in front of him, holding him back. "Get lost," Cort snarled over his shoulder at Rafe, "or I'll find something to bust you for."

Instead of challenging Cort, Rafe surprised them all by simply smiling coldly and then turning away and striding toward the rodeo stands.

"We're done," Cort said to Jed. Then he grabbed Sawyer's arm and said, "Go," pushing him in the opposite direction.

"Are you going to bust me, too?" Sawyer snapped at him when they'd left Jed and his wife behind. He pulled free of Cort's grip, swinging to face his brother.

"I might. Are you gonna take a swing at me, too?"

"I might. Damn it, Cort, I don't need a nursemaid."

"You could've fooled me," Cort said. "How stupid can you get, letting Rafe get to you like that. If you were actually using your brain, you'd know he took that cheap shot on purpose."

Sawyer glared at him. "Really. You think?" he said sarcastically.

Cort blew out a frustrated breath. "He wanted to get you mad enough that you'd blow off any meeting with Garrett. Rafe doesn't want either of us to go through with it."

Sawyer started to tell Cort he was way off base. But he forced himself to think about Rafe's reaction when he'd gone for him and how Rafe had left without even trying to get the last word. "Maybe you're right," he finally told Cort grudgingly.

"There's something going on between him and Jed," Cort said thoughtfully. "And I'm betting it has something to do with the ranch."

"I don't give a damn what their problems are and I don't know why you care so much either."

"I gave up caring a long time ago. I just want to know why, and once I do, then that'll be the end of it."

"This is the end of it as far as I'm concerned." Sawyer paced a few steps away, shoving both hands through his hair, trying to get a grip on the turmoil of emotion bouncing around inside him. "I'm going for a walk. Tell Maya I'll be back soon, will you?"

When Cort found Maya waiting back where they'd left her, she started up off the bench where she'd been sitting next to a sleeping Joey, ready to park Joey's carriage with Val and Paul and go after Sawyer.

"Leave him alone for a while," Cort said, stopping her. He dropped down on the bench beside her. "He needs to get his head together."

Maya chewed her lower lip. "I'm worried about him. No matter what he says, it's pretty obvious he does care."

"Sawyer's always cared too much," Cort said. "You know

how it was for him when we lived with Garrett. And he'll never admit it, but Sawyer half believed all that crap Garrett and then the grandparents threw at him about never measuring up. That's why he's always had to be the best at everything."

"Then why do you keep pushing him to agree to a meeting? You of all people should know how Sawyer feels."

"That's why I push. Because if he doesn't confront Garrett one way or the other, Garrett's always going to be his demon." Cort's expression tightened. His hand flexed on the arm of the bench as if he needed an outlet for the emotion inside. "Sawyer always protected me. You know why Garrett never touched me? Because never once was Sawyer not there for me, even if it meant getting the hell beat out of him. Now it's my turn."

"And what about you?" Maya asked, looking at him. "Why does this meeting with Garrett matter to you?" She was curious because Cort never seemed to let anything touch him. The only other time she'd ever seen him show any hint of a deeper feeling was at the hospital after Sawyer had fallen through the floor of her parents' house. Apart from his relationship with Sawyer, there was something hard and unyielding about Cort.

"Me?" Cort shrugged. He didn't look at her but stared out over the park grounds. "I figured out early on that with the exception of Sawyer, nobody in our family had the time or the inclination to listen to or take an interest in me. So I kept my nose clean and my mouth shut and did exactly as I damned well pleased. Unlike my brother, I've never cared about proving anything to anybody but me. Like I told Sawyer, when it comes to Garrett, I just want to know and then—case solved."

Cort turned to her and seemed to be deciding whether or not to speak. Finally he said, "You're in love with Sawyer, aren't you?"

The personal question surprised her, even more because she wouldn't have thought Cort would have noticed, let alone said anything to her about it. "I guess that's why you're a good cop," she said, avoiding a direct answer.

"I'd have to be blind and stupid not to have figured that out," he said with a laugh. Then he sobered. "You gotta know, Saw-yer's in over his head. He has no damned idea what he's doing. I wouldn't want to see you get burned again."

Maya recognized the warning. Unlike his grandparents, Cort meant well, but it was a warning just the same.

"So you're saying I should walk away first?" she asked Cort, not sure she wanted to hear his answer.

"No, I'm just telling you the way it is." He looked around them, then got to his feet, his unusually serious mood replaced by his usual casual attitude. "I'd better go and find my big brother. I hate to see a grown man sulk. We'll catch up with you."

Maya sat alone after Cort left, her emotions scrambled after all the highs and lows of the day. If it were possible, she felt even more uncertain and confused about her relationship with Saw-yer. Her parents and friends urged her to risk everything because she loved him. Yet Cort and her own fears warned her loving him might not be enough. If she took the chance and acted with her heart, she could end up hurting herself—and worse, hurting Joey. But if she let fear rule her decisions, she could be giving up on love and Joey's chance at having a real father.

Joey started to stir, rousing Maya out of her reverie. With a sigh she went to find Val and Paul.

"Hey, we thought we lost you," Val said as Maya pushed Joey up to where she and Paul sat under the same large tree. Val was getting the girls settled with a snack while Paul gave Johnnie his bottle. She looked around Maya, realizing she was alone. "Where's Sawyer?"

"That's a long story," Maya said. She lifted Joey out of the stroller and settled against the tree trunk to feed him as she filled Val and Paul in on Sawyer and Cort's confrontation with Jed and Rafe.

Paul cursed under his breath when she'd finished. "I told Cort to stop pushing Sawyer to meet with Garrett. I knew it would be a disaster."

"Don't blame Cort," Val chided. "Everyone knows Jed Garrett is a ruthless you-know-what when it comes to getting what he wants. This is his fault for trying to force Sawyer and Cort to talk to him in the first place, but especially here. What was he thinking? Sawyer must be really upset."

"Madder than hell is more like it," Paul muttered, then gave an apologetic shrug when Val poked him in the shoulder and nodded at the girls.

"I think Jed's wife wanted to stop him from pushing Sawyer into a meeting here," Maya said. "But I got the impression Jed wouldn't have listened to her even if she'd tried."

Val's mouth twisted in an expression that said she didn't think much of Jed Garrett's wife. "Del Garrett knew what she was getting when she married him. Jed's her third husband, and she's always been good about taking care of herself first," Val said. "Del will do whatever she can to protect her own son's interests. She's always pushed for Josh to take over the Garrett ranch instead of Rafe. She's probably worried now that Jed will do something that'll jeopardize Josh's inheritance."

"Josh couldn't care less about Garrett's ranch or anything to do about his business," Paul said. He finished feeding the baby and propped him against his shoulder, gently patting his back. "He spends all his time on the rodeo circuit. He's always been a wild thing. Garrett never could control him."

"What about Rafe?" Maya asked. "Jed adopted him, but he never treated him like a son. And Rafe hardly has a warm relationship with Jed, from what I saw."

Paul and Val exchanged a look. Then Paul said in a low voice so the girls wouldn't overhear, "Garrett's a jerk and I doubt he changed after he adopted Rafe. He's always treated Rafe more like a hired hand than anything else, even though without Rafe's father, Garrett would never have gotten that ranch going in the first place."

"I don't understand how Sawyer's mother could have left Rafe behind," Maya said. Sawyer had told her Rafe had a huge chip on his shoulder and she could understand why. "Then again,

I don't understand how she could have stayed with Jed Garrett to begin with."

"You have to ask that after meeting Sawyer's grandparents?" Paul asked. "Sawyer and Cort didn't exactly luck out when it comes to relatives."

"I would think Sawyer and Rafe would have something in common then, both resenting Jed. But they seem to go out of their way to antagonize each other. If Cort hadn't stepped in earlier…"

"Too bad he did. Rafe needs someone to knock some of that attitude out of him," Paul said. "Don't give me that look," he added when Val frowned at him. "I'm sorry Rafe had to grow up with Jed Garrett as an excuse for a parent, but he's had it in for Sawyer ever since Sawyer and Cort moved off the ranch. What's between those two has been building up for a long time."

Val shook her head. "I love Sawyer but he isn't much better. He's always resented Rafe because Garrett adopted him and raised him as his son, but Rafe didn't have anything to do with that or with what Garrett did to Cort and Sawyer."

The twins started squabbling over the last cookie, and Val turned to referee. Paul sat Johnnie on his knee, bouncing him lightly, making his son shriek with delight. "If he pukes on you, don't blame me," Val said over her shoulder.

Maya absently caressed Joey's head as she looked around them hoping to see Sawyer and Cort coming back. Talking with Val and Paul had only intensified her worry and she wanted to talk to Sawyer, to know what he was feeling.

Val reached over and squeezed her hand. "He'll be back. Sawyer just needs time to sort things out."

"I know," Maya said. She made herself smile but inside she ached to do something. Between the argument with his grandparents, the confrontation with Jed and having nearly come to blows with Rafe, Sawyer had to be just about at his limit right now.

Finally, after about a half hour, Maya's anxious watching was rewarded when she saw Sawyer walking toward them.

"We're going to take the twins over to the pony rides," Val said. "Why don't you let Paul and I take Joey along so you can talk to him alone?"

Maya balked and was about to politely refuse, but Paul answered for her. "Hey, we're used to kids. Joey can ride with Johnnie. He'll love it."

"We'll meet you over by the corrals," Val said. Maya was reluctant to leave her son but grateful for the chance to talk to Sawyer alone. She bent and kissed Joey. "Take your time. I've done pretty well with three babies. I think between Paul and me, we can handle one more." With a wink she followed Paul, who was pushing the stroller and the twins in the direction of the pony rides.

Maya watched them for a few moments, then turned her attention to Sawyer, resisting the urge to fidget as he walked up to her. She tried to gauge his mood but his expression gave nothing away. "Hi," she said when he got close.

"Hi." He nodded in the direction of Val and Paul. "Is that a hint?"

"They thought you might not want all the company right now."

Sawyer nodded. "I'm sorry I left you and Joey alone. Although you probably wouldn't have wanted me around right then. Cort accused me of sulking."

Maya glanced behind him. "Where is Cort?" .

"Trying to extricate himself from Trina Hernandez," he said, the corner of his mouth quirking up in a small smile. "She's been after him for years, but Cort's a master at escaping persistent women." He looked down at the rumpled blanket. "You want to sit down?"

Not waiting for her answer, he dropped down against the tree and held out his hand to her, pulling her down beside him.

Maya ran her tongue over her lips, watching him for a moment. Then she asked, "Are you okay?"

"Sure, fine." He didn't look at her.

"Don't do that."

"Do what?"

She put her hand on his jaw and turned him to face her. "Shut me out. It's not fine. I just want to help you," she said, although that insipid word fell far short of her true feelings. "But I can't help if you won't let me get close."

"I let you get as close as possible last night," he said lightly in an obvious attempt to avoid any deeper emotion.

Maya jerked away from him. "So that's all this is to you—great sex and an opportunity to play daddy once in a while?"

He suddenly sobered. Reaching for her hand again, he hung on tightly, ignoring how stiffly she held herself. "You know it isn't."

"Do I?"

Sawyer didn't say anything for a long moment. Then he got to his feet and paced a few steps from her and back before turning to face her again. "I don't mean to shut you out. But right now I just need some space."

He looked so lost that Maya wanted to kick herself for snapping at him. The last thing he needed right now was her pressuring him, too. Getting up, she went to him and put her arms around his waist, laying her head against his heart as she held him. "You don't have to prove anything to me. I just want you."

"I need you," Sawyer said as he wrapped his arms around her and buried his face in the curve of her neck. "Believe that if you can't believe anything else."

She did believe it. Hours later, as she lay in his arms in the midnight darkness of her bedroom while Sawyer dozed, she didn't doubt he needed and wanted her. But she didn't know if he could ever love her wholly and completely, without the shadows of his past coming between them.

Even while he'd made love to her with such passion and tenderness it left her trembling from the power of it, Maya had the feeling he'd been with her in body but not in heart. It felt as if he was trying to leave her from the inside first, shutting her out. What would come next? Would he leave her altogether rather

than risk hurting Joey years later, when being a parent and partner got too complicated? She remembered what Cort had said.
I wouldn't want you to get burned again.

Rather than risk stumbling and maybe making big mistakes,
as most parents do, would he refuse to even to try? Her stomach
clenched; he'd given her no hope of believing anything else.

"You're doing that thinking thing again," Sawyer's voice rum-
bled against her ear. "Didn't your mama warn you that was bad
for your aura?"

She rose up to look at him. "Don't you ever sleep?"

"Not when there are more interesting things to do." With a
quick movement he shifted so she lay under him and could feel
him already aroused, pressing hot and hard against her. His hand
began a leisurely exploration of her body that made her breath
quicken and her blood burn.

"Sawyer, I want to…" She broke off with a soft moan when
his lips and tongue began doing wicked things to her breasts.

"I know what you want, *querida*," he murmured. He kissed
his way lower, nibbling over the soft skin of her belly.

Maya wanted to slow things down enough to talk to him, to
get him to talk about what he was feeling. Except his hand slid
between her thighs, stroking the heat into fire, and her brain
locked.

Then nothing mattered but the way they made each other
feel.

Sawyer held her closely for a long time afterward and Maya
fell asleep in the shelter of his arms.

She awoke in the gray light just before dawn to find him
gone. Maya's heart gave a painful twist. Surely he hadn't just
left her without even a goodbye. She ran her hand over his place
on the bed where the rumpled sheets were still warm and smelled
of him. Sitting up, she could see his shirt tossed on a chair and
his boots kicked in a corner where he'd left them.

Maya got out of bed and, pulling on his shirt, went to Joey's
room, instinct telling her he'd be there. He was, sitting in the

rocker next to Joey's bed, watching Joey sleep. He didn't see her there at first. She could tell by his slight frown and the tension in his shoulders and back he was deep in thought, in a place she couldn't reach him.

He glanced up, rubbing a hand over his face when she lightly touched his shoulder. "Sorry, I didn't mean to wake you," he said quietly. "I couldn't sleep so I thought I'd check on Joey."

"I was afraid you'd left."

Sawyer drew his finger over her cheek and throat, down to the V between her breasts. "Not without my shirt."

"Then good luck getting it back. Come on," Maya said softly, taking his hand.

But before Sawyer followed her out of Joey's room, he paused in the doorway and looked over his shoulder. Maya noticed it was a long, pained look, as though he wasn't going to see Joey for a very long time. It crossed her mind that he was saying goodbye.

No, she was being ridiculous, she chided herself, immediately rejecting the thought as paranoid and replacing it with the idea of luring Sawyer back to bed.

Leading him back to her bedroom, she smiled to herself as he stripped off his jeans and reached for her. She stepped back and shook her head. "Lie down," she told him. "On your stomach."

He eyed her suspiciously before doing as she asked, grumbling, "What is this, torture Sawyer time?"

"No," she said, laughing, as she went to her dresser to get a bottle of scented oil. "But we can try that later if you want. I'm sure I could get Cort to lend me a pair of handcuffs."

"Oh, don't even go there," he groaned.

"How about here?" She knelt down beside him on the bed and, after warming some of the oil in her hands, started to slowly massage his neck and shoulders.

"There's good and—oh, yeah, that's real good," Sawyer said as she worked her hands lower to a particularly tight spot between his shoulder blades.

Maya kept up the slow rhythm of kneading and rubbing, wanting to ease the tension in his body since she couldn't ease his thoughts or the pain in his heart.

After about twenty minutes she felt him relax under her hands and his breathing become deep and even. She slowly pulled back to see he'd fallen asleep.

Gently she brushed the hair back from his forehead and leaned over to touch her lips to his before carefully easing herself off the bed and pulling the sheet up over him. She watched him a few minutes before leaving him to sleep, wishing as she did that she could do more.

That just once she could be everything to him.

"I just don't understand it, Maya. The house is fine. I mean, we're living here, aren't we?"

Maya sighed. She'd been trying for the past four days to explain to her mother why they needed to do some serious repair work to the Rainbow house, but Azure kept insisting no one could make her and Shem move just because of a little mess. Maya had tried appealing to her father, but Shem had basically ignored her, telling her he was too busy with his plans for the herb farm to worry about what some "uptight paper-pusher" said about their house.

The problem was the uptight paper-pusher was the Luna Hermosa building inspector and he'd given Azure and Shem thirty days to make some marked improvement to the house or he promised to issue a condemnation order. Maya knew she had to do something or her parents would end up homeless.

Just like old times, she thought, her trying to fix the trouble her parents had unthinkingly gotten themselves into.

"Look, Mom, do you think you can get a few friends over on Saturday to help?" she asked Azure. "I can call Val and Paul. With enough people we can get a lot done in a day."

"I guess I can do that, although I still think it's a waste of good energy. Tai and Spring are still here, and we're supposed to see

Diego soon…maybe Zel would help us. Isn't Sawyer coming with you?" Azure said abruptly.

"He's working," Maya told her even though she had no idea if it were true. She hadn't seen Sawyer since the picnic. He'd gone back to work Sunday evening, saying he'd agreed to finish off someone else's shift. Maya didn't question him, although she suspected he was using work to avoid dealing with his feelings by going to the one place he felt in control.

He'd called a few times, but their conversations had been brief and unsatisfying and she hadn't been comfortable bringing up the house-repair problem.

"We'll get it done," she told Azure. "Don't worry."

As she hung up to call Val, Maya hoped that was true.

"Of course we'll help," Val said when Maya asked for her and Paul's help. "And wasn't Sawyer going to get Cort and some of the guys from the station to come out before? I'm sure he still can."

Maya wasn't sure what to say since she couldn't give Val the same story about Sawyer working. After a few moments of her silence Val said, "You haven't talked to him about this, have you?"

"No," she admitted. "I've hardly talked to him at all since the picnic. I guess…I guess he needs some space after everything."

"Space, oh please. What he needs is a good kick in the—"

"Val!"

"Well, he does. Typical man, going all macho and pretending like it isn't bothering him while it eats him up inside. You want Paul to talk to him?"

"No, definitely not. I'm serious, Val. I know you mean well, but Sawyer's got enough to deal with right now." Maya loved him too much to put any more pressure on him. Whether or not they had a future, she didn't know. But if she pushed him now, she was certain Sawyer's reaction would be to withdraw from her even more. "Promise me you won't ask Paul to talk to him," she asked Val.

"I promise I won't ask Paul to talk to him," Val said. "And

don't worry, we'll get your parents' house in shape before the bulldozers come calling."

Maya thanked her and hung up, then sat with her elbows propped on the kitchen table, rubbing her temples. It would be nice if for once something could be easy.

Chapter Seventeen

When she pulled up to her parents' house, Maya was surprised to see so many cars parked along the road and in the drive. How had her parents managed to get so many people out here to help on such short notice? She wouldn't complain.

She heard voices coming both from inside the house and out back and decided to try there first. Maybe she could find something to help with there so she wouldn't have to expose Joey to a serious mess of dust, dirt and noise.

Turning the corner, she stopped short.

There, working with Cort to secure a long support beam in place, was Sawyer.

Sawyer finished pounding a nail into the heavy pine beam Cort was holding steady for him. When he was done, he glanced down to see Maya, Joey in her arms, watching him from the foot of the ladder with an expression that said she wasn't quite sure how, or even if, she should approach him.

A twinge of guilt jabbed at him because he knew her hesitancy was his fault. After the fiasco at the picnic he'd been keeping everyone at arm's length, including her. He'd then spent a miserable last week trying to decide if he should make the break with Maya permanent. If he couldn't be everything she and Joey needed, then it was better to end it now, before Joey got any older and too attached and Sawyer ended up hurting both Joey and Maya.

So why did breaking up with Maya feel so wrong? All his life failure had not been an option. But he realized now success was easy when it was only about himself. With Maya and Joey to consider the stakes were much higher. Until his grandparents reminded him how little he had to offer Maya and Joey, he'd been giving it his best. But for the first time in his life he couldn't shake the fear that his best might not be good enough.

"This is a surprise," she said lightly when she caught his eye. "How did you guys find out about this?"

Sawyer jammed his hammer into his leather construction belt. He didn't tell her he'd almost made some excuse not to come today because seeing her would only intensify his need to be with her no matter what the consequences. Looking at her now, he knew he'd been right.

"The town crier, of course—otherwise known as Val," he answered finally. He spied the object of his accusation kissing Paul goodbye at the back door.

Maya shook her head. "I knew she couldn't keep quiet. She told me yesterday she'd have to leave early. She has to take the twins to a ballet practice. Paul said he could stay a few hours, though."

"He was the one who told me about the rebuilding party," Cort said, looking down at the odd array of helpers scattered around. "I couldn't resist joining the circus. Besides—" he flashed her a grin "—I can't let them tear down the love shack. My best high school memory was made here."

"Do I want to know?"

"Let's just say I finally got to see Nova Vargas's tattoo."

Maya laughed. "And all this time I thought you were a good boy."

"Define *good*," Cort said with a wink.

Sawyer looked from Maya to his brother wondering what the hell Cort was playing at. If he didn't know Cort better, he'd say his brother was flirting with her.

"Well, whatever your reasons, I really appreciate the both of you coming out," Maya said as Sawyer and Cort both began backing down their ladders.

Joey squealed and waved his hands when he saw Sawyer. Sawyer waved back. "Hey, there, big guy. You'll have to wait a few years to climb up here."

"Those years will be gone before you know it," Cort said.

Sawyer stopped halfway down the ladder, turned and scowled at his brother, not bothering to bank his irritation. "You have something to say to me?"

Cort shrugged, suddenly the picture of innocence. "Don't get your feathers up. Everyone knows kids grow like weeds, that's all." He beat Sawyer to the ground, hopping backward off the last three rungs.

When Sawyer reached the bottom, Maya hesitated before moving closer and lightly touching his arm. She looked at him with her heart in her eyes, as if there was so much she wanted to say. "This means a lot to me. And to my parents, too."

Without meaning to, Sawyer stiffened a little, her simple touch evoking so many recent memories, a disturbing combination of pleasure and pain. "No problem," he said, not meaning to sound as gruff as he knew he had.

Maya immediately pulled away. She lowered her eyes, but not before Sawyer saw the confused hurt there.

From his lifted brow, Cort had seen it, too, and Sawyer could hear his brother's unspoken question.

"Well, I'll let you get back to work," Maya said, backing up a few steps. "I saw the list the inspector sent and it's going to take nothing short of a miracle to whip this place into shape before the deadline. So I'd better make myself useful."

Cort shot Sawyer an irritated glance. "Don't worry, we won't let your parents get kicked out. We'll have this place in shape in no time." When Sawyer said nothing, Cort nudged him. "Won't we, Sawyer?"

"Yeah, sure. It'll get done, don't worry."

"Well, you've certainly inspired me," Cort said, rolling his eyes at Maya.

She made an attempt to smile. "Let me know if you need anything. I'm going to see how things are inside."

"If you want to end it with her, why don't you just say so?" Cort asked Sawyer after Maya had gone into the house.

"So you can step in and take my place?" Sawyer snapped back without thinking. He regretted it an instant later when Cort grinned wickedly.

"What's the matter, big brother? Jealous?"

Sawyer didn't bother answering, instead hefting another support beam up against the house and starting back up his ladder. Jealous was right—of the easy banter between Maya and his brother, even though he knew Cort had deliberately turned on the charm with Maya just to get a rise out of him.

He decided to try to ignore Cort, and they worked in virtual silence for over an hour until Azure came out back carrying a tray laden with paper cups and a plate of questionable-looking cookies. "Okay, everybody, time for a ginger-tea-and-soy-nut-butter-cookie break," she called to everyone in hearing range.

"Soybean cookies," Cort muttered. "My favorite."

"I took precautions," Sawyer said, keeping his voice low as he came off the ladder for a break. "Beer's in the cooler in my truck."

Several other volunteer workers gathered around Azure to grab a cup and cookies. But he and Cort weren't the only ones less than enthusiastic about soybean cookies and tea, because a few minutes later a scruffy, tattooed bald guy in biker leather lugged in a big cooler filled with beer.

He plunked the cooler down near Azure with a broad smile. "Az, I love you dearly," he said, kissing her on the forehead, "but I'd rather eat broken glass than drink that stuff." He grabbed up a can, popped the tab and held the can high. "Anyone else for a brew?"

A couple of the men took him up on the offer. Laughing, Shem strode over to Azure and draped an arm over her shoulders. "I'll take their shares," he said and downed several cups of the pungent tea in quick succession. "No one makes it like you do, honey. You always know just what I need."

Azure beamed up at him, stretching to kiss his unshaven cheek. "I know my man. Come on, Maya," she called out, gesturing. "There's plenty."

Sawyer turned instinctively in the direction of Azure's wave to see Maya come out of the house with Joey. She met his eyes, then quickly shifted her attention to her parents, smiling at her mother and accepting a cup of tea.

Watching the three of them together with Joey, Sawyer could feel the strength of the bond between them. It was obvious Shem and Azure adored each other even after all the years together. And it was equally obvious they loved Maya and Joey. Maya's face when she was with them said clearly she was secure in the knowledge she was loved. Unconditionally. As he knew Joey would be.

They made it look so easy. But could it really be that simple?

"They know what they're doing," Cort said quietly.

"Yeah, they do." He watched Shem tickle under Joey's chin, making both Maya and Joey laugh. "No wonder Maya's such a great mom. Her parents may be weird, but you know, they're the real thing."

"Actually I wouldn't know," Cort said dryly. "We've always been a little short on the real thing when it comes to parents and grandparents." He paused, then added, "But it doesn't mean you can't have it now."

"Dammit, Cort, don't start. Not today." Sawyer yanked out

his hammer and started back up the ladder again. "I'm not in the mood for another lecture about Garrett."

"I wasn't talking about Garrett."

Sawyer stopped and looked down. "Then what? Whatever it is, spit it out. I can tell you've had something on your mind all day."

Cort climbed up his ladder to look at Sawyer eye to eye. "Contrary to your hostile interpretation of my motives, I never had in mind for you and me and Garrett to be reunited and morph into a loving family."

Sawyer headed to the top of the ladder, Cort at his heels. "Just get to the point," he said.

"The point is, you could have what the Rainbows have. With Maya."

Almost of their own volition, Sawyer's eyes went to Maya standing with her family and laughing with Azure at Shem's antics to amuse Joey. "Just for argument's sake, what makes you think she wants that with me? She's made it clear from the beginning she doesn't need me to take care of her and Joey."

"So?" Cort shook his head. "Not everyone needs to be rescued, Sawyer."

"And my idea of a relationship is me running to the rescue, is that what you're saying?"

"I don't know," Cort said with a shrug, "Is it?"

Sawyer made an exasperated sound. "Stick to being a detective, Cort. The psychiatrist's hat doesn't fit you."

"Clues are clues," Cort said. "So think about this. Maya loves her parents but I doubt she wants to be like them, especially when it comes to raising her kid. Coming back here pregnant and unmarried, with everyone knowing what her parents are like—that had to be tough. You should be proud of her for wanting to stand on her own.".

"I am and she knows it," Sawyer said. "She's done an amazing job of pulling her life together."

"Well, that's a start." Cort reached over and put a hand on Sawyer's shoulder. "But have you told her you love her?"

Sawyer jerked back, nearly dropping his hammer. He glared at his brother. "That's none of your business."

"So you haven't," Cort said casually. "Didn't think so." He let go of Sawyer's shoulder and hoisted a beam from the make-shift scaffolding it had been resting on to push it up to the roof.

Sawyer swiped a nail from his pouch and slammed it into the beam. "This is all leading up to another discussion about Garrett, isn't it? You might as well give it up because I don't believe any of that psychobabble bull about dissecting your past. What good is it going to do?"

Cort shifted his hold on the beam, straightening the angle. "You'll never know, will you?"

"No. And I don't need to. Maya's and my relationship has nothing to do with Garrett."

"Whatever you say, bro. It's your call."

"Since when?" Sawyer muttered. But Cort seemed to have lost interest in the subject and was apparently focused on the job at hand.

Not that Sawyer believed Cort had given up on trying to convince him to meet with Garrett. But for some reason his brother was pushing him on a new issue—his relationship with Maya. That was all he needed, Cort sticking his nose into his personal life.

He slammed another nail into the wood and reached into his pouch for another, then stopped, distracted by the soft sound of singing.

Several yards away, Maya, her hair tied up in a blue bandanna, was busy sweeping up construction waste into a pile. She'd put Joey on a quilt under a tree with another of Azure's mobiles to keep him happy as she worked around him, singing to him. The sweet sight of her grabbed his heart and held him transfixed.

At the same time Cort's question haunted him. *But have you told her you love her?*

Did he love her? His heart gave him the answer his mind had tried so hard to ignore. He'd been calling it *passion* and *concern* and *empathy*. Anything but *love*.

Because he did love her.

She and Joey were the best things that had ever happened to him.

If only he could be the same for them.

"It's quittin' time!" Shem called out over the noisy hum of saws, drills and hammers. "There's a roasted pig out back with our names on it."

Sawyer glanced out the new front window. The sun had already begun its slow, salmon-rayed descent behind the mountains. He'd been so lost in his own thoughts all day, time had slipped away. He turned to where Cort was packing up his toolbox. "I don't know about you, but I could use a break."

"Yeah, but I can't stay," Cort said. "Not that I wouldn't want to join the lovefest, but I have some paperwork to catch up on before tomorrow."

Maya came over to them, two cold beers in hand. "I snagged these for you," she said, handing them the icy cans, avoiding looking directly at Sawyer as she did. "You're staying for the barbecue and bonfire, aren't you?" When they looked at each other, doubtful, she added, "We're having meat, I promise. And potatoes and corn and coleslaw. Normal food. I took control of the menu today."

Sawyer laughed. "You mean you're sacrificing the pig?"

"No," she said, wrinkling her nose. "That was Diego's doing. I don't even want to know how or where he got it. Apparently he's been marinating it for two days in beer. He tells me it's supposed to make the meat tender, but I'm thinking it was just an excuse to buy extra beer."

Cort downed his drink. "Actually I've had roasted pig that way before. It's terrific."

"Great, then you're staying."

"Unfortunately I can't. Like I told Sawyer, I let a lot paperwork go today to be here. If it's not done by tomorrow, the boss'll have my hide."

"We'll miss you," Maya said with a smile. She reached out and hugged him. "Thanks for everything you did today. I think this is the best this house has ever looked. The building inspector should be impressed."

"Let's hope so. Well, enjoy the pagan feast. I've got a date with a computer." He turned to Sawyer. "We ought to work together more often. Think of all the interesting things we'd learn about each other."

"I think you've learned enough interesting things about me."

"Good. Then it's about time you figured me out." Cort slipped Maya a wink and a smile, then headed for the front door. "Tell your folks thanks and ask them for a rain check on the pig, would you?" he called back to her over his shoulder.

When they were alone, Sawyer finished his beer and tossed the can into a garbage pile. Maya went over and fished it out.

"Recycle, right. I forgot," he said.

She looked at him fully for the first time and said softly, "No one's perfect."

Despite the bustle of people cleaning up around them, Sawyer suddenly couldn't see or hear anyone but Maya. He nearly moved to take her in his arms but checked himself. "And what if someone's really imperfect?" he asked.

She smiled and he could see her heart in her eyes, offering him everything he needed—faith, acceptance, passion. Love. "All the more reason to love him," she said.

Sawyer gave up trying to keep any distance between them. He pulled her in his arms, needing to feel her as close as he could get her. How could he have ever thought leaving her would make things right? "I've been an idiot."

"You won't get any argument from me." She pulled back a little to look him in the eye. "I was starting to believe we were over."

"I was starting to believe that would be the best thing for all of us."

"And now?"

"Now I still don't know what the best thing is. I only know I don't want to be without you. I never want to do anything to push you away. Earlier—" he gave a short laugh, almost embarrassed to admit it to her "—I thought I was pushing you at Cort."

Maya reached up and brushed his lips with hers. "Cort who?" she whispered against his mouth, punctuating her words with a kiss full of longing and passion.

Sawyer kissed her back almost desperately, consuming her lips, her mouth in his, aching with need for the feel of her body against his, to know she was truly there with him, for him.

"Okay, that's enough of that." Azure's voice abruptly broke the spell. She bent close to the baby in her arms. "Close your eyes, Joey, you're too young for this. And you two, there'll be plenty of time for that later," she said, smiling broadly as Sawyer reluctantly released Maya. "Right now I need help carrying food. We'll eat while there's still light, then we'll start the bonfire."

Joey squirmed and reached out for Sawyer, making him smile. "Hey, there, buddy, I missed you, too." He took Joey from Azure, earning him a big toothless grin.

"Things are right now," Azure said, looking happily from Sawyer and Joey to Maya.

"So, did Tai and Diego bring their guitars?" Maya asked.

Azure nodded. "And you know your dad had to dig his out, too. And Patia brought her flute and Spring has her tambourine."

"I guess I can expect a sing-along around the campfire," Sawyer said.

Maya and Azure looked at each other and laughed. "What's the matter?" Maya teased. "Don't you know any campfire songs?"

"Don't worry," Azure told him in a confidential whisper, leaning on his arm for a moment. "Shem doesn't either, so he just makes them up as he goes along."

With a last kiss for Joey she turned and started for the kitchen. Sawyer shifted Joey on his hip and put an arm around

Maya, holding the both of them close to him. "Your family's all right, you know?"

Maya smiled up at him. "I know."

"Right now I feel closer to you than I ever have."

It was true, and suddenly he wanted to tell her everything—how much he needed and wanted her. How much he loved her. How he could make it right somehow. But it would never be right if he lost her. "Maya—"

"I'm glad of that, too, that you want us to be together," she said before he could begin. "I missed you so much this week." She abruptly yawned, then looked at him sheepishly. "Sorry. I really want to talk, but it's been such a long day and I haven't been sleeping too well lately."

Sawyer hugged her close. "I know. Me neither. Let me take you and Joey home. We can come get your car in the morning."

"That sounds like heaven," she said. "I'm all yours." And with a dramatically playful wave of her arm she added, "Take me away."

Maya left Sawyer waiting in her living room while she nursed Joey and tucked him in. When she finished, she found him standing by the fireplace, staring into the empty grate. She'd left the lamps off and instead had lit a few candles on the mantel and on a table near the couch, and in the dim light she couldn't see what was in his eyes.

"Sawyer?" she said softly, coming up to touch his shoulder. "I'm awake now."

He started and she wondered why he was so tense. Not tense as in anticipation, but on edge. "Oh, hi. Is Joey asleep?"

"Mmm. Like the angel he is." Comfortable now in her T-shirt and girl boxers, she took his hand and tugged him to the couch to sit next to her. "Nursing helped wake me up. But you must be exhausted."

"What? No, not really."

He seemed a thousand miles away. Gently she reached over and began to rub his shoulders. "Thank you again for your help today."

Sawyer reached up and drew her hands away, holding them in his. "No, I should be thanking you."

She smiled, puzzled by his odd mood. "For what?"

"For being who you are."

"I—I don't know what to say." Maya hesitated as she tried to figure him out. "Sawyer, what's wrong?"

"Nothing. Nothing's wrong. I just—" He stopped, searching her eyes. Then in a rush he said, "Say yes."

"Yes? Yes to what?"

Sawyer gripped her hands tightly. "Say yes to becoming my wife. Maya, will you marry me?"

Chapter Eighteen

Maya was so stunned that for a moment all she could do was stare at him. "Sawyer, I—I don't know what to say," she finally stammered.

"Yes would be good." When she continued to hesitate, he stood up and drew her to her feet. "I love you. I want us to be together, you and Joey and me."

A rush of pure happiness surged through Maya, all the sweeter because part of her believed she'd never hear those words from him. And only now did she realize how much she'd longed for him to say them.

"We're good together, you know we are," Sawyer said. Framing her face in his hands, he kissed her slowly, deeply. "I love you. I need you. The only time things feel right anymore is with you," he murmured against her lips. "I want both of you with me, not just part-time but permanently, as a family. Say yes."

He kissed her again and she clung to him, trying to think when all she wanted to do was push closer and let him take her to that place where her doubts and fears didn't matter.

When he finally pulled back, he smiled, looking as if he was already sure of her answer. "Was that a yes?"

One small word and they could be a family. Maya started to speak with her heart and tell him yes, but her demons of doubt and fear stopped her. She couldn't meet his eyes and stepped out of his arms and took several steps away from him.

Sawyer's smile faded, replaced by a frown of concern and confusion. "What's wrong?"

"Sawyer, I love you," she said in a rush. "More than you can imagine, more than I thought possible." He started toward her but Maya held up her hands to stop him. "I just don't know if that's enough."

"I don't think I'm hearing this right. Why can't it be?"

Maya swallowed hard against the tightness in her throat. "Because all this time you've been telling me you can't trust yourself to be what Joey and I need. Why is it different now? What's changed?"

"Nothing's changed," Sawyer said. He shook his head, turning away from her and then back, holding out a hand to her in appeal. "I don't want to lose you. I need you. And Joey needs a father. Why are you making this more complicated than it is?"

"Because I need to know you're ready. I didn't know…you've never told me how you felt about us. Up until today you acted as if you weren't even sure there should *be* an us. And now all of a sudden you ask me to marry you. Is it truly what you want?"

Sawyer cursed under his breath. "This is about Garrett, isn't it? Apparently Cort has won you over to his side."

"No, it's not about Garrett or choosing sides," Maya cried. "It's about you! I don't care if you never see Garrett again. As long as you can live with that."

"Why couldn't I?" he shot back. "I don't need to confront Garrett to know I love you and Joey. Doesn't that count for anything?"

"Of course it does. But unless you can move forward, we can't move forward."

"And you don't think I can," he said flatly.

"I don't think you have," Maya told him. She looked at him, desperate to make him understand. "Don't you see? Unless you do, we'll just end up hurting each other—and Joey, too. I won't let that happen."

Sawyer stiffened, a muscle in his jaw working. "You don't believe I'm capable of committing to you and Joey, so it's a given I'm going to end up hurting you. Have I got it right?"

"That's not what I'm saying at all! Sawyer, please. I'm not your grandparents or your father. I know what kind of man you are and I know you're already committed to us and that if we made it permanent you'd give your all to us." She paused. "But if things weren't perfect, if raising Joey got complicated or things went wrong for whatever reason, would you blame yourself? And then could you live with that, could you stay after you were convinced it was all your fault even though the mistakes we made were together?"

Looking at her, Sawyer didn't say anything for several long moments. "You know my history. Yeah, of course I'd blame myself," he said at last, his voice cracking with tension. "But I can make this work. I need to make it work."

He hadn't answered her question about leaving, and Maya feared it was because he couldn't.

"Don't think you've moved on either," he said before she could put her fears into words. "You're still afraid of trusting yourself to make the right decisions because you made a mistake with Joey's father. You tell me I'm still living with the past, but you're still living with Evan's ghost. And when you look at me and think about making a commitment, it's him you see."

"I've never compared you to him," Maya said in a voice barely above a whisper. How could he think she would?

"No? Then look at me and tell me you're not afraid."

The intensity in his eyes demanded the truth. "You're right,

I am afraid," she said. "I'm afraid I'm going to screw up Joey's life. I'm afraid of getting hurt again. And I'm scared to death I'm going to lose you."

"Maya," Sawyer said and made a movement toward her, then stopped. "What do you want? How can I make this right for you?"

"It's not about making it right for me. I love you. I don't expect you to be the perfect hero. I don't need to be rescued. I need you. But how can we say forever when we're both afraid it isn't going to work?"

Sawyer swung away from her, his hands fisted so tightly, the knuckles were white. Tears ran down her face unchecked and she hated herself then because she knew she'd hurt him. To Sawyer, her hesitation in accepting his proposal was just another rejection. Another abandonment.

"Sawyer, I'm not giving up on you," she said softly.

"Yeah? That's funny, that's sure what it sounds like to me."

"I meant it when I said I love you. It just—"

"Isn't enough. I got the message." He cut her off with a frustrated gesture, then started for the door. "I need some air."

"Sawyer—" Maya followed after him.

Jerking open the door, he didn't give her time to stop him. "Don't make this any harder," he said and left her standing by the door helpless to do anything except watch him get into his truck, gun the engine and whip out of her driveway.

Maya stayed there a long time, tears streaming down her face. She'd had her chance to hold him and she'd thrown it away. Fear had decided for her and now she didn't know if there ever would be a second chance to make it right.

Sawyer drove without thinking about any destination, suddenly finding himself miles out of Luna Hermosa and not knowing how he got there. Seeing a narrow side road, he made a quick turn onto it and killed the engine.

He leaned his head back, closing his eyes, and tried to figure out how everything had gone from good to completely screwed-up so quickly.

Part of it was he hadn't bothered to think anything through before asking Maya to marry him. His proposal had been an impulse, spurred by an urgent need to hold on to the best thing in his life, the feeling he had being with Maya and Joey.

It seemed so simple, a way to keep her and Joey in his life. He loved her, he loved the kid. And she said she loved him. That had to be enough to make it work.

Except deep down he knew he'd only told himself he believed it while crossing his fingers and hoping it was true.

Maya was right. He needed to move forward. She was afraid of making the wrong choice because she couldn't trust him. And she couldn't trust him until he trusted himself.

Starting the engine again, Sawyer pulled out in the direction of town and Cort's apartment. His brother answered the door almost immediately.

Cort took one look at him and said, "What's wrong?"

"I need your help," Sawyer said, coming inside.

"Name it."

Sawyer faced him squarely, determined now to go through with what he'd started. "I'm ready to meet with Garrett."

Jed Garrett leaned back in his chair and surveyed the four men in front of him with satisfaction. Cort and Rafe had taken chairs, Cort looking deceptively at ease and Rafe like a dark, wild animal being forced to sit in some kind of torture device. Josh, his Stetson pulled low, tilted his chair back and propped his boots on the edge of the couch with an air of being totally disinterested. Sawyer stayed standing, his back ramrod straight, shoulders tense, too edgy to sit.

Jed's eyes settled on him and he laughed. "I can tell you'd like to take a swing at me, boy. Well, maybe I deserve that."

"No maybe about it," Sawyer said, staring straight back. Be-

side him Cort tensed, but Sawyer shook his head. "It's okay. I
want to hear this."

"It won't take long. I've got cancer," Jed said without any pre-
amble. "The doctors say maybe they can fix it and maybe they
can't. Either way, I ain't gettin' any younger and before I die I
intend to square things with my sons.

"I don't much care what you or anyone else thinks of me,"
he said, looking them all over in turn. "I've always been a son
of a bitch and I reckon I'll die that way. But I came from nothing, and since the day me and your daddy—" he nodded at Rafe
"—started this ranch, it's mattered the most to me. I did what I
had to do to make sure I never went back to scraping in the dirt."

Sawyer remembered his mother telling him the only thing
Garrett ever loved was his ranch. It made him ask, "Then why
bother with a family in the first place?"

"The first time, I needed the money," Jed answered without
apology. "Teresa had it and she was a good businesswoman. And
she loved me, although I think most of that was because her parents didn't. It went bad fast, but she stuck it out until she found
out about Maria and the kid."

Sawyer and Cort exchanged glances, and Sawyer knew Cort
was as in the dark as he was. Rafe was frowning, and even Josh
showed a spark of interest, thumbing his hat back to look at Jed
for the first time.

For the first time Jed didn't look directly at them. "Teresa
found out I'd walked out on Maria and the boy to marry her.
Walked out and never looked back. She made me a deal. She let
me keep the money she'd invested in the ranch as long as I gave
up her sons." He nodded to Rafe. "I told her you weren't part of
the bargain. She'd never wanted the adoption in the first place,
so she left you with me."

Rafe's dark glare settled on Sawyer, then Cort. "Why doesn't
that surprise me?"

Jed gestured to Sawyer and Cort. "I know she told you I
kicked the three of you off the ranch, but that ain't exactly the

way things happened. If I hadn't let you two go, I would have lost everything. And you two were probably better off. We never did each other any good."

"You're wrong about that," Sawyer said and everyone in the room looked at him in surprise. "You made me realize I'm nothing like you and that I'll do whatever it takes to make sure I never am."

Jed sized him then Cort up in a look. Then he nodded. "You won't thank me, but I did give you one thing. Because of me you grew up strong and you learned how to watch each other's back."

Sawyer didn't bother to deny him. Maybe in a twisted way it was true. But it was a helluva legacy.

"It's too late to fix what's past," Jed went on. "But I'm gonna do this. You're all gettin' a share of my ranch. You two—" he pointed at Cort and Sawyer "—because it was your mama's money that helped build it. Rafe because his daddy was my partner. And Josh is my son."

"I don't want anything from you," Sawyer said.

Cort got to his feet. "I've heard your story and that's all I wanted."

"I didn't even want that much," Josh muttered. "As far as I'm concerned, you should give it all to Rafe. He's the only one besides you who gives a damn about this place."

Rafe had stood up, too, hands fisted at his sides, but before he could say anything, Jed broke in. "I'm not asking your permission, any of you. And I'll tell you this, I also want my first son to have a share. His name is Cruz Déclan and I aim to find him."

"So how do you feel about having another brother?"

Cort, leaning against the patio wall at Sawyer's house, threw the question out, closely watching Sawyer as he did. Garrett had abruptly ended the meeting after his unexpected announcement by walking out, and Sawyer and Cort had come back here.

"I always figured you were enough of a pain in the ass," Sawyer joked lightly. Then he sobered, thinking it over before saying, "We need to find him. Preferably before Garrett does."

Cort stared, then shook his head. "Man, you can still surprise me."

"What, that it took me this long to get my head on straight?"

A light breeze carried the scent of summer sage and wildflowers to him, stirring memories of Maya. All the time he'd been struggling to figure out how to be father, partner and lover, she had been giving him the answers through her example and those of friends and even her crazy parents. It never mattered to Maya if he got everything right. To her, it was more important he have faith that everything would be right if they loved each other, no matter how many mistakes they made along the way.

"You think you got it straight now, with Garrett?" Cort broke into his thoughts.

"I don't think I'll ever be able to make peace with Garrett," Sawyer answered honestly. "I don't need to. Listening to him today and thinking about all he did to us, I realized we might share the same blood, but that's where the connection ends." He looked pointedly at Cort. "I also realized that it's time I face up to the fact that you and I have brothers we need to know."

"Does that include Rafe?"

Sawyer grimaced. "He got stuck with Garrett because our mother let it happen. I can't imagine ever feeling brotherly toward Rafe, but I think it's time I tried to settle things between us." He stopped, finding it hard to say what he wanted to Cort. They'd always been tight, but neither of them had ever put it into words. "Thanks for not giving up on me. And for pushing me to face Garrett. All these years I've been running from it."

"Yeah, right, Danger Boy," Cort scoffed. "You've never run from anything."

"I have this." Sawyer focused on the trees behind his house. "I was afraid I'd find out I was like him. I made him into some kind of monster. Turns out he was just the son of a bitch he said he was." He turned back to Cort. "Thanks for watching my back, little brother."

"It's one for all the times you watched mine."

Sawyer pulled his brother into a hug, and when they broke apart he said with a grin, "I wish I'd taken that swing at him, though."

Cort clapped a hand to his shoulder. "I was kind of wishing you had, too. Although I'd have had a tough time explaining that one to my boss. So what now?"

"Now?" Sawyer smiled. "Now I move forward."

Maya wondered if she could be any more miserable.

It had been over two weeks since that horrible night she'd turned down Sawyer's proposal, and she hadn't seen him or talked to him since. She'd tried calling him a few times but only gotten his voice mail telling her to leave a message. Twice she did, keeping it brief, asking him to call so they could talk. He never did.

Obviously it was over between them.

She wished with everything in her she could go back and tell him yes, she'd marry him. She'd let her own fears decide then. And Sawyer was right—she'd let her past come between them, too.

She'd hurt him by making him feel she was another person giving up on him, as if she had no faith in him, and now she'd lost her chance to tell him how sorry she was, how much she loved him and wanted to be with him.

In the last weeks of sleepless nights, Maya seriously thought about moving away from Luna Hermosa. Her commitment to Dr. Gonzales and to her parents stopped her from packing up and taking Joey someplace far away from this town and all the memories. That and the fact that she couldn't run away. She'd done that with Evan—she'd run back home to escape everything that had gone wrong, telling herself it was better for her and Joey. She wouldn't do it again.

But she didn't know if her heart could survive living here, in the same town as Sawyer, with the possibility of seeing him again, maybe with someone else, and knowing she could never be with him.

The phone rang and she stared at it a moment before reluctantly answering.

"You and Joey come over to dinner tonight," Val said when Maya admitted to having no plans.

"Oh, I don't know, Val."

"Don't even think about saying no. You need to get out of that house. And besides, we haven't seen either of you for weeks. See you at five," Val said and hung up before Maya could tell her no.

Maya was still muttering over the whole thing later that afternoon as she finished packing up Joey to leave. She was not in the mood to pretend everything was fine and she knew both Val and Paul would probably be bombarding her with questions about what had gone wrong between her and Sawyer, questions she didn't feel like answering even for her two friends.

As she stood at their front door, Maya seriously considered turning tail, driving home and calling to tell them she'd suddenly gotten sick. Instead she forced a smile when Val opened the door and ushered her in—and then froze in complete stunned surprise.

Sawyer stood there, waiting.

"Give me that baby before you drop him," Val said, taking Joey in his seat off Maya's arm and then shouldering his diaper bag. She nudged Maya in Sawyer's direction. "Go on. We'll be in the backyard."

Maya felt paralyzed. There were so many things she wanted to say, but her brain seemed to have stopped functioning.

Sawyer gave her a lopsided smile that brought tears to her eyes. It seemed like forever since she'd seen that smile. "I'm sorry for not calling you," he said. "I got your messages, but I had some things I needed to do before I saw you again."

Maya nodded and brushed hurriedly at her eyes. She wanted to throw herself into his arms and forget the last two weeks had ever happened. Instead she took an unsteady breath and said, "You look good." He did, she thought, and it wasn't just the way his jeans fit. There was a difference about him, as if he'd made peace over something that had been haunting him for a long time. "How have you been?"

He shrugged. "Better."

"Really?"

"I'd say fine but you'd probably throw something at me. I went to see Garrett."

"Did you? How did that go?" she asked cautiously.

"Not great. But it feels like he's in the past for good now. And I don't want to go there again." Sawyer paused. "I sold my house."

Maya stared at him in surprise. "Why would you do that? I mean, it was your mother's and I thought..."

"It was time to move on. I sent most of the stuff back to the grandparents. Except for my chair—I figured they wouldn't want that," he said with a grin.

Bewildered by his mood and decisions that didn't make any sense to her, Maya didn't know what to say. "What are you going to do now?"

"Now? Now I'm going for a drive. Will you come with me?"

"I—" She glanced in the direction where Val had taken Joey.

"Val and Paul will look after him," Sawyer said. And as if on cue, Val called from the other room, "Go, already. Joey will be fine."

Maya looked at Sawyer. "You planned this."

"Guilty," he said, holding up his hands. "I asked for their help. I left my truck down the block in case you saw it and decided to bolt before I had the chance to talk to you. Val's right, Joey will be fine. So will you come with me?"

He held out his hand to her, and after a brief hesitation Maya took it.

"Where are we going?" she asked a few minutes later when she realized Sawyer was heading out of town.

"A place I like," was all he would say, leaving Maya to wonder just what he had in mind.

They drove about fifteen minutes, not saying much other than small talk—Sawyer asking about Joey and her work at the clinic, Maya asking about his job and growing more and more frustrated because she wanted to talk to him about what mattered and he seemed determined to talk about everything but.

Sawyer finally pulled off onto a small side road that eventually led to what looked to Maya like little more than a dirt path leading up into the edge of the mountains. When he stopped the truck, Maya looked around at the dense pines and craggy earth and felt as if they'd come to some secret place, isolated from the rest of the world.

"It's just through here," Sawyer said. Taking her hand again, he led her up through the trees to a clearing that overlooked a small stream and a vista of mountains and turquoise sky.

"It's beautiful," Maya said, not really seeing. Having him so close that she could stretch out a hand and touch the face and body she knew by heart was torture.

"Yes, it is."

She turned and found him watching her with the same longing she felt, so intense, she ached inside.

"I wanted to do things right this time," he said. His smile was rueful. "I've been doing a lot of thinking. Some of it's been painful. There have been days I really missed your massages. All those days, actually."

Trying to smile back, Maya said, "I've missed giving them to you."

Sawyer made a move toward her, then stopped himself. "I missed you. These last few weeks, I felt like part of me was missing—the best part." He looked into her eyes as if searching her soul for answers he needed. "I can't guarantee I won't make mistakes or that I'll be able to be everything to you. And I know you're afraid. No, not yet," he interrupted her when she would have spoken. "I'm still not sure what I'm doing but I know I can figure it out if we're together. I believe that because of you. And I promise you, no matter what, I'll always be there for you and Joey. I promise I'll always love you."

Taking her hand, Sawyer got down on one knee and looked into her eyes, making Maya a believer in that one moment when she saw all the love and promise he offered her. "Will you marry me?"

"I promise I'll always love you and I'll always be there for you, too," she said, and this time the tears were from happiness, washing away the pain and doubt. "The only thing I'm afraid of now is being without you."

"So is that a yes?"

Maya laughed and pulled him closer as Sawyer stood up with her in his arms. "Yes," she said against his mouth a heartbeat before he kissed her until they were both breathless.

"I almost forgot…" Sawyer smiled at her little moan of protest when he put enough space between them for him to reach into his jeans pocket. "This is for you." He took her left hand and slipped a ring on her third finger, an emerald set in a twist of silver. "It's not typical, but neither are you. I wanted something special for you."

"It's beautiful. But you've already given me something special," she said. "You. You're the man I always wanted. I think I've known it from the moment you delivered our son and everything felt so right."

"Our son?"

"Hasn't he been from the beginning?" In his eyes she could see he believed it, too.

"And here I thought you bought all that element-of-surprise stuff." Sawyer laughed and drew her against him again. "Does that mean you'll make room for me and my chair for a while until we can find a place of our own?"

"You and your chair will always have a home with Joey and me. But I still can't believe you gave up that house."

"It wasn't us," Sawyer said simply. "I wanted to go forward. With you. That's why I brought you here. Does this look like a spot you'd want to build our house on? I put a down payment on the land today."

Maya leaned back to look him in the eye. "Pretty sure of yourself, aren't you? What would you have done if I'd said no?"

"Sold the land and slept on Cort's couch." He started nibbling kisses along her ear, sliding lower to her throat. "But I knew you wouldn't."

"Why's that?" Maya said, no longer caring about the answer.

"It's like your mom said," Sawyer told her just before he abandoned words to let his kiss and touch speak for him. "We belong."

* * * * *

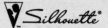

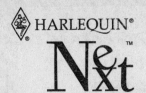

HARLEQUIN®
NeXt™

Coming this September

In the first of Charlotte Douglas's Maggie Skerritt mysteries, an experienced police detective has to predict a serial killer's next move while charting her course for the future. But will Maggie's longtime friend and confidant add another life-altering event to the mix?

PELICAN BAY
Charlotte Douglas

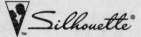

COMING NEXT MONTH

SPECIAL EDITION

#1705 HOME AGAIN—Joan Elliott Pickart
After a miscarriage left her unable to bear children and her high school sweetheart divorced her, child psychologist Cedar Kennedy vowed never to love again. But when humble construction company owner Mark Chandler brought his orphaned nephew, Joey, in for treatment, Cedar sensed she'd met a man who could rebuild her capacity for love....

#1706 THE MEASURE OF A MAN—Marie Ferrarella
Most Likely To...
Divorced mom Jane Jackson took a job at her alma mater to pay the bills...and now used it to access confidential records seeking information about the anonymous benefactor who'd paid for her education. For help getting to the files, she turned to the school's maintenance man, Smith Parker. Did this sensitive but emotionally scarred man hold the key to her past—and her future?

#1707 THE TYCOON'S MARRIAGE BID—
Allison Leigh
When six-months-pregnant Nikki Day collapsed on her vacation, she awoke with former boss Alexander Reed by her bedside. Alex devoted himself to Nikki's care, even in the face of his estranged father's attempts to take over his business. Their feelings for each other grew—but she was carrying his cousin's baby. And Alex had a secret, too....

#1708 THE OTHER SIDE OF PARADISE—Laurie Paige
Seven Devils
The minute Mary McHale arrived for her wrangler job at a ranch in the Seven Devils Mountains, her boss, Jonah Lanigan, had eyes for her. Then Mary, orphaned at an early age, noticed her own striking resemblance to the Daltons on the neighboring ranch. After discovering her true identity—and true love with Jonah—would she have to choose between the two?

#1709 TAMING A DARK HORSE—Stella Bagwell
Men of the West
After suffering serious burns rescuing his horses from a fire, loner Linc Ketchum needed Nevada Ortiz's help. The sassy home nurse brought Linc back to health and kindled a flame in his heart. But ever since his mother had abandoned him as a child, Linc just couldn't trust a woman. Now Nevada needed to find a cure...for Linc's wounded spirit.

#1710 UNDERCOVER NANNY—Wendy Warren
As nanny to restaurateur Maxwell Lotorto's four foster kids, sultry Daisy June "D.J." Holden had ulterior motives—she was really a private eye, hired to find out if her boss was the missing heir to a supermarket dynasty. D.J. fell hard for Max's charms—not to mention the unruly kids. But would her secret bring their newfound happiness to an abrupt end?

SSECNM0805